D

Deception

Zach James

ZACH JAMES

DECEPTION

Zach James

This book is a work of fiction. Any references to historical events, real people, or real places, are used in a fictitious manner. Other names, characters, places, and events are products of the author's imagination. Any resemblance to actual events, places, or persons, living or dead, is entirely coincidental.

ISBN: 978-0-578-83931-8

ISBN: 978-0-578-83932-5 (ebook)

Cover design by Bill Fan | @bandito_bill on Instagram | www.banditobill.com

ZACH JAMES

This book is dedicated to my Grandfather,
Ron Brink.

I miss you, Gunny. Semper Fi.

DECEPTION

"Vive la mort! Vive la guerre! Vive le sacré mercenaire!"

- Michel, "Dogs of War", 1980

ZACH JAMES
Foreword: The DoD and Redactions

This book is a project almost ten years in the making. What began as a nonsensical comedic short story, brainstormed between me and two buddies in the morning study hall of my senior year of high school, eventually became the skeleton and foundation for the thriller you hold in your hands today.

Since I was a kid, I had two dreams. The first was to serve the United States in the armed services. I accomplished this goal at seventeen years old, when I enlisted into the United States Army in May of 2011. The second dream was to write and publish a book. Now, almost ten years later, at twenty-seven years old, I have accomplished that.

Deception is a passion project born of a love of reading, writing, general interests, academic study, and real-world experience. My time serving our country both in and out of uniform has taken me to some amazing places around the globe and allowed me to meet some of the best and brightest in my field.

However, I am not a member of any Special Operations unit. I am not Alex Foaly. I am not Vinny Jensen. I am not Morgan Tyron. I have been lucky enough to be on teams that supported guys like them and have gotten to know many real operators over the years. But I am not one of them, and I have never done anything as remotely 'cool' as they have. I have never taken part in or supported any type of operation or mission that resembles any of the events that occur in this book. It's all made up.

To hammer my point home: none of the content you are about to read has violated any form of operational security or personal security.

DECEPTION

To ensure that, and as a sign of good faith, I submitted the manuscript for Deception to the Department of Defense Office of Pre-Publication and Security Review. This is not a mandatory process for novels, or any work of fiction for that matter. But I figured it was better to be safe than sorry. This book has been 'Cleared as Amended' by the DoD.

'Cleared as Amended' because during the almost year-long review process, the Department of Defense deemed certain terms, phrases, and acronyms too sensitive for public consumption. Those sensitive topics remain in the pages of this novel, blacked out in order to retain OPSEC, as defined by the Department of Defense, and to keep the story intact.

That being said, every single one of these redactions are available through open-source research tools, and many of them are available for consumption through public productions of films, television series, and books, both fiction and non-fiction.

Whether it be a 1986 action film starring Chuck Norris and Lee Marvin; the late Dalton Fury's novel series that ran from 2011 through 2017; Brian Andrews and Jeffrey Wilson's fantastic ongoing action thriller series; copious references to the illusive 'East Coast Command', and it's selection; in shows such as CBS' 'SEAL Team' and the History Channel's 'Six'; as well as nonfiction accounts of significant battles such as Operation Gothic Serpent in 1993; or books that detail the history of the Joint Special Operations Command. All places where the information that DoD deemed too 'sensitive' for my book is available to the public. One such redacted phrase, the unofficial term used for an Army Special Operations unit stationed out of Fort Bragg, North Carolina, was used, unredacted, over nine-hundred times in a nonfiction account that detailed the history of the United States' various Special Operations Commands. My book references this unit nine times, and it remains redacted.

But I have an obligation to follow the guidelines set out by the DoD, and I will maintain the redactions per their guidance. As you read this book, take a moment to sit and think about what the government deemed too sensitive for you to read. Even better, try and figure out which term applies where within the story.

All in all, I hope that the redactions, where they remain, do not detract from your enjoyment of the story. Thank you for your support by purchasing this novel, and I truly hope you enjoy the read.

Zach James
January 24th, 2021
Northern Virginia

DECEPTION

1
April, 2018
El Alto, Bolivia

The two Bell UH-1 Iroquois helicopters flew in a loose formation, with the rear bird behind and to the left of the lead. The two helicopters had been launched ten minutes prior from La Paz-El Alto International Airport and were quickly making their way Northwest to the outskirts of El Alto. They were out hunting.

Each bird was loaded with twelve men from the *Fuerza Especial de Lucha Contra el Narcotráfico*, or FELCN: Bolivia's Special Anti-narcotics Force. Being that this raid would mainly be in urban areas, they had forgone their woodland camouflage uniforms and wore black fatigues. Each FELCN trooper wore matching black body armor and had their faces concealed beneath balaclavas.

Along with the black-clad Bolivian police, each bird also carried a single man dressed more casually than their South American counterparts. In the first bird, a man dressed in a blue polo shirt and brown cargo pants beneath his armored plate carrier vest sat with his back against the rear wall of the helo.

Morgan Tyron wasn't used to sitting in the back of helicopters. He'd grown accustomed to being in the cockpit, hands on the controls and in charge of his bird's destiny. Having spent his career in the United States Army as a pilot in the 160th Special Operations Aviation Regiment, more commonly known as the Nighstalkers, being in the back was something that would take some getting used to.

The American in the second helo had spent much more time in the back of various models of helicopters throughout his own military career, having previously been a member of the Army's elite Special Missions Unit, more commonly known as ▮▮▮▮▮▮▮▮. Alex Foaly, dressed in a pair of jeans and a tan button-up fishing shirt beneath his armor, leaned forward in his seat to get a better view of the city passing below.

"Anything?" Morgan asked, his voice clear through the Peltor headset that Foaly wore over his ears, muffling the otherwise deafening sound of the Huey's rotors.

"Nothing yet." Foaly replied coolly.

In his chopper, Morgan toggled his radio back to the tactical net. Being that Foaly wasn't fluent in Spanish, Tyron was acting as a translator between the FELCN troops and the former operator in the back of the second bird. He listened to the Bolivian pilots for a few moments, then switched back to his team net.

"Vinny, anything?" Morgan asked.

"Negative." Vincent Jensen, the third man of their team, replied. Vinny was on the ground as part of a five-vehicle convoy. The FELCN ground element had departed the airport before the helicopters, coordinating with the air assets to ensure they would link up on the objective at the same time.

The three Americans were private contractors, though that was just the word used in the sterilized world they lived in nowadays. In reality, their jobs fit the old school definition of mercenaries. Morgan was the 'team lead' being that he was the chief executive officer of their three-man corporation, Integral Solutions Consulting. Following their getting out of the military, Morgan had contacted the two former operators and offered them jobs as hired guns. Both men accepted, and they started doing small time gigs here and there, mostly in the Middle East and South America. It had been a surprise when Morgan had been contacted directly by the Bolivian government, and the contract was signed between him and a Bolivian representative at the Consulate General of Bolivia right in Manhattan shortly thereafter.

Integral Solutions had been hired to assist the FELCN in going after Gabriel Lasanta, a Colombian drug and gun runner who had built himself a small army in El Alto. Having been raised by a father who'd been a heavy hitter for the Medellin Cartel during its heyday, Lasanta had followed, and expanded the family business, forming a widespread network to move guns in and out of Colombia to supply the FARC. When the *Compañia Jungla Antinarcóticos*, Colombia's anti-narcotics Jungle Company known simply as JUNGLA, forced Lasanta out of Magangué, he relocated himself to El Alto and started the whole process again.

With drugs and guns flooding into the relatively peaceful region of El Alto and then spilling over into La Paz, the Bolivian government had tried to stamp out Lasanta right away. First they sent in local police, and then *Grupo Especial de Seguridad*, Bolivia's Special Security Group, to oust the fledgling drug lord. When twenty-seven Bolivian police and fifteen civilians were killed, Integral Solutions got the call.

"We're approaching the target site now." Vinny said over the comms. "We're going to dismount and move in on foot. Recommend you guys maintain standoff until we're able to get positive ID on the target."

"Roger." Morgan answered, then switched channels and informed the pilots. He got affirmatives back, and the two helicopters kept their distance as they waited for word to come from the ground element.

2
El Alto, Bolivia

Vinny hopped out of the gray SUV and shut the door behind him as the rest of the troopers he was attached to did the same, spreading out and telling locals to get indoors. Like Morgan and Alex, Vinny was dressed in plainclothes as well, wearing a gray t-shirt and a set of Carhartt cargo pants beneath his tac gear.

"Locals say that they're two blocks to our west." The FELCN ground element commander, Fausto Ramirez, relayed to Vinny.

"Okay. We'll move in on foot and call the helicopters once we're close." Vinny replied. His time with the US Navy SEALs had him deploy to South America multiple times, so he had a basic grasp of the language. What he didn't know, he could pantomime. So far there hadn't been any communication issues.

Vinny did a quick check to ensure his FN Mk-16, more commonly known as the SCAR-L, was loaded. A quick press-check showed his Sig Sauer P226 pistol was also set. With that, he gave a nod to Ramirez and they continued quietly down the street.

The local intel had been correct. The ground unit moved up to see Lasanta leaving the apartment building he resided in. Lasanta had turned the entire upper floor into his own residence, which he'd just exited and was now walking towards a three-vehicle convoy that was waiting for him. The rear vehicle was a dilapidated pickup truck with a .50 caliber machine gun mounted in the bed. *Cocky bastard.* Vinny thought to himself.

The immediate area was filled with Lasanta's local fighters. The fighters ranged in age from as young as fifteen to as old as mid-forties, and it surprised Vinny to see that there were even a few girls and women interspersed through the ranks. Uniformity was no such thing; each wore regular street clothes and old-school web gear or carried their equipment in handmade satchels. Once the shooting started and civilians joined the mix, it would get very difficult to ID targets.

"We've got eyes on the objective." Vinny said into his microphone. "Be advised, at least one technical with a ma-deuce. I'll take out the heavy gunner and you guys fly in."

"Roger that, we're three mikes out." Morgan replied. Vinny could faintly hear the beating rotors of the incoming helicopters. He watched through the optic mounted to the top of his rifle as Lasanta stopped to talk with one fighter, laughing and slapping the younger man on the shoulder.

Lasanta was a short man, coming in at barely five-foot-six, with two hundred and forty pounds of a lot of fat and little muscle packed into his small frame. His stature made him easy to spot among the thinner population of Bolivians, and the bright floral shirt he wore made ID'ing him all that easier. Now the man stopped and kicked a soccer ball back towards a child, who ran out and stopped it with his foot. This got a cheer from Lasanta, and a couple of his goons smiled. It disgusted Vinny.

The cheering stopped as one of the FELCN helicopters roared overhead. When they spied the black-clad troopers sitting in the open doors, legs hanging Ranger-style, Lasanta quickly ordered his men to open fire. The militiaman behind the M2 began rotating the large weapon, but that was quickly put to an end when Vinny popped the guy twice in the head.

Vinny's rifle shots set everything off. FELCN officers stormed from cover, firing their weapons and shouting for the militia to get on the ground. A few complied, and others turned their weapons on the Bolivian police. They were quickly cut down with rapid, well-placed shots. Vinny watched through his rifle's sights as Lasanta took off at a run from the chaos that had exploded around him.

3
El Alto, Bolivia

"Lasanta's making a run for it." Vinny relayed over the radio as Morgan and Foaly both hopped from their helicopters, which had touched down in a barren lot that had been turned into a makeshift soccer field.

"We're on the ground." Morgan replied. Foaly was already moving forward, his Heckler & Koch 416 rifle in his shoulder as he fired at nearby gunmen. Morgan brought his own rifle up and opened fire, then saw Foaly take off at a run when he spotted Lasanta's bright yellow shirt. "Alex, hostiles on the roof!" Morgan yelled, firing. One of them had an RPG launcher on his shoulder. Morgan's rounds tore through the teenager's body and he pitched back, sending the RPG streaking wildly off target. It impacted the ground between three FELCN, sending the men flying through the air. Morgan took off after the others.

Foaly and Vinny rounded a corner and saw Lasanta had stopped a vehicle at gunpoint and was pulling the driver out from behind the wheel. The fat man got into the car and slammed the door shut, peeling away before either could put some rounds through the engine block.

"Shit." Vinny said, stopping behind Foaly who was standing near the man Lasanta had car jacked. Without warning, Foaly whipped around and brought up his rifle, aiming it at an approaching man on a motorcycle. The man hit the throttle and shot past them, turning down an alley.

"Fuck." Foaly said. "Morgan, Lasanta's got a vehicle, we need to get some wheels so-" He stopped when a pickup truck emerged from a side street and plowed into the side of Lasanta's vehicle, pushing the t-boned car until it was pinned against a wall.

Vinny and Foaly ran forward as Morgan climbed out of the truck, putting a dozen rounds into the engine of Lasanta's car to ensure the man wouldn't try to run them down. The driver's side door opened and Lasanta spilled out onto the street, obviously dazed. Foaly kicked Lasanta down before dropping a knee into the small of the man's back and frisking him. Once that was set, he secured Lasanta's wrists behind his back with flex-cuffs and forced the man to his feet. Morgan and Vinny watched the nearby rooftops as Foaly shoved the target into the backseat of the truck.

"Let's go." Foaly said, climbing into the driver's seat. A burst of gunfire rang out and a bullet passed through the top of the truck's cab, narrowly missing Foaly by a few inches.

"Contact!" Morgan called out. Vinny posted up against the side of the truck and returned fire at the group of fighters that had appeared on a rooftop across the street. The inexperienced wannabe-narcos were quickly cut down. Morgan ran around and climbed into the passenger seat while Vinny climbed into the back, forcing Lasanta down behind the seats so he wouldn't catch a stray round. Foaly turned the truck on, fumbled to put it into reverse, and started cursing when it stalled. He quickly started the engine again, and this time was successful in getting them off the street and on their way back towards the airport.

4
El Alto, Bolivia

Morgan had just relayed to the FELCN commander that they had secured Lasanta and were on their way back to the airport.

"Roger. We are heading back with the detainees now." Ramirez replied. While the Americans had gone after Lasanta, the FELCN had kept themselves busy rolling up Lasanta's fighters who hadn't been gunned down.

"VIC from the rear!" Vinny yelled, now facing backwards in his seat. "Looks like three trucks packed with bad guys." He said as he jacked a new mag into his SCAR. Foaly looked at the rearview mirror, then flinched as the mirror disappeared when a round tore through it, sending a spider web of cracks through the windshield.

"Fuck." Foaly grunted, gripping the steering wheel with his left hand, and pushing against the ruined glass with his right. It wasn't budging. "Morgan, give me a hand!"

Morgan leaned back in his chair and brought his leg up, smashing his booted foot into the glass. It shuddered but stayed strong.

"Again!" Foaly yelled. Morgan did it again and it budged a little more. A third kick sent the entire windshield off its frame, slamming forward against the truck's hood. The cracked glass slid sideways and disappeared behind them as they sped away. Both Foaly and Morgan looked confused as the windshield wipers began swiping up and down against the open air where the windshield had been a moment ago. Foaly went to turn them off but saw a bullet had snapped off the wiper controls next to the steering wheel, less than an inch from his torso. He returned his gaze back to the road, concentrating on driving despite the wipers waving uselessly in front of his face.

"Watch out!" Morgan yelled. Foaly looked up at the driver's side mirror as another vehicle peeled out of a side street and impacted with the rear panel on the driver's side, pitting the truck. Before he could recover, another car slammed into the truck, the driver glaring through Foaly's window from behind the wheel. Foaly drew his pistol from the cross-draw holster on his vest and shot the driver and his passengers from his seated position.

"Everyone good?" Foaly asked as he reloaded his sidearm.

"Good!" Morgan said, kicking his own door open.

"Solid back here." Vinny called out.

"What about Lasanta?" Foaly asked as he climbed over the center console to get out through Morgan's door. He cursed as the stick-shift snagged a piece of his kit, and he reached back to free himself.

"He's awake." Vinny said, his left hand curled in Lasanta's shirt as he yanked the man from the truck.

"Hold onto him Vin, I don't want him bolting." Foaly said, checking to make sure his rifle was alright. "We'll continue on foot. Morgan, see if they can get a bird out to us." He looked around and saw the street was rapidly clearing. "And tell them to hurry!" He brought his weapon up as another militia truck turned onto the street, the passengers leaning out of windows to fire at them.

"Cobra, this is Blackbird." Morgan said as he fired at the incoming truck. *"Our vehicle is disabled. We're going to continue on foot and try to reach an LZ for you to pick us up!"*

18

DECEPTION

"Negative, Blackbird. We can't get air support to you at this time." Ramirez replied.

"Why the fuck not?" Morgan yelled, ducking low as a round struck the wall near him and sent a puff of concrete dust into his face.

"The helicopters are refueling, and there's a lot of RPGs on the rooftops." Ramirez said. *"You need to get closer to the airport before we can pick you up."*

"Fuck!" Morgan yelled. "The birds can't pick us up, we need to get closer." Foaly ducked down and looked at the GPS strapped to his left wrist. They still had several blocks between them and the area that was under Bolivian police control.

"Get ready to run!" Foaly said, grabbing a fragmentation grenade from his vest in his right hand, and a smoke in his left. He pulled the pin on the frag and tossed it before doing the same with the smoke, lobbing the second grenade a few seconds after the first.

The fragmentation grenade exploded just as dark gray smoke began to billow from the now-burning container, quickly filling the street and obscuring the view between the two warring groups.

"Go!" Foaly yelled, grabbing Lasanta by the back of the collar and kicking off into a run as they all started towards relative safety, at least compared to their current situation.

5
El Alto, Bolivia

Morgan's entire body was in pain from sprinting the last five 'blocks'. Unlike Manhattan, which had relatively uniform standards for how blocks were laid out, the ones in El Alto varied in shape and size. It had been a workout. His muscles burned as if his veins were pumping battery acid, and his lungs were screaming for air as his feet thudded against the hard ground. He glanced behind him and saw Foaly was only a few feet behind, Lasanta in tow. The large man was stumbling as Foaly struggled to keep the man moving forward, his fat body threatening to send both tumbling to the ground.

Foaly's face was drenched. Sweat poured off him and the shirt beneath his black tactical vest was soaked through. Despite that, and his heavy baggage, Alex was still able to keep pace. Morgan returned his gaze to the front and was surprised to see a crowd of people staring at them as they ran through the streets. Many began clapping and cheering, praising them as Lasanta's captors. The cheers were cut short when the militia opened fire, cutting down several innocents and causing the rest to run for cover.

"Agh, fuck!" Foaly yelled. Morgan whirled around to see Lasanta standing there and Foaly on the ground. Lasanta stared at Foaly for a moment, then met Morgan's gaze before bolting down a side alley. Vinny returned fire while Morgan moved toward their fallen man. Foaly waved them off.

"I'm fine!" Foaly grunted. "Grab Lasanta!" He yelled through gritted teeth. With that, Morgan and Vinny bolted down the alley after their target.

DECEPTION

"Doorway, right side!" Vinny yelled as he watched Lasanta rip open a door and run inside. As much as it sucked, both men pumped their legs harder to catch up. If they lost him in one of the sprawling housing areas, then all of this would have been for nothing.

6
El Alto, Bolivia

Foaly stumbled down an alleyway and fell against the wall beside an overflowing dumpster, gasping for breath. He was struggling to breathe because it felt like someone had hit him with a truck. One of Lasanta's militia had pulled off a lucky shot, and Foaly could feel liquid running down his back. Hoping he wouldn't find blood, he reached back and pressed a gloved hand against his lower spine, feeling the liquid soak into his glove. He looked down and sighed in relief to see it was just water. The round had torn through the CamelBak water bladder attached to his vest but had been stopped by the body armor plate. He took a few more moments to get his breathing under control, then keyed the push-to-talk on his vest.

"Morgan, tell them we're going to need a rooftop extract ASAP." He said. Things were getting hairy down there.

"What's your position?" Morgan asked. He looked down at his GPS and relayed his relative position. Morgan grunted. "Alright, I'll see what we can do."

Foaly was about to reply but was interrupted when a militiaman ran around the dumpster and slammed into him. Foaly clamped his hands around his attacker's wrists, struggling to keep the man from sinking the large knife he held into his throat.

7
El Alto, Bolivia

Morgan slammed his attacker against the stucco wall and shot him twice in the stomach before throwing him down the stairs of the small house they'd charged into after Foaly's call had been interrupted. Vinny had Lasanta by the arm, his pistol jammed into the man's back.

"Extract is on the way; we need to get to the roof!" Morgan yelled, running up a flight of stairs that felt like they were made of Balsa Wood before kicking open the small door that opened to the rooftop. He watched as a helicopter approached.

"That's us on the rooftop to your one o' clock!" Morgan yelled as he waved his left arm. The Huey slowed and flared, lowering itself toward the roof. A few FELCN troopers sat in the back, firing down at the fighters on the street. A crew chief, dressed in a tan flight suit, waved for them to approach. The bird was hovering a few feet from the edge of the roof, the pilots knowing that if they set down it would collapse beneath them. Morgan jumped for it and was caught by the crew chief, who pulled him out of the way as Lasanta landed in the bird. Vinny landed on top of Lasanta a few seconds later, pinning the man to the decking. Neither American stopped the few FELCN that rained blows down on Lasanta before another crew chief waved them off and dragged the man towards the cockpit.

"We're clear!" The crew chief yelled as he and the other chief secured the target. The man tried to struggle and was rewarded with a pistol smashed across his face by one of the Bolivians. Morgan slid himself to the door, seated between two FELCN. His eyes grew wide at the literal wave of people that was rushing down the street.

23

"Alex, come in!" He yelled over the radio. A moment passed and he got no response. "Alex!"

"RPG!" One of the troopers yelled. The pilot pitched the bird to the right and Morgan lost his balance, tumbling forward. His ass left the decking of the helo, and he was staring at nothing but air between him and the ground. It was then he remembered he hadn't snapped in his safety line.

He frantically reached out to grab ahold of something, anything, that would keep him from plunging back to Earth. Then his back slammed into something hard. He looked and saw several gloved hands wrapped around his arms and gripping his vest as Vinny, the FELCN, and a crew chief pulled him back into the bird. Once inside, Morgan snapped his safety line into place as he got his breathing under control, then he radioed for Alex again.

8
El Alto, Bolivia

Foaly ran down the street as fast as he could. Gunshots rang out from behind as the militia tried to gun him down, stray bullets whizzing all around him. Some of the closer calls kicked up dirt around his feet and *snapped* just past his ears.

"Alex, what is your position?" Morgan yelled over the radio for the third time.

"I don't know!" Foaly replied. "Have the bird circle until I get to a roof!" He saw an open door to one of the complexes and dove inside. He landed on his back and kicked the door closed, scooting backwards. Bullets tore through the door and the sounds of the yelling militia grew closer. Foaly flipped onto his stomach and got to his feet, looking for a way onto the roof.

There was a ladder against one of the walls with a hatch in the ceiling. He quickly climbed the rickety ladder, which creaked and strained beneath his weight. When he was through the hatch, he kicked the ladder down before closing the small opening behind him. The helicopter flew overhead, and Foaly saw Morgan sitting between the Bolivian troops. Their weapons snapped up, and they began firing into the crowded gunmen below.

"Hurry!" Morgan yelled. Foaly didn't dare turn around as he sprinted across the corrugated metal rooftops. He reached the edge of the roof and jumped, clearing the gap between the two rooftops. Once he was in the air, it occurred to him that the thin metal might not be able to handle the impact of his landing and could threaten to send him plummeting right back inside. Straight into the hornet's nest.

25

He landed on the roof and rolled, popping right to his feet and continuing in a dead sprint towards the edge of the roof as the bird lowered itself until it was hovering near the edge.

"Move!" Vinny yelled over the radio. Foaly could see Vinny standing in the helo, waving Foaly on. Alex grunted and pumped his legs with every ounce of energy he had. Morgan, Vinny, the FELCN, and the crew chiefs were now all firing, and Foaly could hear the rounds *snapping* past him.

He reached the edge of the rooftop and used the last of his energy to jump for the helicopter, which was drifting away from the roof at the same time. Foaly realized too late that he hadn't jumped hard enough. He wasn't going to make it.

Then Morgan was hanging halfway out of the helicopter, one hand latched around the shoulder-strap of Foaly's vest. Foaly reached up and grabbed the hand of the FELCN trooper beside Morgan, and the two of them pulled the man inside. Foaly tumbled into the crew bay, panting. He looked to see a flex cuffed Lasanta sitting there with a bag over his head.

"You're one lucky son of a bitch!" One of the FELCN men yelled. The words were lost to Foaly, but he got the general gist of what the guy was saying. Foaly nodded, panting as he raised a fist and bumped the Bolivian's waiting hand. He scooted back and leaned against the fuselage of the helo, watching as El Alto retreated into the distance.

9
Murray Hill, New York

Morgan opened the door to his apartment and saw the lights were off. He'd called his wife, Julia, when he'd landed at Newark. She'd said that she wouldn't be home until around six o' clock that evening. He looked around the small place and saw that she'd tidied up in his absence. The living room/dining room/office had been a mess when he'd left for South America, with papers scattered about. Now it actually resembled what it was supposed to be.

Thankfully, traffic from Newark to Murray Hill hadn't been terrible, so he'd made it home with a minimal headache. He set his bags down and sat in front of his computer, booting it up. While he waited for the machine to start, he pulled off his shoes and set them on a mat beside the door. He then shrugged off his jacket and hung it in the closet, before sliding his Springfield Operator M1911 from the holster on his belt and set it on the desk, the barrel facing the wall.

Still waiting on the computer, which seemed to be moving extra slow today, Morgan looked at the stack of mail in a plastic tray labeled 'inbox'. The stack was tall enough that it was beginning to lean to one side, threatening to spill everywhere if it was disturbed.

With the computer finally booted up, he opened his email and began sifting through the messages. Most of them were junk, but there were a few that he flagged for thorough reading. The one that interested him the most was from one Ian MacMiller. Morgan had met Ian, a former Marine sniper, at a bar a few months prior in Middletown, New York, where both had been attending a local gun show held at the Orange County fairgrounds.

The two hit it off after discovering they were both gun nuts.

Ian had worked for both Heckler & Koch as well as Remington before leaving to begin his Associate of Science in firearms technology from Sonoran Desert Institute. During their discussions, Ian had expressed interest in some of the ideas that Morgan had, and business cards were quickly swapped.

Nowadays, Ian kept Morgan in the loop on what was going on in the private sector of the global defense world, as well as changes that many of the world's militaries were making weapon-wise to keep them ahead of the market for research and development.

After sorting through the rest of his emails and ordering a G-Shock wristwatch from Amazon to replace the watch that had ended up getting broken in Bolivia, he turned on some music and picked up his pistol. He carried the .45 with one hand as he sat down on the couch. The pistol went across his lap as he rolled out a large, oil-stained towel on the coffee table, along with a cleaning kit. Once that was all laid out, he turned on the news and began to disassemble the handgun. He couldn't wait to see what mindless bullshit the mainstream media would be focused on today, knowing full well that their efforts and success with the Bolivian government would go without mention.

DECEPTION

10
Upper East Side, New York

Foaly stepped into his apartment and sat his bags by the door. He was happy to be back home. He grunted in pain as he stood back up. Getting shot was never fun, and he'd been lucky that his plate had stopped it. He hadn't been so lucky in the past, and he had scars that showed he'd paid that price.

He walked into the kitchen and saw a stack of mail waiting for him on the counter. This got a smirk out of him. *Seems I only get mail whenever I'm gone.* He thought to himself. They'd only been in Bolivia for nine days, but the stack looked like more mail than he'd gotten during the previous two months home. Foaly ignored the mail and opened his liquor cabinet, pulling out a bottle of scotch and a glass tumbler. He placed three ice cubes in the glass and poured himself two fingers, replacing the bottle and grabbing the mail as he went to the living room.

The first piece of mail was from Foaly's mentor and adoptive father; Richard Gray. Foaly put the envelope to the side, planning on reading it before he inevitably fell asleep in a few hours. The next was from Foaly's cousin, Blake. It was a save-the-date card for Blake's wedding. Foaly frisbee'd the card into the garbage. There was no way he'd be attending the wedding. Blake was a prick who thought the world revolved around him and hadn't had the decency or respect to show up to either of Foaly's parents' burials, or his wedding.

Alex sifted through the rest of the mail and set it on the side table before leaning forward and unlacing his boots, sliding them off and setting them beside the couch.

He picked up the remote and turned on the television, flipping the channels until he was on BBC International.

"...and as the civil war in Angola rages on, many sources are saying that the actions from paramilitary companies, such as Saber Security International, have only added fuel to the already-burning wildfire. Their mostly-unwanted involvement in the conflict supporting President Osman has caused the Angolan rebel forces to increase their attacks. Over a dozen civilian casualties were reported from the last conflict between Saber Security and rebel forces, and President Osman is being urged to expel the paramilitary fighters from the country lest he suffer losing support from pro-Osman regimes whose families have been caught in the crossfire..." The reporter continued. Foaly sighed and leaned back as the report went on.

Private firms like Saber Security International and the Jolly Roger Corporation had come up during the Second Gulf War as guns-for-hire in Iraq and Afghanistan. Despite the backlash that PMCs faced after the witch hunt that almost put Blackwater out of business, the companies continued to grow and force their way into other conflicts around the world. Nowadays, one would be hard pressed to look at any conflict without seeing contractors of some type being involved, and most were causing more harm than help.

Foaly looked at the table when the screen of his phone lit up. He picked it up and the Caller ID showed it was Morgan calling. The picture displayed was of Morgan and Foaly's grinning faces, covered in dirt and grime. Vinny had snapped the picture of them after a firefight on their first job together down in Nicaragua.

"Yeah." Foaly said as he put the phone to his ear.

"You watching the news?" Morgan asked.

"Yep." Foaly said as he set his now-empty scotch glass on the table. "Looks like Saber is screwing the pooch down in Angola."

"And to think they beat us out for that job." Morgan said, disgusted. "It's a total clusterfuck thanks to those idiots."

"Who knows. If Osman kicks them out, the contract might be up for a rebid." Foaly replied, grunting as he stretched his injured back. He'd already scheduled an appointment with his chiropractor in two days.

"The last thing that place needs is more white dudes running around killing whoever the 'government' tells them to." Morgan said. Foaly nodded, glad they were of the same mindset. The way the conflict was going, Angola was on a fast track to become Africa's west-coast Somalia.

11
Two Bridges, New York

Foaly pulled his truck into the mostly empty lot and put it in park, zipping up his windbreaker before stepping out into the rain. A tropical storm had come up the coast and was hitting New York City hard. Rain pattered loudly against his windbreaker's hood as he retrieved his bags from the back seat. He looked up to see Morgan's truck and Vinny's Jeep pull up and park beside his black Toyota Tacoma.

"Morning, guys." Foaly said with a smile. They returned the greeting as they retrieved their own bags and began walking towards the large storage container marked C-137. They were at the Two Bridges Storage Company, located in a large lot right off Pike Slip and South Street. Two Bridges Storage Company was identical to any one of the cookie-cutter self-storage facilities located throughout the United States, with rows of large metal containers side-by-side with rolling doors on the front and smaller doors on the sides. Container C-137 was unlike the rest though.

After putting down the initial security deposit, the three contractors had measured out the dimensions of the container's interior. That information had been sent to a company that custom-made vaults, safe rooms, and panic rooms. They built, transported, and installed the vault inside the container. Now the rolling door revealed nothing but a steel wall, and the side door opened to another door that could only be opened through biometrics and a passcode that was only known by the three contractors. Morgan had gone through and wired an additional alarm that had to be disarmed within a minute of the door being opened. If not, an alert would be blasted out to them as well as to the NYPD and State Police if someone did manage to get in but didn't know the seven-digit code to punch into the keypad set beside the door on the inside of the vault.

"Welcome home, boys." Morgan said as he pressed the tip of his index finger against the biometric scanner and the heavy locks disengaged with an audible click. He pushed the door inwards and stepped in, turning on the lights as he punched in the secondary code.

It took a moment for the track lighting to illuminate completely, lighting up the interior of the fifteen-foot-wide by twenty-foot-long vault. After the vault had been installed, they'd moved metal wall lockers and installed shelves that held Pelican cases so that everything could be stored in a proper fashion. Sitting in the center of the vault was a large steel table. Along with their weapons and equipment, they also kept three full sleeping systems that consisted of camping cots, sleeping bags, field blankets, and pillows. There were also a few cases of MREs and freeze-dried foods as a contingency in case they needed to hunker down in the vault for a few days.

Foaly walked over to his locker and unlocked it, pulling open the double doors. Hanging on the rack inside was the MultiCam vest that he'd worn while he was in the military. It was the same model as the black one he wore as a contractor, and still had his old pouches mounted on it, as well as the large three-by-five-inch full-color American Flag patch affixed to the front. Foaly pulled his black vest out and hung it on a heavy-duty hanger beside his old carrier.

The interior of the locker was a smaller version of the ones he'd had in the 'cages' of the locker room back in the ███ compound on Fort Bragg. On the shelf above his vests rested two helmets, one ballistic and one non-ballistic bump helmet, both made by OPS-Core. On other shelves sat containers that held spare sets of gloves, magazines, batteries for equipment, pouches, and other items that he needed as a private mercenary.

His eyes rested on the two strips of Velcro tape he'd attached to the inside of one of the locker doors and the patches affixed to them. The first two were two of his call sign patches from his last assignment as a team lead, and under that was the worn, subdued American flag patch he'd worn on his shoulder. Looking at the patches brought him back to thinking about his old team.

"Alex, you with us?" Vinny asked, breaking Foaly's concentration.

"Yeah, yeah." Foaly said, turning around and reaching back into his duffel bag on the table. Morgan and Vinny were keeping themselves busy going back and forth between their bags and lockers. Morgan opened his rifle case and retrieved the Daniel Defense Mk18 short-barreled rifle, setting it to the side so he could clean it once everything else was put away. Cleaning and stowing the equipment was a ritual they always did the day after they returned from a job, no matter how tired or crappy they felt. They all understood the importance of maintaining their gear. Whether it had been pre-flights and maintenance for Morgan or kitting up for raids like Vinny and Alex. If their gear failed them in the field, it more than likely meant death.

Foaly remembered that he had to replace the plate in his vest and pulled the plate carrier back out. He grabbed a new plate from a box next to his locker and set it on the table beside his vest.

DECEPTION

"We really should invest in some multi-strike plates." Foaly said as he undid the Velcro and pulled the plate out from the bottom of the carrier. He'd used multi-strike plates when in the Unit, and they'd saved his ass on more than one occasion.

"I'll look into it, but the things are just so damned expensive." Morgan said as he detached the chest rig from the front of his vest and smacked it to get any dirt from the tan pouches. Foaly held up the plate that had saved his life, turning it from side to side. He was looking at the three large cracks that ran from the bullet's point of impact, which would have likely severed his spine. He tossed the ruined plate to the side and it broke into three separate pieces, breaking along the cracks. With that done, he put the new plate in place and returned the vest to the locker.

Next, he went to cleaning his weapon. Alex picked up his HK 416 and broke it open, laying out the individual components on a large towel. The 416 had been Foaly's weapon of choice after passing ████ selection in 2009. Following his discharge and being hired on by Morgan, Foaly put in an order for the weapon along with a couple of replacement barrels. Once it was in his hands, he couldn't even tell that it wasn't the same one he'd carried across the mountains of Afghanistan so many times before.

Lost in thought while cleaning, Foaly took a moment and looked up to see how the rest of the guys were doing. Vinny was cleaning his Sig Sauer P226, and Morgan had just reassembled his rifle and was now field stripping his pistol, bobbing his head to the sound of Metallica's *For Whom the Bell Tolls* playing from his phone.

"Ow!" Vinny said. Foaly and Morgan looked up to see Vinny waving his hand. "Son of a bitch!" Foaly

35

noticed that the slide of Vinny's pistol had closed, probably down onto the man's thumb. Both men gave sarcastic remarks to their friend, whose thumb was already beginning to bruise, before returning to their weapons. There was a lull between songs and Vinny decided to spark up a conversation.

"Sooo, how are the wives?" Vinny asked, mimicking the speech patterns of a Long Island hairdresser. Morgan rolled his eyes while Foaly chuckled and shook his head. Goofy bastard.

"Julia was happy." Morgan said, popping the bubble of his gum on the first word. "Ended up going out and meeting with some old friends up in Newburgh. Dinner on the waterfront, all that jazz."

"Nice." Vinny said. "Alex?"

"Shannon's been swamped with work, so we just stayed in. The usual." Foaly said. His wife, Shannon, was an attorney at a Lenox Hill-based firm. Alex would always be the first to admit that Shannon had the more difficult job between the two of them. "How about yourself, Vin?"

"I fed Juniper and fell asleep on the couch." Vinny said as he locked the slide of his rifle back. Foaly smirked. Vinny was a divorcee from his time in the SEALs, so he filled his free time with working out, going on few and far between dates, and taking care of the scorpion he'd successfully smuggled out of Iran. Foaly wasn't a fan of creepy crawlies, and the *Hemiscorpius acanthocercus* that was Vinny's roommate in his studio apartment made the hairs on the back of Foaly's neck stand on end. That damned tail was the worst part.

"Anything lined up for the next job?" Foaly asked as he set his weapons on the table following the final application of lubricant to the parts that needed it.

"None yet." Morgan said, not looking up as he ran a rag along the slide of his 1911. It was already clean, polishing the slide was just something he did out of habit now. "I'll check for RFIs and RFPs and send out a few emails sometime next week to see what comes back. I'd like to relax a little before we take another assignment, considering how sideways Bolivia went." *Especially for you, Alex*. Morgan omitted.

"You're telling me." Foaly chuckled. His back was bruised and sore as hell. Shannon had not been pleased when she saw the bruising the night prior. "Sounds like a plan." The checks from the Bolivian government had come through, and with that padding their bank accounts, they wouldn't be hurting for work in the near future. With his weapons and equipment taken care of, Foaly placed them in their respective slots in his locker before retrieving his Glock 19 and press-checking it. Satisfied to see the brass of the hollow-point round in the chamber, he let the slide forward and slipped the handgun into the holster on his belt, covering it all with his windbreaker. "I've got some things to take care of. I'll catch you guys later."

"See ya." Morgan said. Vinny smiled and waved. Foaly returned the gesture before stepping out into the lot. He spotted a homeless man lingering near Morgan's truck.

"Careful old timer, the guy who owns that is likely to shoot first and ask questions later." Foaly said, only half-joking.

"It's a nice ride!" The old man replied, smiling with yellowed teeth. "Don't s'pose you'd spare an old man some change?" Foaly stopped in front of his truck and reached into his pocket, pulling out a loose five-dollar bill.

"Here." Foaly said, holding the folded and wrinkled bill towards the man. The vagrant reached forward with tattered, fingerless gloves and took the money.

"God bless you, sir." The man said, taking a bow.

"Alright, alright. Take it easy." Foaly chuckled as he started towards his own ride. "And seriously, my friend catches you around his truck he won't hesitate to pop your old ass!" The man replied with a loud grumble and started walking away. *Takes care of my good deed for the day.* Foaly thought to himself as he pulled away from the lot.

12
Murray Hill, New York

Morgan came home to the sound of lo-fi music and the smell of something cooking wafting from the kitchen. He closed the front door and peeked into the kitchen to see Julia dancing to the music as she cooked what appeared to be stir fry. Her dirty-blonde hair hung down past her shoulders, and she was dressed in a t-shirt and a pair of shorts that showed off her toned legs and the bottom of the dream catcher tattoo she had on her right thigh.

"Hey babe." He said as he walked in. She turned to him and smiled.

"Hey you." She said, her soft features smiling at him. He smiled back and brushed a stray golden lock of hair from her face before she kissed him. "Everything all set?" She asked.

Julia was a real estate agent that he'd met while on leave visiting a friend in West Chester, Pennsylvania. She didn't understand too much about the world of private contracting, so she always kept her questions about his work to a minimum. That didn't mean she wasn't worried about him though, especially when he came home injured.

"Yep, everything's set." He said.

"How are Alex and Vinny?"

"They're good, glad to be home." Morgan hadn't told Julia about how Foaly had been shot on the last job. He didn't need her worrying more than she already did. That, and he knew she'd hear it from Shannon eventually.

"I'm just glad you're all home and safe." She said. "We should all go out sometime. It's been a while."

"I think that's an excellent idea." Morgan said. "How long until dinner's ready? Smells awesome."

"Probably another twenty minutes or so. Go relax, I'll let you know when it's all set." She said, then kissed him again. He replied with a kiss on her cheek and a smack on her ass before walking over to their shared desk. He sat in the chair and watched as the images of their screensaver scrolled past, switching every fifteen seconds.

The one currently on the screen had been snapped on their wedding day four years prior. Morgan had been dressed in the Army's old Class A 'pickle suit' uniform with his maroon beret on his head. Four years felt like yesterday on some days, and a lifetime on others.

The next photo was of Morgan. He stood shirtless on a rocky cliff, his arms out to his sides and a big smile on his face. That had been taken when he'd been doing some training flights around Fort Huachuca. He'd taken every opportunity to hike the Arizona mountains surrounding the Army's Military Intelligence Training Center with his fellow pilots, and they'd loved every minute of it.

His throat went dry at the next photo. It was a screenshot grabbed from helmet cam footage from a GoPro that one of the Rangers had been wearing that day. In the picture, Morgan was dressed in his camouflage flight fatigues and MultiCam vest, being supported between Foaly and Vinny. That was the day that Morgan's helicopter had been shot down. Foaly had spearheaded the recovery effort and Vinny's team had been absorbed into the larger group that had gone to the crash site.

Staring at the picture, a slight pain began to radiate up Morgan's left leg, and the smell of burning aviation fuel filled his nostrils as he thought back to that day.

13
Englewood, New Jersey

Foaly walked through the large double doors of Heartfield Retirement Home and made a beeline towards the receptionist's desk.

"Good morning." The cheery receptionist, a cute blonde in her mid-twenties, said with a smile. "How may I help you today?"

"Alex Foaly here to see Richard Gray." Foaly said, handing her his driver's license. She looked at the photo on his ID, then at his face, before she tapped away at her keyboard. A moment later the compact printer beside the keyboard spat out a small visitor's pass with his name on it.

"Okay Mister Foaly, you're all set. You know what room he's in?" She asked as she held the sticker towards him. She must have been new.

"Yep, I'm all set. Thanks." Foaly said, returning her smile as he stuck the pass to the front of his jacket before starting down the hall.

Richard Gray was a retired Gunnery Sergeant and CIA operative that had fought beside Foaly's father, Thomas Foaly, during Vietnam. Foaly's father had been an Infantryman while Gray had been deployed with the Military Assistance Command, Vietnam - Studies and Observations Group, more commonly known as MACV-SOG. It had been Gray who'd recruited Thomas Foaly into the Central Intelligence Agency following Vietnam, and the two worked together all over Eastern Europe and the Middle East during the Cold War. Their final assignment together had been in Iraq during the First Gulf War in

1991. It was there that Gray had been injured, resulting in the loss of use in his legs.

When Thomas Foaly had been killed in Afghanistan in December of 2001, Gray took Alex Foaly in as his adoptive son, providing for the young man until he graduated high school. It was only after Alex had finished school, joined the Army, and gone off to war that Gray decided to officially retire, moving to New Jersey to live out his golden years in one of the few states his government-paid pension would afford.

Foaly stepped up to Gray's door and knocked.

"Who is it?" Gray called from inside. Foaly smiled and tried the doorknob, surprised to find the front door unlocked. He poked his head past the threshold.

"Hey old man." Foaly said when he saw Gray sitting in his wheelchair in the middle of the living room, glaring towards the door.

"Hey kid!" Gray's eyes lit up when he realized it was Alex, and he started wheeling himself towards Foaly.

"You keep the door unlocked? You must be slipping." Foaly said with a sly smile.

"Fuck that. Assholes made a new rule where we can only lock the doors at night." Gray said as he stopped before Foaly and took his adoptive son's hand, giving it a hearty shake. Despite being eighty-six years old and restricted to a wheelchair, Gray still retained the strength and intensity from his days in the field, made apparent by his vice-like grip. It still didn't compare to that of Foaly's though. "How the hell are ya?"

"I'm doing good. Yourself?" Foaly asked as he walked over to the couch and sat down. He reached into his jacket pocket and pulled out a pack of Marlboro Red cigarettes, tossing them to Gray. The old man caught the pack with one-hand as he wheeled himself to the coffee table.

"Same shit different day, ya know?" The old man laughed. "What about yourself? Keeping busy with the job?" Foaly nodded.

"Yeah, just got back from Bolivia a few days ago." He said.

"Bolivia? That place is going to shit." Gray said as he lit one of his cigarettes.

"Yeah, I know." Foaly said with a smirk.

"Well you don't look too fucked up. Everything went well?" Gray asked, cigarette bouncing between his lips.

"For the most part." Foaly adjusted how he was sitting on the couch. "We got the guy we were going after, and no one bought it." Foaly paused a moment, looking at his old mentor. "I took one to the back, but my plate caught it." Gray's eyes widened with surprise and concern. "Like I said, my plate caught it. Left one hell of a bruise, but other than that I'm good." He said reassuringly.

"You're just like your old man." Gray laughed. "You boys got another job on deck?"

"Nah, not right now. We decided we're gonna take a bit of a break after the last one." Foaly looked down as his phone started to buzz. It was Shannon. "I gotta take this, it's Shannon." Gray waved Foaly to take it, smiling as he listened to one side of the conversation.

Gray had taken an almost instant liking to Shannon. She wasn't the usual beret-chaser, and actually had a personality. Her quick and snarky responses the first time Gray had met her had won him over, and when Foaly had told Gray that he was going to propose, Gray had chided Alex for waiting so long.

43

14
Upper East Side, New York

The punch caught Morgan off guard, sending him flying backwards as the breath exploded from his lungs. His back hit the wall of the octagon and he just barely managed to get his arms back up as Vinny moved in to deliver a barrage of strikes to Morgan's arms and stomach. Vinny backed off as Morgan fell to a knee, staying down for a moment before he regained his footing, wheezing as he rose.

"Come on dude, you've taken worse." Vinny said, smacking his hands together. The clapping sound was made louder by the black UFC gloves he wore. Morgan shook his head and raised his hands.

Vinny pivoted just in time to see Foaly charging him, but it was too late. Foaly wrapped his arms around Vinny's legs and performed a textbook double leg takedown. Both men crashed to the ground, with Vinny breaking Foaly's fall. Foaly then hopped up, arms raised, and bounced on his toes as he allowed Vinny to stand. Alex was focused on ground work today.

They were at Eastside Training, the mixed martial arts gym where they held their weekly beat-the-crap-out-of-each-other sessions while in the states. They would practice boxing, grappling, and other methods of hand-to-hand to make sure they were ready to go toe-to-toe with anyone while on a job. Morgan had limited experience as an amateur boxer in college, but his ground game was almost nonexistent. Both Foaly and Vinny were experienced in Muay Thai and Brazilian Jiu Jitsu since they both styles were used by SEALs and Green Berets, and they were happy to teach Morgan. Foaly also had the advantage of a basic knowledge of Krav Maga, having spent some time cross-training and working alongside certain Commando Units within the Israeli Defense Force.

Vinny sprung forward, swinging a right hook towards Foaly's head. Foaly rushed forward into the punch, letting Vinny's fist connect with his shoulder. The next thing Vinny saw was the ceiling, then the floor, then the ceiling. It was his turn to have the air expelled from his lungs. Despite being unable to breathe, Vinny clamped his arms around Foaly's torso and tried to flip them so he could get the mount. Foaly hammered his gloved fists into Vinny's head, neck and sides as Vinny continued to try and get any advantage.

Just as Vinny was starting to make some progress, Foaly rolled them over and broke Vinny's grip. The former SEAL scrambled, but the lack of oxygen had slowed him enough that Foaly was able to slap a rear naked choke on his teammate, applying just enough pressure to turn Vinny's face beet-red. They both knew Vinny wouldn't tap. Morgan barreled into Foaly's side, breaking the choke, and knocking him away from Vinny.

Morgan's efforts resulted in him ending up in Foaly's grasp, and that quickly turned into another rear-naked choke. Morgan gagged as he tried to raise his hips in an effort to throw Foaly's center of gravity off, but it was in vain. Shortly after, he passed out.

He woke up a moment later with Foaly slapping him on the cheek and Vinny splashing some water on his face. Morgan coughed explosively, sitting up and rubbing his throat.

"There he is!" Foaly said with a smile. Morgan continued coughing as he sat up. The small crowd that had gathered around the training octagon applauded before returning to their workouts. Both former operators helped Morgan to his feet.

"I think that's all she wrote for today." Vinny said, patting Morgan on the back. "I'm pretty sure that's the longest you've lasted so far." Morgan shrugged his shoulders, not wanting to speak just yet.

"Definitely improving. That's all that matters." Foaly said as he held the door open for his teammates. "Come on, let's go get cleaned up." Foaly turned and saw a group of five teenagers gawking at them, so he gave them a smile before heading into the locker room.

15
Murray Hill, New York

The guys were all sitting in Morgan's living room, drinks in-hand. Morgan had broken out his bottle of Johnnie Walker Odyssey, which had been passed down, unopened, to him from his father upon Morgan's selection into the 160th. JW Odyssey was an ultra-rare blend, with only two hundred and fifty bottles having been produced and ran for about three-thousand dollars apiece. It had become tradition for the team to have two fingers after each successful job, and they were beginning to put a significant dent into the amber liquor.

Resting on the coffee table were four framed copies of a group photo that the three Americans had taken with their FELCN counterparts following the successful mission in Bolivia. The photos, along with individual letters of thanks and recognition from the Bolivian government, had arrived in the mail that morning. Morgan saw that as reason enough to have their post-mission drink and had called the boys over.

It felt good to finally relax. The first few days post-job were always busy: weapons cleaning, equipment maintenance, etcetera, etcetera. It always delayed the time they could take to actually decompress, which was just as important as everything else in this line of work. Even more so following the several near-misses they'd had in Bolivia.

Foaly couldn't help but smile. After his discharge from the military, he'd fallen into a depression. Morgan's offer of coming into contracting had alleviated that feeling a little, but after their first job together he felt like himself again.

ZACH JAMES

Having joined the Army when he was seventeen, and the years after that being filled with constant training and combat rotations, adjusting to life outside the uniform had been something so foreign to Foaly that it had beat him down worse than anything he'd endured while in uniform. Luckily, he'd had Shannon there to keep him sane. Without her and the guys, he didn't know what he'd do. Foaly glanced down at his watch and saw it was a quarter to noon.

"Well, I'm gonna get going." Foaly said, finishing his drink before standing up. He was heading out to meet with Shannon for a quick lunch while she was on a rare break from work, and he didn't want to be late. His work kept him away from his wife enough, so he didn't want to waste any opportunities to see her.

"See you later." Morgan said with a wave. "Don't forget your stuff."

"Oh yeah, thanks." Foaly said, having almost forgotten to grab his framed photo and letter.

"Tell Shannon we say hi." Vinny waved, now speaking like a Jewish Grandmother.

"See ya, guys." Foaly said before leaving the apartment.

16
Yorkville, New York

Foaly sat in one of the booths in Monster Sushi at the corner of East 82nd and 2nd. He'd already ordered a plate of California Rolls and some Dancing Eel rolls, which were by far his favorite type of sushi. There was also a bowl of wonton soup waiting on Shannon's side of the booth, and he triple-checked his watch to make sure he was on time and hadn't forgotten to adjust the time back from Bolivia.

A smile broke across his face when he saw the door open and Shannon walked in. She was pointed in his direction by one of the wait staff.

"Hi." She said with a smile. He slid out of the booth and met her at the side of the table, kissing her. She was almost a full foot shorter than Foaly, which was only slightly alleviated with her heels. She wore her dark brown hair in a neat bun, and her chocolate-colored eyes were still hidden behind the pair of Ray Ban Clubmaster Metal sunglasses. She removed the glasses and placed them in her purse. Shannon wore a slate-colored suit and matching skirt, with a dark blue undershirt. Foaly took in every detail about his wife as she slid into the booth across from him, smiling at him with slightly-pursed lips. Good Lord she was beautiful.

"How's work going?" He asked. Her smile disappeared with a sigh.

"It's been a busy day. I have to head over to Long Island this afternoon to meet with a client, so it's going to be a late night for me." She said before partaking in her soup. "How about you?"

"So far so good." Foaly said. "Got our workout in. Choked Morgan's ass out."

"Poor Morgan." Shannon said with a chuckle.

"Hey, he's getting better." Foaly said with a smile. He took pride in being able to help instruct Morgan to be more deadly with his hands and feet. "We went and had a drink at his place after. Got a picture and letter from our last client; I'll show you those when you get home."

"Speaking of *clients*." Shannon said, amused that her husband had started using that term to help her understand his work better. "Are you planning on travelling again anytime soon?"

"No nothing yet. Morgan is looking but he hasn't found anything that's a good fit for us." Shannon visibly relaxed at his answer. "Other than that, I've got nothing planned. Vinny invited us over to watch the fight tonight."

"I'm probably not going to be able to make it." Shannon said. "Depending on how late I'm in Long Island I may just get a hotel room and work out of there for the night." She saw Foaly opening his mouth and cut him off. "You go have a good time with the guys, don't worry about me." She said, answering his question before he could get it out. She smiled before biting into a California Roll.

The two of them continued talking and eating, trying to fit the most that they could into the hour and a half they had together. With his background in Special Operations, Foaly was all too familiar with how high the divorce rates for men like him were. Hell, Vinny was a prime example, having come from the SEAL side of the house. It was no secret to Alex that he was one of the rare ones who'd managed to keep his marriage together. He also knew that only a fraction of the success in their marriage was because of him; the rest all came from the sheer patience and understanding that Shannon had towards him and what he did. She knew he was most comfortable when behind the sights of a rifle, and she was fine with that. That being said, he always made sure to spend as much time with her as possible to let her know that he loved her. The effort from both sides had made it easy for them to stay together over the past seven years, when a lesser woman would have left him after seven months.

And all too quickly, their time together came to an end.

"I'll be home sometime tomorrow." Shannon said as she wiped her mouth before sliding out of the booth. Alex left cash on their table to cover the check and tip, and the two of them held hands as they walked out onto the busy street. Shannon felt a buzz in her purse and pulled out her cell phone. The client was calling. "That's the client, I have to get going." She stepped up and kissed him. "I love you; I'll see you tomorrow!"

"Love you too, babe." Foaly said with a smile. She squeezed his hand, then started walking away as she held the phone up to her ear. Foaly watched her walk away for a few moments, then turned and started down the opposite end of the street. It was his turn to pick up beer for the fight.

17
Pearl River, New York

The gunfire was deafening. Or, it would have been, had they not all been wearing hearing protection. The only three lanes that were occupied were side-by-side, each man taking full advantage of this range's nonexistent rules about rapid fire. The pistol and carbine shots all sounded off, blending into a cacophony that reverberating off of the solid walls and concrete floor.

Foaly sighted down his Glock 17 nine-millimeter and finished firing at the target that now stood twenty-meters away. He transitioned from center-mass to the target's head, popping three rounds in quick succession, then swapped back and kept firing center-mass until the pistol's slide locked back. He lowered the handgun and was glad to see there weren't any stray rounds. Satisfied with his carry pistol, he ejected the mag and set it and the weapon on the bench before him, reaching for the Glock 34 long-slide nine-mil for his next firing iteration. In the lane to his left, Foaly heard the loud reports of Morgan's 1911, mixed in with the sharper report of Vinny's Sig P226, which he had chambered in nine.

They'd been lucky that they'd showed up on one of the range's slower days. Without anyone else to gawk or otherwise bother them, they would be able to break out their bigger guns. Nothing irritated Morgan more than when some off-duty cop harassed them about having the proper paperwork, then stood by drooling over the hardware until inevitably asking to put a mag through.

As Foaly began popping shots off with his long slide at a target thirty-five meters away, Morgan swapped from his Springfield to his Browning Hi Power Mark III, and waited for the target to settle into place at fifteen meters. Similar in design to the 1911, the Hi Power was chambered in nine-millimeter, and was a favorite of Morgan's when he wasn't packing the powerful .45. As soon as the paper target stopped moving, he brought the pistol up and fired six shots in rapid succession. He pulled the trigger again and was met with a *click*. A quick glance showed that the slide had locked back for some reason, leaving the next round in the magazine waiting to be chambered.

"Shit." He said, ejecting the mag and angling the weapon to ensure that the chamber was clear. He pulled the slide back and let it go, but it caught itself and remained in the rear position. "What the fuck?" He said as he hit the target return button and pulled back on the slide again. The HP had been a gift from his father and had never given him any kind of issues before.

While Morgan was fiddling with his pistol, Vinny had stepped up from pistols and was now aiming down the sights of his SCAR-L. When the target settled at fifty meters, he gave three double-taps: two to the chest and one to the head. The normally loud report of the rifle was reduced thanks to the new suppressor and sub-sonic ammunition he was trying out. It wasn't the same stuff he'd used while on the Teams, but it seemed to get the job done well. Against paper at least. He moved the target back to sixty meters and repeated the drill, then seventy, then seventy-five, continuing to move the target back and repeating the drill until he expended the magazine.

While the three men practiced on their weapons, the range master and owner of the rifle club, Fred Dillons, sat quietly and watched. He was impressed as each man put their rounds exactly where they needed to be, doing smooth transitions from one weapon system to the next. Of the scores of rounds fired, not one was off target. Dillons, a Vietnam combat veteran with the First Marine Division, hadn't seen shooting like that in a long time. He'd gotten to know these three over the past few months and loved to watch them work.

Alex went empty with his 416 and transitioned to shooting his Sig Sauer P228 with his left hand in a one-handed grip. The P228 was the compact baby brother to the P226 that Vinny used, and Foaly had used both along with Glocks and a couple of 1911s during his time in the Unit.

Morgan was in the middle of reloading his Mk18 and stopped, looking back at the old range master. Fred was sitting there with a small smile on his face, oversized ear protection sitting around his black Vietnam vet hat. Morgan safed the weapon and placed it on the bench before walking to the range station.

"Want to give them a try?" Morgan asked. Fred's smile grew and he nodded. The contractors had quickly taking a liking to the old vet that allowed them to practice at his range unmolested and were more than happy to let him play with the hardware. Fred took Morgan's place in Lane Five and picked up the Mk18, slapping the magazine and the bolt release with quick, practiced efficiency. He'd used the original M16s in Vietnam, and apart from a few bells and whistles, they were practically the same as the thing he held in his hands now. The only thing he wasn't used to were the fancy optics that the youngster had bolted onto the top of the carbine, but he was relieved when Morgan reached over and popped the flip-up sights. Fred was instantly comfortable; nothing like good ol' iron sights.

DECEPTION

Soon the rapid-fire reports of the Mk18 in the Vietnam vet's hands joined those of Vinny's and Alex's rifles.

18
Murray Hill, New York

Morgan tossed his keys into the bowl sitting on the small table beside the front door and kicked his shoes off into the closet. Once again, he sat down in front of the computer and wiggled the mouse to kill the screen saver. Moments later he was logged into his email and looking over the ever-growing list of government contract requests for proposals. The majority that he seemed to come across were requests for one- or two-person financial analyst jobs, intelligence analysis positions, or vastly underpaying security jobs. Long gone were the days where contractors could make two-thousand dollars a day like they did when Iraq was in full swing. There was no way he would subject himself or the others to the dangers of Afghanistan for a measly sixty grand a year. A quick search showed zero requests for private helo pilots. Now that was where there was some money to be made.

Morgan had almost given up on today's search when something caught his eye. There was a lone request for a cargo ship security detail. They weren't accepting submissions yet, so he clicked the link to be put on the mailing list. Hopefully, it would open soon; a ship detail would be cake for him and the guys, especially with the hardware they could bring along. And with their small crew and vast experience, he could undercut the shit out of the competition and still make a healthy profit.

After he finished with that, he stumbled across another job, this one requesting a security consultation team for a mining operation out in Zambia. *Two in one day, might have to go buy a lottery ticket.* Morgan thought to himself. The request was by a company called Paoli

Industries, and they were taking submissions. Morgan clicked the link, filled out the requisite forms, then sent off a capabilities brief along with his, Alex, and Vinny's resumes.

Riding high on having found two possible easy jobs in one day, Morgan continued searching for another fifteen minutes. Unfortunately, the well had run dry, and so he decided to get up and pour himself a drink. He was startled to turn around and see Julia sitting on the couch, staring at him.

"Hey." He said. "I didn't hear you walk in."

"I was napping." She said with a sleepy smile. "Did you find anything?"

"Yep." Morgan said, happy to share the news of two possibly easy jobs. "Just sent in a submission for a security consultation in Zambia." He walked over to the liquor cabinet and grabbed the bottle of Maker's Mark, placing two whiskey stones in a tumbler before pouring himself a few fingers. He held the bottle up and looked at his wife, but she waved him off.

"Zambia?" She said, thinking. "Isn't there a civil war happening there?" Morgan couldn't help but chuckle. What African nation didn't have a civil war raging at the moment?

"Yeah, but that's mostly near the capital. These guys are running a mining operation, so they're going to be well out in the bush." Morgan said, half-lying. He had no idea where Paoli's operation was. For all he knew this would be a consultation for their HQ, which very well may be in...whatever Zambia's capital was. He was going to have to study up on the country's geography. Those details would be addressed in the contract negotiations if the company decided to pick them up.

"Okay, as long as you'll be safe." Julia said with a smile. He returned the smile and sat down on the couch beside her. They spent ten minutes scrolling through Hulu before she decided to put on a romantic comedy. While she laughed and snuggled against her husband, Morgan stared blankly at the screen, oblivious to the antics of a fat suit-wearing Ryan Reynolds. His mind was already racing as he went into planning and preparation mode for the Zambia job.

19
Upper East Side, New York

Foaly grunted and pulled the tie undone again, attempting to properly re-tie it for the third time. Shannon chuckled with her back to him as she pulled on the black dress she would be wearing for the night's event. Foaly found himself staring at the dress, which was tight in all the right places and clung to her toned body as she pulled the straps up over her shoulders, then turned to face him.

They would be joining Morgan, Julia, and Vinny in attending a high-class business dinner event, and the plan was for all of them to work the floor for investors and possible contracting opportunities. It was a black-tie event, and they would be bringing their a-games.

"Enjoying the show?" She asked with a smile.

"I could be asking you the same thing." Foaly said, finally getting the tie how he wanted. With that done, he turned around to where Shannon waited for him and zipped up the back of her dress while she draped a sterling necklace around her neck and then placed small diamond earrings in her ears. She had just pulled on her shoes when there was a knock at the door. A quick glance over showed Alex was still fussing with his cuff links. "I'll get it, you finish getting ready."

Shannon walked across the living room and pulled open the door to see Morgan and Julia standing there, both dressed for the evening. Julia wore a dark blue, near-floor length dress that was accented by the gold jewelry on her wrists, neck, and ears. Morgan was in a black-on-black suit with a matching tie. His lapel was adorned with a miniature 160th Nightstalkers pin.

"Hi guys." Shannon said with a smile.

"Hey! Long time no see!" Julia said excitedly, stepping forward and embracing Shannon. "You look fantastic."

"I was about to say the same about you." Shannon replied sincerely. "Come in, please. Alex is finishing up and should be out in a few."

Foaly couldn't help but smirk as he heard his wife excitedly chatting away with Julia as he pulled on his suit jacket, smoothing the front to make sure there weren't any creases. With everything set, he exited the bedroom to greet the Tyrons.

"Hi guys." Alex said with a warm smile.

"Hey Alex." Julia said, standing. "Good to see you."

"It's good to see you too, Julia. Been too long." Alex said as he embraced his friend's wife. "Fancy a drink?"

"Yes please." Julia smiled. "What do you have?"

"Here, follow me." Shannon said as she got up from the couch and walked into the small kitchen. Shannon poured herself and Julia a glass of pinot noir each, and they both went back to the living room to pick up the conversation that had been sidelined by Foaly's entrance.

"They sure are excited to see each other." Morgan said.

"No different from when we were in uniform." Foaly said as he started digging into his liquor cabinet. Morgan nodded, and a moment later Foaly retrieved his arm, holding a bottle of Johnnie Walker Platinum. Both men were big fans of JW. "Care for a glass?"

"Absolutely." Morgan said. Foaly grabbed two glasses and opened the bottle, pouring each of them a drink. "When the hell is Vinny planning on showing up?" Alex asked as he handed Morgan one of the glasses.

"Who knows with him, you know how he plays it fast and loose." Morgan said, taking a sip. *Damn that's good.* He thought to himself. Foaly looked down at his black Seiko Astron wristwatch.

It impressed Morgan how quickly Foaly was switching from super-soldier ex-commando to suave black-tie businessman. Well, he at least had the look down. Other than the small scars that stitched across the right side of his face, breaking up the uniformly trimmed sideburns and stubble that clung to his jaw, one would think Foaly was a high-level executive. His actual business skills left a lot to be desired, and that's why Morgan took the helm as CEO.

"This Platinum Label is damn good." Morgan said, swirling his drink around in its glass. He'd never had that particular blend before.

They continued to talk shop and eventually joined their wives out in the living room while waiting on Vinny.

20
Upper East Side, New York

Forty minutes later there was a knock at the door. Alex got up and opened it to find Vinny standing there in a black suit that matched his and Morgan's. Vinny's hair was gelled in a side-part, and his face was clean shaven.

"Hey dude, sorry I'm late." Vinny said with a smile as he shook Foaly's hand before walking in.

"Well look who finally showed up." Morgan said from the couch, his second glass of booze in-hand. He almost didn't recognize Vinny, having never seen him fresh-faced before. "You look like a twelve-year-old without the beard."

"What can I say? I like to keep people on their toes." Vinny said with a smile and a shrug. "Ladies." He said with a sparkling smile. Both Shannon and Julia got up to greet and hug Vinny. Morgan rolled his eyes while Alex shook his head and chuckled. Vinny was most definitely a SEAL.

"Want a drink?" Foaly asked.

"Nah, I've already made us late enough as is. Don't want to be the reason we miss anything important." Vinny said. "I did get us a ride though. This thing has valet, right?" Morgan nodded.

"Alrighty then, let's hit it." Foaly said, downing the last of his drink. Morgan threw back the rest of his and set the glass on a coaster before getting up. The five of them walked down the hall to the bank of elevators, and Vinny made a show of graciously holding open the door for the others.

They reached the ground floor and Vinny handed the building's valet his parking ticket. The man disappeared, leaving the five well-dressed people standing there with hands in their pockets or clutching their purses.

"Gonna be cramped in your Jeep." Morgan said. Vinny scoffed.

"I told you I got a ride." Vinny said. As if on cue, the valet rolled up in a chromed-out Hummer H3 and handed Vinny the keys.

"You always were the modest one, Vinny." Foaly chuckled as he opened the back door of the monstrous vehicle for Shannon and Julia. "When the hell did you get this?"

"Unfortunately, it's not mine. It's on loan from one of my team buddies who owed me a favor." Vinny said as he climbed into the driver's seat. Foaly looked at Morgan, who climbed into the back with the wives. Foaly took shotgun.

Half an hour later they pulled in front of the Sheraton New York Hotel & Towers for the event. There were a surprising number of eyes on them as they got out of their enormous, and obnoxious, vehicle, which stood out among the BMWs, Mercedes, and other high-end cars that everyone else was arriving in. Vinny stepped out and handed the keys, along with a crisp fifty-dollar bill, to the valet. Foaly looked around, his chest tight. His time in SOF had had him shroud himself from the public eye, whether it was on or around Bragg, or downrange. His anxiety was broken when he saw Vinny stepping towards him, fixing something to his lapel. Foaly couldn't help but let out a groan and roll his eyes when he saw what it was: a miniature SEAL trident pin.

"Almost left it in the car." Vinny said with a mischievous smile. With that the five of them started up the stairs, mixing in with scores of others making their way to the banquet hall. They reached the top and stopped in front of one of the doormen.

"Good evening ladies and gentlemen." The man said. "May I see your invitations?" Morgan held up the three invitations for himself, Alex, and Vinny, and showed that Julia and Shannon were plus ones. "Thank you very much. Enjoy your evening." The doorman said as he held open one of the large double doors.

The banquet hall was huge. Dark red tapestry and matching carpets accented the white walls and clusters of lights in complicated chandeliers that lit the large space. Scores of tables were set out for the hundreds in attendance, all of whom were dressed just as formally, and many more so, as the three contractors and their wives.

"Champagne?" A waiter asked, balancing a tray of flutes on one hand. They each took a drink and thanked the man. He gave a gracious nod before jetting off to provide drinks for someone else.

"Well this is different." Vinny said before sipping his drink.

"We keep this up and we're going to have to start acting like social elites." Morgan said. "That or get into pulling security for gigs like this. Cush, plainclothes deals."

"Or just become bodyguards." Foaly deadpanned.

"Hi folks!" Someone said from behind the group. They all turned to see an older man with silver hair dressed in a visibly expensive suit walking towards them. "So glad you could make it, I'm Marcus Hollifield, CFO of Hartmund Industries." Marcus smiled and extended a hand towards the closest person, which happened to be Foaly. Hartmund Industries was the host of the event.

"Alex Foaly, nice to meet you." Foaly said with a smile. "This is my wife, Shannon."

"Pleasure." Shannon said with a warm smile.

"The pleasure is all mine, ma'am." Marcus said respectfully, even though he was at least twenty years Shannon's senior. Marcus went down the rest of the line, introducing himself to the others and giving them all equally friendly and respectful greetings. "Is it safe to assume you all work together?" He asked following pleasantries.

"The three of us do." Morgan said, pointing to Vinny and Alex. "I'm the CEO of Integral Solutions. Vinny is our Chief Medical Officer, and Alex is Chief of Operations."

"Integral Solutions? I don't think I've heard of them. What is it that you do?" Marcus asked. Foaly could see that the man was not hamming it up and was genuinely curious.

"We mainly do overseas security consultations." Morgan said. Marcus' eyes lit up at this.

"How exciting! I'm sure you have some stories to share." The older man said. "And what do you lovely ladies do?"

"I'm a lawyer." Shannon said as she finished her drink.

"And I work in real estate." Julia replied.

"Oh wow, quite the variety you have!" Marcus said, then turned back to Morgan. "I have to ask, how did gentlemen in such a...niche industry, find out about this event? Normally, it's all business types that come here; oil, automotive, etcetera."

"LinkedIn, actually." Morgan said with a half-embarrassed smile. Marcus stared at him, wondering if he was joking. When he realized Morgan wasn't, he laughed even harder.

"Networking is a hell of a thing!" Marcus said. "I'd be honored if you would all join me at my table. If you don't mind, I have some more questions about the work you do." Morgan glanced over his shoulder, and everyone else nodded.

"Absolutely." Morgan said with a smile. They followed Marcus to a larger table that was empty, and all sat with him.

"So, where have you worked?" Marcus asked, settling into his chair.

"We've had a few small contracts here and there." Morgan said. "If I'm being honest, you're looking at the entire company. It's just the three of us. We've done work in Nicaragua, along the New Mexico-Mexico Border, and just recently wrapped up a job in Bolivia. We have some work possibly lined up in Africa, but we're still waiting to hear back on that." Morgan rattled off the information as if he'd practiced it for hours in front of the mirror. For all the others knew, that was what he did. Surprisingly, to himself more than anyone else, he hadn't.

"And what are your backgrounds? Military? Police?" Marcus asked, his attention now one hundred percent focused on Morgan.

"I was a pilot in the Army. Vinny was a Navy SEAL, and Alex was in Special Forces." Morgan pointed to his two friends respectively. Both were relieved Morgan had given him the 'white-side' rundown of their careers, considering that both ███████████ and ███ didn't officially exist like the regular SEALs and Green Berets did. Marcus looked at them all in awe.

DECEPTION

"You guys are like real-life G.I. Joes." Marcus said, admiration in his voice. "I truly envy that and respect the hell out of all of your sacrifices." He stood and gave each man a hearty handshake. "I mean that from the bottom of my heart."

"Did you ever serve, sir?" Vinny asked. The admiration gave way to sadness for just a moment.

"Unfortunately, not." Marcus said, then his face turned to a forced smile. "Born with a bad valve, got turned down when I tried to enlist." He tapped a finger against his chest. "Ever since then I always lived vicariously however I could. Comics, movies, books, and all that. It's an honor to be sharing a table with men like you." None of them knew how to take the compliment, so they gave polite thanks. After a moment, Marcus reached into the inner pocket of his suit coat. "I tell you what. If you guys ever get bored globetrotting, I could use men like you on my security staff."

Seeing what Marcus was doing, Morgan quickly reached into his own jacket and retrieved a business card. "And if you're ever travelling somewhere and need a consultation, or a protective detail, call us. We don't mind travelling." The two swapped business cards. Unlike Marcus', which was just for him, the Integral Solutions card had email addresses for all three men, as well as a business phone number that went directly to Morgan's cell.

Marcus continued chatting with the contractors and their wives, enthralled as Vinny told a story from his time with SEAL Team Seven. The group was joined by Marcus' wife, Deborah, the CEO of Hartmund Industries, Adam Hartmund III, Navy Admiral Tony Adames, Correa Mining COO Miguel Hernandez, retired NYPD

Commissioner Lawrence McGinley, and former New Jersey Representative James Olfeld. Foaly couldn't believe the heavyweights that had joined them at the table, particularly the four-star Naval Officer. Hollifield had some high-level connections, and by pure luck and a good first impression, the men of Integral Solutions sat right in the middle of them.

What impressed him even more was watching Morgan work the entire table. When he was in business mode, there wasn't a more charismatic person in the entire building. Watching Morgan explain the business, detail current events, and use buzz-words that were plucked right out of the Wall Street Journal, one couldn't be blamed for thinking he'd grown up working in high-rise offices around Manhattan instead of having flown helicopters in every warzone the United States had been involved in over the past seventeen years. Morgan's voice carried such passion and conviction that he had the attention of everyone around them, and they couldn't help but hear him out, even if they were anti-gun pacifists.

Following Morgan working the table and everyone enjoying yet another large course of exquisite cuisine, Admiral Adames cleared his throat as he dabbed at his mouth with a napkin.

"Being that I'm a squid, you know I'm obligated to ask about that." The Admiral said to Vinny, pointing at the trident pin on his lapel. Vinny finished chewing his filet mignon before answering.

"Team Seven, sir." Vinny said politely, omitting his full service from the conversation.

"You Frogmen are a tough bunch. Never got the opportunity to work with any of you during my time though." Adames said with a wistful smile.

DECEPTION

"Were you a mustang, or commissioned right off the bat?" Vinny asked. Mustang was military-speak for service members who started their careers off on the enlisted side before becoming a commissioned officer through either ROTC or Officer Candidate School.

"Commissioned right off the bat." Admiral Adames said, using Vinny's colloquialism. "Got my degree and Ensign bars through NROTC at Georgetown. Didn't even get the opportunity to try for BUD/S. Instead, they slated me for carrier work. That's how I ended up commanding the Carrier Group that was in the Persian Gulf when we first went to Iran." The three contractors perked up at this, and Vinny's eyes grew wide.

"That's where I know you from!" Vinny said excitedly. "When we first got there, my team flew in off of the America!" This got a smile from the Admiral. He'd been in command of that group from the bridge of the America herself.

"I think I stopped on the America to refuel a couple of times." Morgan said. Adames looked at him. "I was in the Nightstalkers."

"We had more than a few of your birds stop on there to pick up and drop off the likes of him." Adames said, nodding towards Vinny.

"Were you there during the Shahid Sadoogi Airfield Seizure?" Foaly asked.

"I was. Most of the fast movers that provided air support for that were launched from my group." Adames said. Morgan, Vinny, and Alex all looked at each other for a moment, then all eyes returned to the Admiral. "What? Did I say something wrong?"

"No, sir." Vinny said. "All three of us were on the ground during that airfield seizure."

"You probably sent in the CAS that saved our asses." Foaly added. This further piqued the Admiral's interest. The four of them were so enthralled in their conversation that they didn't notice the rest of the table had fallen silent, everyone soaking in the details of the exchange.

"Talk about a small world." Vinny said.

"What was it like on the ground there?" The Admiral asked. From the way he'd spoken to Vinny earlier, it was obvious he was just as star-struck to talk to ground-pounders as Marcus had been. Everyone at the table looked at the three men with admiration and respect as they began to tell what they could about the events of the previous year.

21
May, 2018
Mutwale, Zambia

The white jeep came to a stop and the driver hopped out, followed by the three contractors. The visitors grabbed their bags from the open back of the vehicle and carried them towards a small group of approaching people wearing matching uniforms.

The team had arrived in Zambia about an hour beforehand, having landed at a small airport in Lesa where they were met by the Paoli Industries jeep that brought them to the mining complex in Mutwale.

"Morning, gents!" A cheery British-accented voice said. They turned to see a man wearing khaki cargo pants and a dark blue polo approaching.

"Hi there." Morgan said, slinging his bag over one shoulder and extending his free hand. "Morgan Tyron."

"Ah yes, we've spoken over the phone." The man said as he shook Morgan's hand. "I'm Jack Greenwood, project manager of this complex." He continued to shake the rest of their hands. The others introduced themselves.

"Looks like you've got one hell of an operation here." Vinny said, adjusting the Ray-Bans over his eyes as he looked out over the massive hole in the ground that the complex was built around.

"Quite the understatement, I assure you." Greenwood said with a smile. "Follow me, I'll show you your quarters and then give you the tour." He waved for them to follow and led them into the interior of the complex. All three men were grateful for the wave of cold air that washed over them. They knew Africa was going to be hot, but it was still going to take some time to acclimate compared to New York temperatures. They followed Greenwood up a set of stairs and down a hallway with doors on both sides. "This is where you'll be staying during your time with us." The manager said as he stopped in front of one of the doors.

The interior of the complex was interesting to say the least. The clean white walls and rubbered floor had a hospital-like sterility to them. The inside of the place felt completely alien to the warm and rolling environment outside. Large windows opened up to look out over the expansive flats around the complex, flooding the halls with natural light. It felt as if it was meant to be part of a space station, or a research vessel at the bottom of the ocean, rather than in the middle of the African savanna.

The three men walked in and looked around. It was a surprisingly spacious room; three beds, footlockers, and wall lockers; two desks, a kitchenette, and a bathroom. The white walls and paneled faux-hardwood flooring gave it an open feel. It was definitely not what they'd expected while helping an industrial mining operation.

Foaly set his bag down and quickly slid his holster onto his belt, chambering a round in his sidearm. Two spare mags went in his cargo pocket; he would put the carriers for them on his belt later. Once they were all set, he followed Morgan and Vinny into the hall where Greenwood was waiting. The Brit didn't even glance at their sidearms as he led them back outside into the oppressive heat. They climbed into a waiting four-seater Polaris Pursuit Ranger utility vehicle. Morgan, being the lead man, took shotgun, while Alex and Vinny climbed into the back and closed the strap-doors behind them.

"I don't know how much research you've done on it, but this is the largest Cobalt deposit discovered in

Zambia so far." Greenwood said over the engine as he began driving the small vehicle. "Paoli Industries happened upon it during a survey and managed to secure exclusive rights with the Zambian government." As they drove closer to the mine, Foaly noticed more and more locals mixed in with Paoli employees.

"You guys hire locally?" Foaly asked.

"We do. Paoli offers local job opportunities working in the mines and as support staff around the complex as a form of reparation for the land that is used and lost to the mining. We provide steady employment, food, and healthcare to them and their families. And we pay them much more than they'd make if they stayed farming." The manager's answer impressed everyone. Not many companies took the livelihood of those they pushed out into account.

As they continued to drive, Morgan noticed many uniformed security personnel walking around. They wore khaki pants and dark polos that matched Greenwood's 'uniform' but also had plate carrier vests strapped to their chests and carried AR-style rifles. Most wore ballcaps to keep the sun out of their faces, though a few wore wide-brimmed boonie caps instead.

"What's the story with your security?" Morgan asked.

"Paoli Industries has its own internal security branch that we use at all of our facilities, from small satellite offices to large projects such as this, and especially our headquarters in London." Greenwood said as he pulled the Polaris off to the side of the dirt 'road' and parked it behind one of the white Jeeps that looked identical to the one they'd arrived at the facility in. "Our security is good, but we wanted to bring in some external consultants to assess the current situation due to the recent escalations of the civil war." They all turned to see a lone security officer approaching. "Gents, this is Kurt Dalyel, head of the Mutwale Complex security team."

"Hi guys." Dalyel said. He was American, with just a hint of a Boston accent. "Nice to meet you. Jack told me we were bringing in some consultants to help out. Glad you're here." He shook each of their hands.

"Can you give us a rundown of the current situation?" Morgan asked.

"Since the civil war kicked off, we've been spread pretty thin to keep up security. Here, follow me." He said, gesturing for them to walk with him. He led them up a set of stairs that went to the top of the complex, which was ringed with a waist-high wall. Armed guards patrolled along the roof, looking out over the plains that surrounded their temporary home. "About a month ago the rebels started operating in this area. We're not sure how many there are or what their full capabilities are because they've only done a few probing attacks. Mostly just small arms fire, but I'm worried that they might be planning something big in order to storm the complex and take it over for themselves."

"Wouldn't they want to take you guys hostage and demand a ransom?" Morgan asked.

"That's the best-case scenario." Dalyel said. "But this particular group has been reported to be pretty brutal. If they find out one of our workers is employed by us, there's more than a good chance that the rebels will track down the family and butcher them, if not raze the entire village. It's happened to about half a dozen guys so far."

"What's the strength of the security here?" Foaly asked, pushing past the crimes against humanity they were being told about. He stopped and looked out over the tall brush and sporadic trees that surrounded the facility. Africa had a natural beauty about it that the United States did not possess. And it sure as hell beat the Moon-like landscape that was Afghanistan.

"We usually have thirty-six armed personnel on watch at any time, with shifts rotating every eight hours. I've got three in the infirmary at the moment; two that are sick and one that was wounded in the last attack." Dalyel explained.

"How was he wounded?" Vinny asked.

"Caught a bullet to the arm." Dalyel pointed to his left bicep. "Docs stabilized him and said he'll be clear to come back on light duty in about a week or so. They hit us with small arms fire and a single RPG that ended up being a dud…" Dalyel trailed off, his head slightly tilted. Foaly knew this all too well as the body language of someone who was listening to their radio earpiece. Dalyel then reached down and pressed the transmit button on his radio. "Copy that. Keep them separated until I get down there." He turned his attention back to the group he was showing around. "Sorry about that, one of my guys just radioed in. Apparently, some of the locals started getting into it down in the mine. Gotta go take a report. I'll catch up with you later." Then he took off at a jog down the stairs and towards the mine.

"Never an easy day here." Greenwood said with a wan smile. "I'm sure you're pretty tired from the flight. What do you say we head in for a quick bite to eat and then I'll let you get settled? I can give you a tour of the mine tomorrow, as well as a full security brief from Kurt, and then we can move on from there." They all nodded in agreement and followed Greenwood back downstairs and inside, where he led them to the cafeteria.

22
Mutwale, Zambia

The next morning the three contractors joined with Greenwood and Dalyel within the complex for breakfast before they were taken down into the mines. They were now dressed in polos and cargo pants, with Foaly and Vinny wearing their pistols on their belts while Morgan had his in a drop-leg holster on his thigh. Vinny also wore an IFAK on the back of his belt as a blowout kit in case the need for it came up.

The Mutwale Mining Complex was essentially built in a seventh-eights circle around the mine itself, with the sliver between the two ends of the complex used as an access road for incoming and outgoing vehicles transporting new personnel into and mined ore out of the facility. The road led to the airstrip that the contractors had landed at the previous day.

It was impressive; the facility had two large cafeterias on either end of the 'horseshoe', housing for the Paoli employees, a fully-stocked infirmary with two surgical suites and an isolation room, and a couple of day rooms for employees to relax in when not on shift. The upper level of the facility housed administrative offices, server rooms, a couple of laboratories, the security office, and the armory. The armory held racks of FN 15 rifles, Glock 22 pistols, and the six M240-Lima machine guns, which were only to be used in the event the complex came under sustained attack.

"In the next year and a half, we're slated to enclose the facility entirely, which will give us added security with a man-trap for vehicles. Once that's done, we will add an additional floor which will expand housing for Paoli employees and open the bottom floor up to allow for our local employees to move in rather than having to live in the housing units outside." Greenwood said, pointing to the rows of containers that the off-duty Zambians were milling around. At the moment, the locals lived four to a room in containerized housing units, CHUs, which were basically shipping containers with the interior converted into living quarters to provide a bed, electricity, and air conditioning. All things considered, CHUs weren't bad. Morgan, Vinny, and Alex had all spent their fair share living in them in the past.

They reached one of the balconies that surrounded the mine and Greenwood motioned for them to take a look. Foaly leaned over the railing and looked down. The mine was at least four hundred feet deep, tiered at about every thirty feet to allow the traffic of workers, carts, and Polaris vehicles to move back and forth unimpeded. The lower levels of the mine were smaller, but had tunnels branching off them that burrowed deep into the ground towards the cobalt veins hidden beneath the earth. Workers, both Paoli and Zambian, worked side-by-side as they picked, dug, carved, and blasted their way through dirt and stone towards the precious mineral that was paying their salaries.

"When our surveyors first came across the cobalt deposits back in 2014, we sent out a small crew to break ground. At first, it was just twenty of us, working and living out of containers just like those behind us." Greenwood motioned towards the Zambian living quarters, and Vinny saw a game of soccer had broken out between a dozen of the off-duty miners. "My office was my part of the CHU; using a wi-fi puck to try and pick up a signal to send in reports and coordinate moving equipment and personnel into the area. We've come a long way in four years." Greenwood paused and thanked a Zambian boy who came over with a bucket of water bottles that sat in a bed of rapidly-melting ice. The boy was maybe ten years old and looked up at the large Americans with wonder in his eyes and a large grin on his face. Foaly returned the smile and pulled out his wallet, handing the boy a five-dollar bill before taking a bottle. The boy's grin grew larger and he said something in his rapid-fire native tongue before taking off to continue his duties. "The facility has grown large enough that it's now visible on satellite imagery. The current crew on the ISS even pointed us out!" Greenwood said with pride.

"What do you do about environmental activists? I'm sure they can't be too happy about this." Vinny said, wiping some sweat from his brow. It wasn't even ten in the morning, but it was already hot as hell.

"We have a land reclamation project in place. We take a portion of the income from our cobalt exports and put it into humanitarian assistance towards the Zambian people; mainly in helping the local farmers in the areas around the mines, but we've also dug about thirty wells and helped build six schools. We also give them money for cattle, help plant more trees and crops, things like that." Greenwood said before finishing his water bottle and tossing it into the nearby recycling bin. "We understand that once we finish here, we get to go home, but Zambia will always bear the scar of our presence here. We want to reduce that scar as much as possible and support our hosts, because at the end of the day Paoli is just a guest here."

"It was a good system until the civil war found its way here." Dalyel said, approaching the group. "When the rebels rolled into this area, they started taking farms, crops and cattle as their own. If the farmers refused to help,

79

they'd kill the family and burn the crops. A few brave souls stood their ground at first, but the rest caved after seeing what the rebels did to them."

"So, you've been helping the bad guys?" Morgan asked.

"For a time, yes. It was unfortunate. When we heard news of what was happening, we began redirecting funds to pay our workers more, as well as offer them and their families incentives on bonuses and education through some of Paoli's outreach programs. Two of the day rooms on the first floor are used as classrooms on certain evenings, and we're currently looking at the logistics to put more CHUs on the east side of the complex for workers who want to move their families closer. The locals are in a bad situation now, and it won't improve anytime soon until the rebels leave the area." The British foreman looked down at his watch. "I have a meeting to go to. Kurt, continue showing them around please?"

"You got it." Dalyel said with a nod. As Greenwood walked away, Kurt turned to the group. "Come on, I'll show you our security at the access road."

"Now that your boss is gone, can you give us a no-shit assessment on the rebels?" Foaly asked.

"They moved into the area because they want the mine for themselves." Dalyel said, walking with his hands resting loosely on the rifle slung across his chest. "That's why they're probing us; they want to see what kind of security this place has to see if they'll be able to waltz right in, or if they're going to have to light us up beforehand. Like I said yesterday, we've had a few small incidents where one or two would fire off a couple of pot-shots and then disappear into the nearby brush. The last one was a semi-coordinated attack with small arms, and that RPG I mentioned. Other than one guy being hit, the only thing the rebels really accomplished was scaring the hell out of most of the employees. Harkens!" Dalyel called out. One of the guards near the security shack by the access road got up from his chair and jogged over.

Dalyel introduced them to Ricky Harkens, one of the newest members of the security team. Harkens was a kid in his early twenties, dressed in the standard Paoli security uniform with a black baseball cap on his head.

"Ricky, these guys are the security consultants Mister Greenwood hired." Dalyel said as the younger man shook their hands.

"Awesome, nice to meet you guys." Ricky said.

"Nice to meet you as well." Morgan said. "Former military?"

"Yup, oh-three-eleven." Ricky said with pride. That was the military occupational specialty code for Marine Infantryman. "Did a tour over in Iraq and finished out my contract before I found these guys."

"Ricky was on duty the night of the attack, and he was part of the assessment and recovery team the morning after. We went to check out where the rebels had come from, and that's when we found out that our security had tagged three of them during the fighting. They also found two other blood trails, but those guys couldn't be found." Dalyel looked at the junior security officer. "Grab Daniels and get us a jeep. Tell Rollins I want him to help Gerard cover the front while we show these guys where you popped the rebels." Ricky nodded and jogged off to take care of what he'd been instructed to do.

Ten minutes later one of the white jeeps pulled up. Ricky was driving and another guard with close-cut blonde hair sat in the back. He looked bored.

"Daniels, take shotgun." Dalyel said as he climbed into the open back.

"Sir." Daniels replied, climbing over the partition, and dropping into the passenger's seat. Vinny, Alex, and Morgan all climbed into the back. Once they were set, Dalyel told Ricky to drive and they rolled up to the entry control point. The guard, who they assumed was Rollins from the earlier conversation, lifted the gate for them.

Harkens drove them to the nearby wood line, which was more like a couple of trees and some waist- and chest-high brush. He parked the jeep, and everyone hopped out.

"This is the main site that they attacked us from." Dalyel pointed at some spent shell casings sitting among the grass, then to the patch of burnt grass that had ignited from the RPG's back blast. Morgan knelt and picked one of the casings up, turning it between his fingers.

"Seven-six-two by three-nine." He said to himself before looking up at Dalyel. "Did you recover any weapons with the bodies?" Dalyel looked at Harkens.

"Yep." Ricky said. "Along with some other gear they had on. I guess their friends were too spooked by the counterattack to grab them."

"AKs?" Morgan asked as he stood up, shell casing still in-hand.

"Yeah, but not the shitty ones you'd think. They're some kind of modern version; rails and everything." Ricky replied. Morgan nodded and picked up a few more shell casings, dropping them into his right cargo pocket.

After visiting the second site that the rebels had attacked from, Morgan collected a few more casings before the group made their way back to the complex. Dalyel dismissed the junior officers back to their posts and led the contractors to the armory. He swiped his badge to open the door and had them sign the logbook while he walked into the caged area that held the security weapons. When he came back, he held one of the rebel weapons, which he passed off to Morgan.

"This is an AK-103." Morgan said as he looked the rifle over before working the action. "It's one of the newer variants of the AK, and a hell of a lot more expensive than the knockoffs rebel groups usually get." Morgan looked up at Dalyel.

"That means these rebels have some serious cash." Vinny commented.

"Or someone with some good connections." Foaly chimed in. "What about equipment? Anything of interest recovered off the bodies?" He asked as Morgan passed Vinny the AK.

"I've got forensic photos taken of the bodies and their gear on the computer in my office." Dalyel paused and looked over at Vinny, who had shouldered the AK-103 and was aiming it at the ceiling. "I'm going to need that back."

"Yep, here ya go." Vinny said, handing the rifle back to the security chief. Vinny had always had an affinity for AKs, and he liked how that one felt compared to the dozens of different variants he'd used while running plainclothes ops with the SEALs.

With the weapon locked away and the armory secured, the contractors followed Dalyel up to his office. He logged into the Paoli cloud service and opened the forensic files, pulling up the photographs of the rebels his staff had killed and displaying them on the television that was mounted to the wall.

The first rebel was a guy in his mid-thirties. He was dressed in a pair of jeans and a red tank top, with a pair of sneakers on his feet. What interested the contractors was the military-style chest rig that the rebel wore to hold his magazines. It was similar to the rig that Morgan wore over his armor, but the rebel's mag pouches were larger to accommodate the AK 'banana mags'. These guys were running around with high-end equipment and weaponry, comparable to the contractors and Paoli staff minus the bonus of armored plates.

The next photo showed a teenage rebel whose skull had been partially caved in by a high-velocity round. He'd gone into combat wearing shorts and sandals, but he also wore the same style chest rig that the first guy had been wearing. This kid also had a CamelBak water bladder, and a Century Arms Canik TP9SA pistol tucked into a holster mounted to his vest.

The third photo could have been a reprint of the first, with the biggest difference being that this rebel had been wearing a baggy soccer jersey rather than a tank top. He too had a chest rig, and this one was brimming with extra pouches that had been stuffed with everything from loose bullets to dried jerky, according to the photos that had the contents of each rig laid out beside them after they'd been taken off the bodies.

"What do you guys think?" Dalyel asked, leaving the photo of the three rigs and their contents laid out on the screen.

"I'm thinking these guys have one hell of a financier." Foaly said. "I've seen groups like this before, out in the Horn of Africa, but those guys were running around with AKs that were held together with duct tape and carried their mags and grenades in handmade satchels.

These guys here are packing some serious hardware. The vests aren't terribly expensive, but from the looks of it, someone high up in this organization is a frequent flyer to some Ranger Joe's knockoff. And they're buying enough so that even guys out here in the bush are getting the good stuff." He paused for a moment before looking at his guys, then back at Dalyel. "I think that we should run some recon in the area around the complex tonight, see if we can find anything or anyone that might help prep against the next attack. They've probably got a good idea of your defensive capabilities now, so they're likely going to make their big move sooner rather than later."

"Okay." Dalyel said after a moment of silent thought. "Alright, you guys do what you need to do. I'll let the night crew know not to just light up anything they see. If there's any equipment I can help with, just ask and I'll get it to you."

"Thanks for the offer. We'll report to you with our findings in the morning." Foaly said. With that, they left for their quarters to prepare their gear.

They were going hunting.

23
Mutwale, Zambia

The moon sat high in the sky as Foaly and Vinny stalked through the high brush. Alex stopped and held up a closed fist, which Vinny responded to by stopping in place. After lowering himself into a crouch, Foaly checked his watch. It was fifteen minutes after midnight.

"Anything?" Foaly asked quietly into his radio.

"Standby, looping back around." Morgan replied. He was back at the complex, sitting on the roof while he piloted the RQ-11 Raven drone that they had brought with them and monitored its scopes through his tablet. Alex knew that he and Vinny were damn near invisible to the naked eye as they waited in the tall brush, thanks to both being dressed in MultiCam Arid and desert digital AOR1 combat fatigues respectively. Combine that with the soft ground eliminating the noise of their footsteps, and they may as well have been ghosts. That being said, they both knew that the Forward Looking Infrared, FLIR, cameras on the Raven would pick them up clear as day against the cool earth beneath them. That was good though, because that meant the drone could pick up anyone else that the two men on the ground might miss.

Foaly reached up and adjusted the tubular night vision device that sat over his right eye, cleaning up the picture a bit. They were out looking for any signs of rebel activity in the nearby area. With Morgan watching from the sky, he could pick out anything of interest and direct the ground team to move in for a closer look.

"Possible contact." Morgan said. "Heat signature one-two-seven meters to your one o'clock. Doesn't look like wildlife." This region of Zambia didn't have too much local fauna, so anything giving off a heat signature other than them was a point of interest. With a hand motion between the two of them, Vinny followed Alex as they continued moving through the brush, suppressed pistols at the ready.

Upon exiting the brush, Vinny spied what had come up on the Raven's FLIR. It was the remnants of a small campfire that had burned down to smoldering coals.

"Morgan, we've got a campfire here." Vinny said, kneeling and picking something up off the ground. He turned it over in his hands before showing it to Foaly. "AK mag." Foaly nodded.

"Morgan, see if you can get the Raven up to a higher altitude to find where the guys who made this are camping out. Can't be too far from here." Foaly said.

"Alright. Hold tight while I get the drone into position." Morgan said. As they waited, the former operators backed into the tall brush and sat back-to-back, sipping from their CamelBaks, and passing a stick of beef jerky between each other. While they waited, Foaly removed the NOD from his eye, blinked to clear his vision, then looked up at the starry sky above.

He loved places like this, where the stars could easily be seen. The only light pollution around here came from the mining complex, whose high-powered floodlights were kept on all night to make sure no one fell into the mine while wandering around at night. Staring up at the sky, Alex thought back to one of his first deployments to Southeast Afghanistan. Up in the mountains, the sky had been so clear that he'd been able see a belt of the Milky Way, along with beautiful twinkling stars, and at least four shooting stars every night.

"Okay." Morgan said a few moments later, startling Vinny awake from his power nap. "I've got two contacts: two-four-zero meters to your two o' clock. Stationary."

"Roger. We're moving." Foaly said, replacing the NOD over his eye and getting to his feet. Vinny was only a second behind him, instantly alert and awake.

They pushed from the brush in the heading that Morgan had given them. Soon enough they eventually picked out two unnatural shapes lying on the ground. They'd found the contacts.

At fifteen meters, Foaly confirmed that it was two rebels who were fast asleep on roll-out sleeping mats. He signaled to Vinny, who nodded in response. They slowly and quietly approached the rebels. Just as they were about to be on top of them, a twig snapped underneath Vinny's boot. This caused one of the rebels to open his eyes to see what had caused the noise, while the other just rolled over and grunted. The first rebel blinked for a moment, then his eyes shot wide open when he realized he was staring at two men in tactical gear creeping up on them in the dark.

Before the rebel could alert his friend, both contractors pounced. Mouths were covered to prevent any noise as Vinny wrapped his arm around the struggling man's throat and he applied a rear-naked choke that knocked the guy out almost instantly. Foaly's struggled a bit more, thrashing his body to try and break away from the larger and heavier American. Fed up, Foaly slapped his hand over the guy's throat and choked him out by pressing his thumb and fingers against the arteries in the man's neck, cutting off blood circulation and causing him to lose consciousness.

DECEPTION

With both rebels taken care of, Foaly and Vinny waited while Morgan did a quick scan and confirmed that those were the only contacts in the area. Knowing they were in the clear, the two contractors looked around and saw that the rebels had been sleeping with their rifles in the dirt beside them, along with chest rigs and small bags. Without a word, both men gathered up the weapons and equipment, flex cuffed the prisoners, and sanitized the area of any signs of a struggle before hauling their quarry back towards the Paoli complex.

24
Mutwale, Zambia

Dalyel sat in his chair, listening intently as the contractors filled him in on what they'd found the previous night, as well as why there were now two Zambian rebels occupying two empty offices in the complex.

They'd laid out the items retrieved from the two captured rebels across the conference table. The items of most interest were a set of binoculars, a compass, and a topographic map of the area where the mine sat, which had alarmingly-accurate penciled-in drawings of the mine and the surrounding buildings. There were also notes and numbers scribbled down the margins, with specific grid coordinates written beside red X's and arrows that pointed towards the Paoli complex.

"That map is French." Dalyel said, looking at the scale and additional information that was printed along the bottom of the map. "So, they're using Russian weapons, American-made tac gear, and French maps. How the hell does any of that work?"

"Rebel leadership must be in bed with some pretty good black-market dealers to get this stuff." Morgan said, his arms crossed against his chest.

"Did the guys you brought in give you any information?" Dalyel asked, re-folding the map and setting it on the table.

"Nothing yet. We worked them over a bit this morning, but neither of them would budge." Vinny said. "Figured we'd let them sweat it out a bit while we grabbed a bite to eat before briefing you and Greenwood."
Following the initial meeting, Greenwood had gone back

to his office to phone the Paoli headquarters and inform them about the latest developments.

"We should go down and talk with our 'friends' again. I'm pretty sure I can get the younger one to cave." Foaly said from the side of the room.

"Alright." Dalyel said, smoothing the front of his shirt as he stood. "I'll let Greenwood know so he can stop by if he wants. I'm sure he'll want to hear whatever information these guys give firsthand." They all waited as Dalyel called his boss and informed him they would be questioning the two detainees. Greenwood told his security chief that he would be on his way and asked that they not begin the questioning until he arrived. This was answered with nods from the contractors.

The guard next to the door of the room holding the younger rebel pulled it open, and all five men walked in without a word. Dalyel had his rifle with him to add to the intimidation factor. Foaly grabbed the back of the chair and rotated it so the detainee would be able to see them, then pulled the bag from the guy's head. This detainee was the younger of the two, and he was sixteen or seventeen years old at the most. He looked scared shitless as he stared up at Foaly with wide eyes as the large American bore down on him.

"Are you ready to cooperate?" Alex asked after staring down for a few moments. The best part of them being in Zambia was that the local population spoke and understood English thanks to it being a primary language during colonial times. Not needing an interpreter made things a hundred times easier.

Vinny and Dalyel both took meticulous notes as the kid, who revealed his name to be Kabwe, spilled his guts on the recon plan for the base. While he claimed that he didn't know when the attack was planned, he did confirm that the rebels intended to storm the complex, kill everyone inside, and keep it as their own to mine whatever they could before holding the place ransom. Kabwe wasn't sure if the attack would be moved up, delayed, or cancelled because of their disappearance, and apologized profusely when he had no more information to give.

"Alright then, here's what we're going to do." Alex said. "When I start yelling and slam my hands on the table, you start screaming. Make it sound like I'm hurting you."

Everyone in the room jumped when Foaly picked up the chair beside him and threw it against the wall, then slammed his open palms against a metal table and screamed at Kabwe to give him answers. The boy replied with yells of genuine fear, and Morgan noticed that the sudden noise had caused the young man to piss his pants. To anyone not in the room, including the guard outside, it sounded like Foaly had absolutely lost his shit as he demanded information from the boy. The finale was Foaly flipping the metal table, then smashing the chair he'd used before against the wall that connected to the room the other rebel was in. The boy went quiet as soon as Foaly held up a finger to his lips. Foaly patted him on the shoulder, then whispered for him to stay quiet before they exited the room. He was glad that the kid had decided to cooperate; he had no desire to hurt a teenager who had likely gotten drawn into the conflict to provide for his family.

They all walked into the second room and the older rebel, a guy in his mid-twenties, looked like he'd just about pissed himself. His breathing became quicker when he saw Foaly, who had sweat beading on his forehead and was panting thanks to the theatrics in the other room. For all this guy knew, this large man had just beaten his friend to death.

"You ready to talk?" Morgan asked. The rebel replied with a muffled 'fuck you' through his gag. Morgan shrugged and took a step back, allowing Alex to come forward. He grabbed the rebel by the shirt and slammed him against the table, bouncing his head off the metal surface before slamming the guy to the ground with an ippon seoi nage throw.

"Holy shit." Greenwood said, surprised Foaly was actually putting his hands on this guy. He'd honestly been hoping that this would have gone like the first, but it was obvious that a different approach was needed and being taken.

"What were you looking for?" Foaly yelled as he grabbed two fistfuls of the rebel's shirt. The guy mumbled something against his gag so Foaly pulled it down from the rebel's mouth, only for the captive to spit in his face. This was answered with a hard punch to the face before Foaly launched the smaller man over his shoulder, sending him crashing into the chair he'd been sitting in before.

Using his booted foot, Foaly rolled the rebel onto his back.

"Vinny, water." Foaly said, tossing a spare towel over the man's face. Without missing a beat, Vinny had a bottle of water and stood with his feet on the towel to secure it in place while Foaly secured the captive's arms and torso. With a nod from Alex, Vinny began pouring. After what must have been a terrifying forty-seconds of gagging and choking, Foaly pulled the cloth away from the rebel's face.

"What were you looking for?" Foaly asked again. The guy they'd just waterboarded coughed up water but said nothing as he glared up at the two men above him. "Hit him again." Foaly said as he replaced the towel.

"No, no, no, wait! Please!" The rebel panicked. "No more!"

"Sit him up." Foaly said, taking a knee so he would be eye-level with their guest as Vinny pulled the man into a sitting position. The rebel was still gasping, his shirt soaked through with both sweat and water, which made his dark skin shine under the fluorescent lights in the room. "Where did you get the weapons from?"

"The weapons are from our commander, up to the North near Mapunga." He said, his breathing still labored. "We get shipments every month, and they gave us the new rifles before they sent us out."

"And the maps?" Vinny asked.

"Given to us from our regional commander. He handed them to us and walked away, we were given instructions later."

"Who is 'we'?" Morgan asked.

"Myself, and Kabwe." The rebel jerked his head towards the other room. "We were given the maps, compasses, and binoculars to observe the base and report back on security. And then you…" He blinked for a moment. "Kabwe was just a boy, he joined us only a few weeks ago because he wanted to help his family. He did not deserve to die!" That confirmed their suspicions that he thought the younger rebel was dead.

"When is the attack happening?" Foaly asked. The rebel looked down at the floor, defeated. He'd already given up too much information, he would be killed either way. "Hey." Foaly snapped his fingers. "I'm talking to you. When is the attack happening?" Still, he said nothing.

"I think we're done here." Dalyel finally chimed in. Foaly stared at the man for a few moments before standing. They exited the room, leaving the broken rebel sitting in the middle of the floor. Once the door was closed, Foaly turned to Greenwood.

"Sorry if that caught you off guard, but he wasn't going to give us anything without being roughed up first." Foaly had picked that up once the guy had come to during their first round of questioning.

"No need to apologize." Greenwood said. "I didn't see anything other than you giving some water to a thirsty rebel defector." The manager smirked, and Foaly reciprocated.

"I think that you guys should plus-up your security. With these guys scouting you out and them not knowing the timetable of the attack, it would be better to prepare now rather than being caught with your pants down." Foaly stated as he cracked open a fresh bottle of water, downing half of it in one swig.

"Sounds good, I'll get started on that right away." Dalyel said, breaking off from the group.

"Gentlemen." Greenwood said. The three Americans turned to face him. "I can't thank you enough for the effort you've put forth in helping protect my people. You've truly gone above and beyond expectations, and I will ensure that you are paid healthy bonuses in addition to your originally negotiated terms for what you've done." Vinny looked at Foaly, who smirked.

"We like to be thorough." Morgan said, CEO-mode engaged. "And we take pride in what we do. Repeat business is always a plus, too." He smirked.

"I'm sure Paoli will be happy to hear that." Greenwood said. "You'll have to excuse me; I have to prepare a report to send back to corporate detailing the current situation and the discoveries made by your findings and 'discussions' with the captured rebels. Hopefully, this will allow me to request more security be flown in until the current situation has blown over."

"Very good, Mister Greenwood." Morgan said. With a small wave, the Brit disappeared from view.

25
Mutwale, Zambia

The contractors were relaxing in their quarters as the day wound down. While Morgan and Alex tapped away at their laptops, Vinny was lying on his bed, lightly snoring with his arm covering his eyes. Foaly's rapid-fire typing as he wrote up a report for company records was mostly silent thanks to the Air Pods Morgan had nestled in his ears, listening to Metallica as he watched the Raven's footage on his screen.

In the three days since they'd interrogated the two detainees, the older of which who was still in custody, they had kept the drone up during the night hours. The younger rebel, Kabwe, had been rewarded for his cooperation by being released from custody and allowed to assist the employees around the complex. That being said, he had been given a bright-yellow safety vest as well as a white hard hat, both of which he was to wear at all times. The security staff had been given his description, and there was a shoot-on-sight order if he was found trying to leave the complex. So far, he had been quick to follow every order given to him and expressed his gratitude over and over for them not injuring him and allowing him to work rather than arresting him. He was particularly on the spot with bringing Foaly a new, sealed bottle of water whenever his current one ran dry.

Morgan perked up and leaned forward when he saw something that didn't look right on the UAV feed. He tapped an arrow key and the Raven banked left as he rotated the camera to cover the spot again. After a moment, he was staring at several bright spots standing out against the cooling ground on the thermal image.

"Got something on the feed." Morgan said as he popped the pods from his ears. Foaly closed his laptop and walked over to the desk, leaning down and looking over Morgan's shoulder. With the Raven's flight pattern fixed, they were both seeing at least twenty foot-mobiles heading towards the complex from the North. The drone continued on its current heading and showed another group behind the first, then another to the Northeast.

"Shit." Foaly said, leaning in closer to the screen. The movements of the contacts on the screen made it obvious they were attempting to move without being seen from the sentries posted on the complex's roof. "Those are rebels, they're attacking tonight." Alex broke away from the desk and slapped Vinny's leg as he passed. "Kit up, we're in for a fight."

As Alex and Vinny began to don their equipment, Morgan put the Raven in a holding pattern and synced up his tablet to the computer so he could view the drone's feed from the mobile device before heading to his bed and pulling out his vest and helmet.

Vinny was just pulling the straps of his medical bag tight over his vest when a fully geared-up Foaly ran out, heading down the hall towards Dalyel's room.

"Dalyel!" Foaly yelled, pounding his open hand against the door. "Kurt, wake up!' He took a step back as a tired-looking Dalyel pulled the door open, rubbing his eyes with one hand.

"What's up?" Dalyel asked, then blinked and stared at Foaly, who was clipping his helmet strap under his chin. Then his eyes went wide.

"The rebels are moving to attack, they're already on their way towards the complex from the North. Get all of your guys armed and ready." Without a word, Dalyel reached over and hit the alarm button beside his door. Red lights began flashing, accompanied by a loud klaxon a few moments later.

"All units, this is One-One." Dalyel said into his radio. "This is not a drill. Get armed and topside to defensive positions immediately. Say again, get to defensive positions immediately. We have an imminent threat." He looked up at Foaly. "I'll be out in two."

"We're headed up now." Foaly said, watching as Morgan and Vinny, both wearing their kits over whatever they'd been wearing while relaxing, jogged down the hall.

The three ran outside, surrounded by Paoli security officers who were scrambling to get to their posts. The ones who had been on duty were in full uniform, while those who had been off were in a mix of regular clothes and relaxed wear, with some being just in their boxers and boots beneath their vests and helmets.

"They're coming from the North side, get the crew-served up there!" Foaly yelled to a passing group carrying a couple of 240s and extra ammo cans. They nodded and started up the stairs.

"Guys, hold on a second." Vinny said. They all stopped and looked at him as he glanced towards the sky as the security and mining staff ran around them.

"Incoming!" Morgan yelled when he heard the whistling. They all dove for cover as the whistling became louder and then turned into an explosion when the mortar shell impacted in one of the lower levels of the mine.

"You guys good?" Vinny asked.

"I'm good." Morgan replied.

"I'm up." Foaly said as he got to his feet. The rest of the staff were yelling to each other to check if there were any injuries. Thankfully, there were none.

"Hey!" They all turned to see Dalyel running out, dressed in a t-shirt and cargo pants under his gear. "Hey, get inside!" Dalyel barked at some of the mining staff, who were standing out in the open, shocked at what was happening. "Inside, now!" He waved for them to move towards the door, and after a moment they bolted inside towards safety. Once they were clear, he started towards the contractors. "Hey, you guys good?"

"Yeah, we're up." Vinny said.

"Here, look." Morgan pulled the tablet from his pocket and brought up the UAV feed. The bird was slowly circling over the area that was now full of the white-hot silhouettes of the approaching hostiles. There were a few groups that weren't moving, which was likely where the mortars were set up.

"We need to hold fire and maintain cover." Foaly said, pulling Dalyel's attention away from the drone feed. "They're going to try and soften us up with mortars before launching the main assault."

"So, we just sit here and wait?" Dalyel asked, not expecting that answer from their security advisors.

"Once they come at us, we'll be up on that wall with your guys to hold them off in a counterattack. It's what we're here for." Vinny said, having read Foaly's mind. That was the beauty of them both having been █████ █████; they knew this shit like the back of their hand. Dalyel looked at them for a moment before nodding.

"Okay, let's get up there and-"

"Incoming!" Dalyel was interrupted by the yells of the security personnel as more mortars whistled overhead. Dalyel and Morgan dropped to the ground while Vinny and Foaly dropped to a knee, hunkered down, and covered their faces before the mortars impacted. This volley impacted outside the walls of the compound. When the ringing from the explosions went away, they heard screaming.

Someone was hit.

26
Mutwale, Zambia

Vinny broke away from the group at a run, taking the stairs two at a time as his SOCM instincts kicked in. He reached the top of the complex and saw one of the security officers on his back, surrounded by two others who were kneeling over him.

"Out of the way!" Vinny barked, taking a knee beside the injured man. He'd caught some shrapnel from one of the mortars in the upper chest and face. Most of the cuts were superficial, but there was one piece that was dangerously close to the man's jugular. "Listen, you two." He pointed at the officers that had been kneeling around their wounded man. "Go get a backboard and secure him, then carry him, carefully, to the infirmary. Make sure whoever is in charge gets this." He tore away the piece of paper he'd scribbled down his hasty assessment on and stuffed it into one of the officer's hands while the other called for a backboard. Soon they had one and the man was loaded, his neck secured in a cervical collar after Vinny ensured that it would not disturb the metal protruding from his neck. "Wait." Vinny said. They stopped, and he reached in and began pulling magazines from the wounded man's vest. "We need all the ammo we can use up here." They nodded, and once he was done, they began carrying the casualty downstairs.

While that had transpired, Morgan, Alex, and Dalyel had made their way to the roof, moving towards the waist-high wall that ringed the outer perimeter. Morgan pulled out the tablet and consulted it with Alex, who nodded and conferred with Dalyel.

DECEPTION

"Alright, light up the tree line!" Dalyel ordered. Vinny moved forward, his SCAR shouldered, and pulled the trigger. The outpouring of fire was enormous and would surely stave off another volley for a bit.

Morgan stopped firing his rifle and took a knee to look at the Raven feed. He ducked his head when the rebels returned fire from the tree line, and everyone else went to take cover. Two Paoli security weren't fast enough. One was shot through the head, snapping him backwards and killing him instantly. The other took two rounds to his left arm and was struck once in his plate, sending him toppling over the edge of the roof to the ground inside the complex below.

"Shit!" One of the officers yelled, staring down wide-eyed at the dead man who'd crumpled where he'd been shot, blood pouring down his forehead. Vinny ran over and did a quick assessment, already knowing the guy was gone.

"Hey!" Vinny yelled. "Hey, return fire!" That snapped the man out of his stupor, and he shifted his gaze from his dead friend to behind the sights of his rifle. With that taken care of, Vinny swung himself over the edge of the wall and dropped down beside the wounded man who'd fallen. On top of his gunshot wounds, he'd also landed badly, giving him a compound fracture in his right tibia. The white bone starkly contrasted with the blood-soaked uniform it was poking through. "Yo!" Vinny called out to the two guards who had carried the shrapnel casualty in before, who were just exiting the complex. "We're going to need medical personnel out here to triage and treat the wounded. If we have to move them to the infirmary, they're going to die. Go!" With that they ran back inside to relay the information while Vinny went to work stabilizing the man in front of him.

27
Mutwale, Zambia

Alex dropped to a knee to reload his rifle. Just as he'd slapped the bolt-release and popped up to begin firing again, he saw the flash of a mortar tube from the tree line. At least now he had an idea of where they were firing from.

"Incoming!" His voice joined the others as everyone on the roof dove for cover. The mortar impacted the roof on the south side of the complex, punching through and detonating inside the second story. "Morgan!" Foaly called out.

"Yeah?" Morgan replied from down the line.

"I need the launcher!" Alex yelled as he opened fire at a group of charging rebels. The contractors had brought along a Heckler & Koch HK169 forty-millimeter grenade launcher with them on this job.

Morgan picked himself up and ran over to Foaly, bullets *snapping* overhead as he moved past the Paoli security forces. He'd almost left the launcher back in the room when they'd first ran out after seeing the incoming rebels, but had stopped just long enough to grab the launcher and bandolier of grenades from his bag. He was just happy he wasn't running all the way back to retrieve them now.

"Here!" Morgan said, sliding the launcher and bandolier from his shoulder and handing them to Foaly. Alex popped open the chamber and loaded an illumination round. He aimed high and let rip. When the round reached its apex, the flare lit and a small parachute deployed, bathing the surrounding area in a light comparable to the daytime sun. This revealed even more rebels than what had previously been seen, all of whom were momentarily stunned as they looked up at the bright light in the sky. The Paoli forces quickly focused fire on their now-visible attackers, breaking those who weren't immediately cut down from their flare-induced trance.

With the added illumination, Foaly could actually see the mortar crews. They were quickly adjusting their tubes and getting ready for another volley. He popped the spent illum round and slid a high-explosive shell into the launcher before shouldering and aiming it. He squeezed the trigger just as the crew held up another mortar to hang before letting it fire. The grenade impacted, and the explosion seemed normal for a moment, then doubled and tripled in size. Secondary detonations; a direct hit.

"Truck coming towards the main gate!" Someone yelled, cutting the cheered celebrations short. Both Morgan and Foaly turned to see a pickup truck with pieces of metal welded to it as makeshift armor speeding down the main access road towards the main gate.

"Focus fire on that truck!" Dalyel shouted. A number of the security staff turned and opened fire, while the two machine gunners held down their triggers, allowing their weapons to go cyclic as they walked their rounds onto the target. Foaly reloaded the launcher and placed the sights well in front of the truck, knowing he'd have to lead the target. His finger was just about to pull the trigger when his ears picked up the whistling of another incoming mortar.

28
Mutwale, Zambia

Vinny kicked down the locks on one of the metal gurneys that had been wheeled out by the medical staff before helping lift a wounded security officer onto it. She was unconscious, having taken a round to the helmet that had knocked her out cold. Vin hadn't even checked yet but knew she was more than likely concussed.

"Incoming!" The security staff on the roof yelled. Vinny leaned over, shielding as much of the wounded officer as he could with his own body to protect her from the incoming round. He braced himself for the impact and was shaken to the bone when the shell landed inside the complex. A wave of heat and dirt flew over him, and a moment later the ringing from the impact was replaced by screaming.

Vinny turned around and saw that one of the Zambian workers had been caught by the blast. He was gripping his leg as he screamed and writhed in pain.

"Stay here, I'll get him!" Vinny barked at one of the Paoli medical staff, who seemed stunned by the order from a random volunteer.

Vinny took off towards the injured man, pumping his legs as fast as he could. He reached the worker and knelt beside him, his eyes instantly catching the sight of the arterial bleed squirting from the man's severed left femoral. The guy's left leg had been shredded by shrapnel.

"Sit back." Vinny ordered as he took the screaming man's hands away from the leg. He reached down to his battle belt and pulled a Combat Application Tourniquet from one of the many holsters he had and opened it up, applying it above the wound and near the man's crotch to ensure it would stop the bleeding. Vinny looped the strap over itself and then cranked down the windlass, which drew another scream from the worker. "I know, I know." Vinny said as he secured the windlass and looked down at his watch. The face was covered with blood, so he wiped it away with his thumb to get a read on the time before writing it on the CAT's time tab. With that done, Vinny carefully picked the man up and carried him over to the treatment area. "Hey, Doc." Vinny said, getting the attention of a nearby Paoli doctor. "This guy's got an arterial bleed; left femoral. I put a tourniquet on it, but the artery was shredded by that mortar."

"Okay, okay." The doctor said, peeling off a pair of nitrile gloves from her hands and tossing them to the ground before grabbing a fresh pair while Vinny laid the worker down on a gurney. The doctor grabbed one of the pre-packed surgical kids and tore it open while another member of the med staff began cutting away the worker's pants as Vinny hooked an IV into the guy's arm.

"Hey, we need a medic!" Someone called. Vinny turned to see two security officers carrying a third between them.

"You got him?" Vinny asked the doctor, who nodded. She was busy sterilizing the Zambian's leg. Vinny ran towards the security officers. The guy between them was limp; his head down and feet dragging. There was a blood trail following him. "On the gurney, here!" Vinny pointed. They brought him over and Vinny secured the guy's neck as the others lifted him up. "What happened?" He checked for a pulse. There was one, but it was weak.

"Dunno." One of the guys said. "He was good, then he dropped." Vinny nodded as he checked the man over. He was bleeding steadily, but Vinny couldn't find the wound. He began tearing the guy's vest away, then grabbed his trauma shears and started cutting away clothing. The guy's breathing was shallow, and he was losing a lot of blood. Vinny knew he had to work fast.

29
Mutwale, Zambia

Morgan slapped a new mag into his rifle before checking the tablet again. He hit the power button and the screen came to life, jumping right to the Raven's feed.

The screen showed heat signatures all over the place, with at least two other mortar positions set up among the sparse trees. Those would have to be taken out before they could successfully stage a counterattack.

"Alex!" Morgan called out as he slid the tablet back into his cargo pocket.

"Yeah?" Foaly replied from down the line, his voice almost lost among the rapid gunfire. Morgan wished they'd been able to dial in their radios before the shit kicked off as he ducked down and made his way towards his fellow contractor. There was another explosion, and the access road to the complex was lit up as a grenade impacted with and took out a second incoming vehicle. Morgan stopped beside Foaly, who was reloading the launcher and watching to make sure the vehicle he'd just hit was out of commission.

"Here, look." Morgan said, pulling out the tablet again. "They've got more mortars set up here, and here, with another large group moving in from the North." He traced his gloved index finger to each point of interest to make sure Foaly got the picture. Alex nodded, then looked behind Morgan.

"Dalyel!" Alex called. "Kurt, over-" Both ducked down when Foaly was interrupted by the sound of a heavy machine gun opening fire. Large tracer rounds shot over their heads moments later, accompanied by the loud reports. "Stay down!" Foaly yelled to both Morgan and the surrounding Paoli staff. After a moment, there was a lull in the gunfire, and Foaly slowly raised himself up so just his eyes were peering above the rooftop wall.

The gunfire resumed, focused on a different portion of the wall. From the muzzle flashes, sound, and constant jamming, Foaly figured it was a Browning M2 .50 caliber machine gun, though thankfully the rebels had fucked up the headspace and timing. The large gun jammed again, then started firing. And that's when they heard the frantic calls of 'man down' and 'medic' coming from down the line.

"Fuck this." Foaly said, popping out the HE grenade he'd put in the launcher and loading one of the few incendiary rounds they'd brought with them. "Cover!" He called out. Morgan and the rest of the surrounding staff popped up and opened fire, laying into the tree line. Foaly stood up and shouldered the launcher, aiming in the direction of the .50's muzzle flashes. A few moments later the area where the .50 was exploded, which quickly caught fire, the flames rapidly spreading through the dry grass and brush of the savanna.

The flames continued to spread well beyond the initial impact point. The illumination from the fire backlit the few dozen rebels still standing after their initial attack. Realizing they couldn't retreat, the rebels began screeching as they charged forward, weapons firing at the complex. Foaly planted another incendiary grenade in the middle of them.

"Hit 'em!" Dalyel yelled, firing at the hostiles. Foaly let the sling catch the launcher as he shouldered his rifle and joined Morgan in putting down the remnants of the attacking force. The rebels who weren't immediately cut down ran out of the burning tree line, their clothes and skin alight. Paoli gunfire quickly brought an end to their suffering. Everyone on the wall watched and waited, swapping magazines, eyes scanning over and through rifle sights as they waited for the next wave. To their collective relief, none came.

The fire continued to burn until it reached the trimmed grass surrounding the complex, stopping its forward motion. The tall grass around the outskirts of the perimeter continued to go up until the entire complex sat in a ring of fire.

"Get the fire suppression system up!" Dalyel called out. Two minutes later a loud klaxon began blaring, followed by high-pressure streams of water and fire-retardant foam shooting from nozzles set in the complex's outer walls. The orange-red foaming gel dampened the fire around the immediate perimeter but did nothing to stop the outer flames that continued their swath through the brush and small trees further from the walls.

Dalyel sighed and looked over at Morgan and Foaly, both of whom were staring out at the burning landscape. They both blinked, then turned to face the weary security chief. They were all tired and glad to be alive.

"Come on." Morgan said, slinging his rifle. "Let's go see how Vinny is doing."

30
Mutwale, Zambia

"Hold his legs!" Vinny barked at the assisting Paoli security officer, who locked his arms around the flailing legs of the wounded man while Vinny popped the cover of a syringe with his teeth. "Dude, I need you to hold still so I can give you this, it'll take the pain away." The officer on the gurney answered with a guttural cry of pain, his eyes wide and staring up at Vinny. "Hey, someone hold this guy's shoulders!" Vinny barked. One of the nearby Paoli medical staff ran over and placed her hands on the guy's exposed shoulders.

The officer had been nicked by a piece of shrapnel when the truck had exploded. Now there was a piece of metal half the size of a credit card lodged in his left pectoral. It wasn't deep enough to do any damage to his heart or lungs, but it was obvious that it hurt like a bitch. With the officer's shoulder secure, Vinny swabbed the injection site before administering the shot. It would take a few minutes, but the guy would relax once the Ativan kicked in.

"Alright buddy, you're going to be fine. Just try to relax until the meds kick in." He said before looking over at the nurse, who gave him a nod. Vinny stood and *snapped* the gloves from his hands before taking a swig of water from the bottle he'd shoved into his cargo pocket at some point. He paused and took a moment to look around the de-facto surgical center that had been set up under one of the entrance awnings. It wasn't pretty.

"Vinny!" Someone called out. He turned to see Alex, Morgan, and Dalyel approaching. They were all drenched in sweat. He raised a hand and waved, swishing the water around his mouth before spitting into the dirt.

"Hey guys." He said. Morgan walked up and clasped his hand.

"Glad you're alright." Foaly said.

"Likewise." Vinny extended the bottle towards Foaly, who took a swig before passing it to Morgan. Dalyel was looking over the injured Paoli officers on the gurneys, then those who were sitting on the ground. Then the eight that were lined up on the ground, covered by sheets. "We tried everything we could." Vinny said. Dalyel just nodded, lips pressed together.

"Shit." Dalyel said quietly. He walked past the contractors and stopped at one of the gurneys.

Lying on his back, blood covering his exposed chest and legs, was Ricky Harkens. He had taken a round to the upper arm, one to the shoulder, and one through his thigh. A piece of shrapnel had punched through his chest, collapsing his right lung. The med staff had fought to keep him alive, and now he was asleep thanks to the morphine drip the medics had given him. He still looked rough though. With things getting as hectic as they had, the medics had done what they could to stabilize him before moving onto more priority wounded. Dalyel saw there was a large '2' written on Ricky's forehead in Sharpie.

Vinny and the medical staff had triaged their patients into three categories: 1's were walking wounded; they weren't going to die if they didn't receive attention right away, and were mostly met with gauze and pressure bandages, as well as orders to keep pressure on theirs or someone else's wounds until the medics got to them. There were more than a few 1's posted on the roof, having returned back to the fight. 2's were priority, and went right onto a gurney when they arrived, receiving the most attention from the staff. 3's were past the point of no return. If they were still alive when they arrived at the medical station, they were given an assessment, determined to be a category 3, and given a shot of Ativan to ease whatever pain they were in until the inevitable happened.

Dalyel gently placed a hand on Ricky's bloody shoulder and bowed his head in silent prayer for a few moments before moving to the next gurney and doing the same. He continued this for each of his wounded staff, and then for those who hadn't made it.

"Sorry I wasn't up there with you guys." Vinny said.

"Don't sweat it. You did more down here than you would've up there." Foaly said. "Half of these guys would be under sheets if you hadn't loaned a hand." Vinny nodded, giving a shallow smile to his friend.

"So, what happened? You get them to retreat?" Vinny asked. Foaly shrugged.

"I don't see any movement." Morgan said as he checked his tablet. "Though it's hard to make out what's what with all that heat. And the thermals are fucking with the Raven's flight." He began tapping in the recall order for the small drone.

"Thermals?" Vinny asked.

"Come check this shit out." Foaly said. Vinny followed Alex up the stairs to the roof. He didn't have anything to say as he observed the burning countryside that now surrounded the complex.

31
Mutwale, Zambia

They stood on the roof in the early morning. Dalyel smoked a cigarette as he looked over the charred and blackened ground that had been savanna and trees the day prior. His eyes joined the three contractors' as they watched a Paoli helicopter fly overhead, dumping another load of water on the field to the North.

The fire had ended up spreading over two miles out from the complex, burning through everything in its path. Luckily, Greenwood had been able to radio the airfield and got the Paoli birds up. Eighteen hours of continuous flight operations later, they'd managed to contain the fire and prevent it from spreading to the outlying croplands that belonged to local farmers. To the surprise of the contractors and the security chief, the airfield hadn't been attacked at all.

"I really can't thank you guys enough for what you did." Dalyel finally broke the silence. "We wouldn't have seen that attack coming, and it probably would've been too late once we realized what was happening. You grabbing those two really saved our asses." The contractors looked at him, gave either a small smile or nod, then returned their gaze to the now-barren land. None of them really had anything to say about it, being that they'd failed to prevent the injuries or deaths of the Paoli staff. The total death count was thirteen, and that included Ricky, who was one of five that had succumbed to their injuries during surgery. Another seven were still critical, and fourteen more were on light duty due to their injuries.

They all watched as one of the recovery teams, who'd been dispatched outside of the complex to recover and clear each and every body they found from the botched attack, lifted up the charred remains of a rebel. They swung the body twice before releasing it, where it landed in the back of a pickup truck on top of other bodies that had been recovered so far.

Foaly finished his coffee and patted his cargo pocket for a bottle of water, but his current one was empty. As if on cue, Kabwe came up the stairs and stood on the roof behind them, toting a bucket full of water bottles resting on a rapidly-melting bed of ice. Foaly turned around and was caught off guard by the young man standing there in his bright-yellow vest and white hard hat.

"Water?" Kabwe asked.

"Sure, thanks." Foaly said. The young Zambian retrieved a bottle from near the bottom and handed the dripping drink to the American, who cracked in and took a swig. "Put that down and look at this." The boy did, then went to stand beside Foaly at the wall of the roof.

As Kabwe took in the ruined landscape, his eyes widened, and a knot formed in his stomach. That knot threatened to turn to nausea as one of the teams picked up another burned body. This one came apart at the waist when they went to toss it in the truck.

"You would have been one of those bodies had Mister Greenwood not kept you here." Foaly stated bluntly.

"Y...yes sir." Kabwe said, his voice shaking. "Thank you. Thank you for saving me." The boy looked up at Foaly with wide, tearful eyes. "Thank you, thank you!" He repeated as he went down the line to Morgan and Vinny, then practically fell to his knees as he thanked Dalyel over and over.

"Enough. Go see if anyone else needs water." Dalyel growled. It was obvious he held no fond feelings towards Kabwe, being that the boy could have easily been another gun firing at his men.

"So, what happens now?" Morgan asked, breaking another silence after Kabwe made himself scarce. Dalyel finished his own coffee and crushed the Styrofoam cup.

"Greenwood's on a video conference with the Paoli higher-ups right now. He wanted me to bring you guys in for a meeting around noon. Not sure what it's about, but that's all he told me. Can't imagine they want to shut this place down, but who knows after last night." Dalyel turned and sat on one of the folding lawn chairs that a guard had set out at some point. It was obvious that the loss of so many of his people was hitting him hard, but Dalyel was holding it together. It was natural to be angry; they were all too familiar with that.

"What do you say we grab something to eat?" Vinny asked.

"Sounds good to me." Morgan said. They all looked towards Dalyel, who exhaled and looked up at them.

"You've got a one-track mind, Jensen." Dalyel smirked. "Alright, let's go." He slapped his knees as he stood, leading them to the cafeteria.

The four of them walked into the cafeteria and were met with applause from the Paoli staff sitting for a mid-morning meal. It caught them by surprise, so they all stood there awkwardly until the moment passed.

"Looks like security aren't the only ones who appreciate what you guys did." Dalyel said.

"Just doing our job." Morgan said with a shrug. They continued towards the buffet line, where they were met with handshakes, back-slaps, and smiles from almost every person they passed.

32
Mutwale, Zambia

Following breakfast, the contractors went back to their quarters to continue cleaning weapons and gear before their meeting with Greenwood. While Morgan was typing up another report on the events of the attack, an email popped up on his screen. He double-clicked the message, and his jaw clenched when he saw it was from the Department of State.

"Ah shit." He said as he scrolled down, his eyes flicking back and forth over the body of the message. He read it twice before looking over the top of his laptop towards where Alex and Vinny sat on the floor, their weapons disassembled in front of them. "Hey guys, just got an email from the State Department."

"What do they want?" Vinny asked, scrubbing away at his rifle's bolt carrier.

"Looks like we're slated to fly back to DC and give them a debrief on what happened here." Morgan leaned back and picked up the half-eaten power bar from his desk, taking another bite out of it.

"How the fuck do they know about this already?" Foaly asked.

"Probably Instagram or Facebook from one of the security guys." Vinny replied.

"They're going to want to know what we dealt with regarding the rebels. Should be real interesting for them to see the weapons and gear these guys were carrying out in the bush." Foaly said as he snapped the upper and lower receivers of his rifle together. "When we meet with Greenwood, we should request a copy of all of his documents as well. Maybe even request to take some of the evidence back with us."

"What about Kabwe and the other guy?" Vinny asked. None of them had taken the time to learn the other rebel's name.

"What about him?" Morgan asked through a mouthful of power bar.

"We could bring them back with us. We already know Kabwe will cooperate and give up whatever information they want. The other guy might not be so keen to talk, but throw him in a cell at Guantanamo for a few weeks so the Agency interrogators can work him over for a bit, and he'll be singing like a bird in no time." Vinny said matter-of-factly.

"I don't think it works like that." Foaly said. "Especially for some low-level rebel targeting a foreign company's mining operation." Vinny paused for a moment. He hadn't thought of that. "And if State does want to talk with them, I'm sure they'll send their own plane to collect them. The gear and weapons should be fine for us to take back though."

"I'll shoot them a quick confirmation for the meeting and let them know about Kabwe and the other guy." Morgan looked down at his watch. "And then we'll head to Greenwood's office." He quickly typed up the email and sent it back, then stood and slid his pistol into its thigh holster.

The three of them made their way to Greenwood's office on the second floor. Dalyel was already sitting in one of the chairs, waiting with the manager. A tired-looking Jack Greenwood greeted them, coffee cups and paperwork scattered around. It was obvious they weren't the only ones moving non-stop since the attack began.

"Mister Greenwood, good to see you again." Morgan said as they all shook the man's hand.

"Good to see you as well, gents." Greenwood said wearily. Having kept busy coordinating the fire-control efforts with the airfield, as well as having dozens of different teleconferences with Paoli executives regarding what happened, Greenwood hadn't left his office since he'd hunkered down there after the first shots had been fired. He stood and rubbed a hand across his unshaven chin before stretching his arms above his head, resulting in multiple pops from his back. "Anyone want some coffee?" He asked as he walked over to the coffee pot plugged into the wall. They all declined, so he poured himself a cup, mixing in some honey before returning to his seat.

"So, what's the story?" Morgan asked. Greenwood closed his eyes and sighed.

"After all the meetings, the Paoli executives have decided that it's in our best interest to close your contracts early in light of recent events. Long story short: they don't want anyone not insured by them to be injured or killed. You'll be paid in full, and I've negotiated a healthy bonus be added as a thank you for all of the work you've done to support and protect Paoli's interests. The money will be wired to your accounts by close of business today; London Time." He glanced at his watch for a moment, then gave up. He was too tired to calculate the time difference right now.

Silently, the three contractors stole glances to one another. Not only were they being cut loose to go home early, but they were getting paid more money. It was like finding a unicorn.

"That's a shame to hear we can't stay. But please extend our thanks to your executives. I'll be sure to write in our reports and testimonials that Paoli Industries, particularly your staff, have been excellent to work with." Morgan said. "We do have one final request though."

"What's that?" Greenwood asked, flinching as he almost knocked over a stack of papers when setting his coffee mug down.

"We're to give a debrief to the US State Department regarding the Zambian rebels. We'd like to request a copy of your documents regarding the rebels in both hard copy and digital, at the least. If possible, we'd also like to take one or two of the captured weapons and some equipment back, as physical evidence." Greenwood stared up at them for a moment, and none of the men knew which direction this would go in.

"Consider it done." Greenwood said after a moments' thought. "It's the least we can do after all you've done for us." The phone on the manager's desk rang, and he sighed. "That's another conference call. You gentlemen can see yourselves out. Thanks again."

"I hope this State meeting goes quick. I want to get home and sleep in my own bed." Vinny said as they walked down the hall back towards their quarters.

"You mean that mattress sitting on your floor?" Morgan chided as they entered the room and began to prep their things for travel back home.

"Hey, box springs are expensive!" Vinny shot back in mock-defense. Unlike the larger apartments that Morgan and Alex lived in, Vinny had settled into a small studio apartment on East 85th and First. While his living conditions were spartan, they were more than enough to keep him comfortable. The biggest quality of life improvement he'd made was purchasing a couch to put in front of the TV for Morgan and Alex to sit on when they'd come over to watch the fights.

As he packed his bags, Foaly's phone *dinged* in his pocket. He looked to see it was a text from Shannon. While it wasn't an actual text from her, the message did contain a link to some realtor agency. He clicked it and saw images of a two-bedroom apartment with a large living room, kitchen, and concrete patio pop up. He swiped through the images, then texted back *How much?* As he waited for a response, he pulled up the address and saw it was on East 78th and York; a step up from their current gigs.

Twenty-two a month. Julia got us the hookup. Shannon replied. Foaly whistled; it was almost a thousand more than what they were currently paying. *We can afford it.* The second text came seconds later, almost as if to reassure him even though he hadn't asked. He smirked.

Flying to DC first. Get the paperwork started. See you in a few days. Love you. He typed out before tossing the phone back to the bed.

There was a knock on the door and Morgan went to open it. Dalyel stood there with another member of his staff, both carrying weapons and equipment 'liberated' from the rebels.

"Here you go, guys." Dalyel said, laying three of the AK-103s down on the table, along with a hard case for the weapons. "The bag has three of the vests and everything that was in them, each individually packed and sealed.

"Thanks, Kurt." Morgan said. Dalyel nodded and smiled.

"I'm the one who should be thanking you guys." The security chief gave each of them a nod.

"You handled yourself well out there. They made a good choice putting you in charge of security here." Morgan replied.

"Yeah, well." Dalyel shrugged. "Thinking I might go back to doing stateside work after this. Take it easy and see my kids, ya know?" He smiled. "But listen fellas, you three definitely have your shit together. If you ever decide to expand, or just need an extra gun, please give me a call." He pulled out three business cards and handed one to Morgan before laying the others beside the wrapped AKs.

"We'll definitely keep you in mind." Foaly said with a smile.

"Alright guys, be safe." Dalyel gave a faux salute. "Greenwood got you set with a ride to the airfield?"

"Yeah, he's got one of the jeeps fueled up. We'll be driving ourselves out. That way you can keep all your people here." Morgan picked up one of the AKs and inspected the paperwork.

"Well, good luck guys. I owe you a round of drinks if we ever get together in the states." Dalyel said. With that, he bid them a final farewell and exited the room, leaving the consultants to finish packing for their trip back home.

33
Arlington, Virginia

Foaly woke with a start as the government-provided Gulfstream G650 touched down. After the Paoli flight dropped them off at Gatwick Airport in London, they were met by two black SUVs with government plates and were escorted to a private hangar that held two of the G6 planes. The contractors were given an opportunity to eat and shower before hopping onto the smaller plane that would take them the rest of the way for their meeting with State.

"Gentlemen, we're here." One of the otherwise-quiet pilots said from the cockpit. Foaly stretched his arms above his head, his lower back cracking as he did. A glance at his watch showed he'd gotten about eight and a half hours of sleep, but he was still groggy.

As Alex continued stretching to wake himself up, Morgan and Vinny got up as well. The three men were silent as they went about to ensure they didn't leave anything behind on the plane as the aircraft taxied to one of the smaller hangars to the north of Ronald Reagan National Airport's main terminals.

"Thought Reagan didn't do flights over the pond." Vinny grunted as he cracked his neck from side to side.

"Guess they do when it involves meetings like this." Morgan said as he bent over to look out the window. "Typical cloak-and-dagger shit I'm sure. But at least it's a quicker drive than it would've been from Dulles." Vinny grunted in response as he zipped up his backpack before slinging it over one shoulder. None of them were morning people.

DECEPTION

About ten minutes later the G6 was parked and the engines were powering down as the stairway opened. A rush of warm summer air flooded into the cabin, and Morgan squinted before putting his sunglasses on and stepping out onto the narrow stairway.

There were three SUVs sitting on the tarmac, with suited State Department employees standing around. As the three contractors descended the stairs, one of the SUVs opened and a man wearing a gray suit stepped out.

"Morgan Tyron?" The man asked, buttoning his suit jacket as he approached Morgan.

"That's me." Morgan replied.

"Scott Reinhardt, State Department." Reinhardt shook Morgan's hand. While the State employees wore suits and ties, the three contractors looked much more relaxed. Morgan was the only one in a suit, though he wore his collar open. Vinny wore a polo shirt untucked over a pair of slacks, and Alex wore a button-down fishing shirt with the sleeves rolled to his elbows, and a pair of nondescript cargo pants. "Glad to have you back in the states. We're looking forward to hearing your report on the situation in Zambia." Reinhardt said as he shook the rest of their hands.

"USAID?" Foaly asked as he lit the remaining half of the cigar he'd started back in London.

"Yes sir. Are you Foaly or Jensen?" Reinhardt asked. Alex finished lighting the cigar and puffed a few times.

"Alex Foaly." Reinhardt gave a half-smile towards the scruffy-looking contractor. Foaly was in no rush to get to this debrief, and even contemplated offering a stogie to Morgan to prolong their trip.

"Once they're done offloading your bags, we can get underway." Reinhardt said in a passive-aggressive manner towards Foaly's smoking. Alex was just about finished by the time the airport personnel had unloaded the bags and tough boxes and transferred them into the waiting vehicles. Morgan checked his watch, and Vinny chuckled as Foaly took one last exaggerated pull before letting the cigar butt drop to the hangar floor and crushing it beneath the heel of his boot.

Twenty minutes later they all sat around a large conference table inside the Harry S. Truman building. The table was almost full, with only one chair left free. Reinhardt had been joined by other Department of State staffers, all of whom were conferring quietly while shooting curious glances towards the three men with visitor passes hanging around their necks. The contents of the bags that had been provided by Paoli were now strewn out on the table, with the weapons having been rendered safe by Morgan.

"Hey, sorry I'm late." Someone said as the door opened. "Traffic from Langley is at a freaking standstill." *Langley?* Foaly thought with a frown. So, these 'State' guys were actually from State then, and the Agency had sent one of their own.

The man from the Central Intelligence Agency was dressed in a dark blue suit with an open collar white shirt. His dark hair was gelled back, and his silver wristwatch and wedding band glinted in the bright lights set in the ceiling.

"Hi, Tom Donnelly." Thomas Donnelly introduced himself to Reinhardt and the other staffers.

"Scott Reinhardt, State Department." Reinhardt said as he shook Donnelly's hand. Morgan frowned. He'd never understood why these State guys felt the need to announce who they worked for every time they met someone new. This one was especially egregious considering they were sitting in the *headquarters* building of the State Department. "And those three are Morgan Tyron, Vincent Jensen, and Alex F-"

"Oh, don't worry, I know all about these three, particularly Alex." Donnelly gave a knowing smile even though he'd never met the three in person. "Their reputations precede them." This made Foaly's stomach knot up.

"Have we met before?" Morgan asked.

"I was on the ground around the same time as you three last year." Donnelly said. That was enough to have them all wide-eyed.

34
June, 2017
Yazd Province, Iran

Captain Alex Foaly leaned forward on the bench-seat of the MH-6L Little Bird helicopter. He squinted behind the goggles that protected his eyes from the wind as they approached their target, his ears tuned to the chatter of pilots and other team-leads through the headset that protected his eardrums from the screaming helicopter engines just feet above his head. Foaly and the rest of his team, callsign Solid, filled out the Little Bird, and were joined by other helos loaded by Metal, Kilo, and Vector Teams. They were also joined by four Blackhawks loaded with troops from the Seventy Fifth Ranger Regiment's First Battalion, and there was an armored convoy of MRAPs carrying more Rangers below.

The task force was moving to secure the Yazd Sadooghi Airport, which was currently being used as a stronghold by the Islamic Republic of Iran Army to defend sorties being launched against Tehran by the Iranian Air Force, or IRIAF. While most IRIAF bases had been bombarded during the initial invasion, US Navy F-35's had engaged Iranian F-4's over the Yazd Sadooghi Airport, and signals intelligence had corroborated the fact that the Iranians had shifted over to using civilian airports to launch air missions against US forces.

Iran had finally forced the United States into a full-on war following a rocket attack that hit Camp Shorabak in Afghanistan's Helmand Province. The attack killed fourteen US service members and ten Afghan National Army soldiers and wounded an additional forty base personnel. It had been discovered that the point of origin of the rocket attack had been in Gosht, Iran. While the Iranian government initially played coy about the whole event, the straw that broke the camel's back was when a Marine Corps CH-53E Super Stallion helicopter was shot down while on patrol Northwest of Chakhansur, Afghanistan. The helicopter went down in Hamun Lake, where the two Marines who'd survived the initial explosion drowned. Forensic analysis came back and revealed that the helo had been downed by an Iranian Qaem-M ground-to-air missile. In the next week, President Samuel Gooding had the Navy's Fifth Fleet parked in the Gulf of Oman, where the US had begun its shock-and-awe campaign against Iran, taking a page from the strategy used during the invasion of Iraq fourteen years prior.

With the initial shock-and-awe phase concluded, the US had moved in and secured strategic locations throughout Iran. Now they had moved onto phase two, which was simply dubbed the 'Thunder Run', another callback to a strategy once again used in Iraq. Both had been essential in taking Tehran, which still had certain portions of the city being contested by Iranian forces attempting to beat back the Americans. Foaly and his team had been in Tehran helping roll-up high value targets until tasking had come down for them to join 'Task Force Eleven' to assist in the seizure of the Yazd Airfield. From there, they would push into the nearby city of Zarach, where it was reported that Iranian's Minister of Defense, Brigadier General Hossein Ghorbani, was holed up following his evacuation from the capital city. The secondary objective was to secure the Yazd International Airport to utilize as a staging area for all Special Operations Forces in the area, giving them a centralized location to launch from until outlying bases could be secured.

"One mike." The pilot of the Little Bird carrying Foaly's team said. Foaly looked back over his shoulder and raised his index finger towards Master Sergeant Mike Hicks, his second-in-command. Hicks nodded, and both men faced forward, their rifles shouldered. Foaly was staring just over the holographic sight affixed to the top of his HK rifle when the air around them was suddenly filled with incoming small-arms fire. The pilots reacted by adding elevation, rending the AK fire basically useless. Then a loud, incessant beeping started through their comms.

"Flares, flares, flares." The co-pilot said coolly, setting off the helicopter's countermeasures. All the other helos in the flight did the same, causing the incoming surface-to-air missiles to fly harmlessly past. One managed to cut through the interference generated by the flares and clipped the tail boom of one of the Blackhawks, but mercifully didn't detonate. The operators of Solid Team watched with wide eyes as the Rangers inside the bird held on as black smoke began pumping from the rear rotor, causing the helicopter to pitch from side to side.

"Six-Two is hit." The Blackhawk pilot grunted into the radio. "I think I can get us...nope, no I'm losing pressure in the pedals. Six-Two is lame duck. Say again, Six-Two is lame duck." The winged Blackhawk broke from formation and the pilot managed to hold it in a wobbly hover about thirty feet over the ground, allowing the Rangers inside to kick out the ropes and fast rope into the dusty streets below. It gnawed at Foaly knowing that those Rangers would be on their own until the column coming through Yazd reached them, but there was no room in any other birds to take them in.

"This is Hunter Two-One, we're going to hold position until the convoy reaches us." The Ranger Squad Leader on the ground radioed in.

"Copy Two-One. Six-Three, break off and provide overwatch with Two-Three until the ground element arrives to pick up Two-One." Hunter Two, the Ranger Platoon Leader, ordered.

"Hunter Two-One this is Jester Six, we're en-route to Objective Clancy. Mark location on BFT and we'll pick you up." Foaly was surprised to hear the Green Beret Captain radio in. This brought a smile to his face. Having come from the Green Berets, Foaly was always happy to have Special Forces on his six.

"All call signs be advised, there is heavy RPG and small-arms coming from the airport." Major General Bradley Walters said over the radio. *Yeah, no shit.* Foaly thought to himself. Leave it to some REMF, Rear Echelon Motherfucker, to clog up their comms with redundant bullshit.

"Yeah, no shit!" The co-pilot barked as sparks flew across the canopy, AK fire hitting the front of the bird. "Fifteen seconds!" The bird did a wide loop of the airfield. The co-pilot, pissed at the concentration of fire directed towards them, leaned out and fired his H&K MP7 personal defense weapon at a group of Iranians that were leveling a launcher toward the bird. They collapsed under the combined fire of the co-pilot, Foaly, and Hicks. As the bird moved to touch down, each operator stuck their legs out and were unhooked and unloaded within seconds of the skids reaching tarmac.

"We're clear!" The team medic, Sergeant First Class Dwayne Hudson, called out over the radio.

"Copy Zero-Three." The pilot said as he began to lift his helo off. It got about twenty feet in the air before a rocket slammed down into its main rotor. The explosion sent the ruined bird back to Earth, almost killing the four shooters it had just discharged. A piece of shrapnel from the shattered rotors embedded itself in Hicks' goggles, causing him to bark out in surprise.

"Star Three is down! Say again, Star Three is down!" Foaly yelled over the radio. Hicks took a moment to remove his goggles and saw that he'd come about three quarters of an inch from losing his right eye. He stuffed the ruined goggles into the dump pouch on his battle belt and moved to meet his team lead at the crashed bird. Neither of the pilots had survived. "Be advised, both Star Three pilots are KIA." They began a hasty extrication of the bodies, wanting to get them clear before the wreckage caught fire.

"Copy Solid Zero One, Angel One-One is thirty seconds out." The lead of an Air Force Pararescue Squad chimed in over the radio. Twenty-Nine seconds later, a Blackhawk had set down and the elite Air Force medics took the two bodies and had them loaded up. "You boys need a lift?" Air Force Master Sergeant Jamal Phillips asked over the radio.

"Nah, we're good. You guys watch yourselves!" Foaly replied. The two bumped fists, then went their separate ways.

35
Yazd Province, Iran

Chief Special Warfare Operator Vincent Jensen stared out of the window in the back of the MRAP, watching passing rooftops as their armored column passed through the nearby city of Yazd towards the airfield. Jensen would have preferred riding in one of the smaller and more nimble Joint Light Tactical Vehicles, but the only one of those from ███ Squadron that had been loaned out for this operation was being commanded by their Task Unit commander.

"This land route is bullshit." Jensen's buddy, SO1 Jeff Dennison, commented. Dennison had become a SEAL because he liked the excitement of boats and helicopters, not being shoved in the back of a tin can as they drove through a city.

"What are you complaining about? We got to do an amphibious infil *and* a combat jump. Let the Army have their airfield seizure." Jensen knocked his fist against Dennison's knee before re-checking the straps of the medical pack he wore on his back. Jensen was their team's Special Operations Medic, which meant he carried a shit ton of extra gear to ensure he kept his people alive.

"Lima Actual, be advised." The pilot of the Command-and-Control bird orbiting high above the battlefield came over the radio. "Forward element is taking heavy AA fire from the airfield, two birds down and multiple KIA."

"Lima Actual copies, C2." General Walters replied. Jensen grunted and stood up, bouncing on his toes in anticipation for a fight. The Army Specialist sitting behind the console that controlled the remote M2 .50 Cal mounted to the top of the vehicle looked at him with wide eyes. The kid was maybe nineteen years old.

"Anything on the scope?" Vinny asked, pointing to the screen.

"Rooftops are clear." Specialist Miles Copre said. As if on cue, there was a loud 'pinging' as rounds impacted the left side of the armored vehicle. One round smacked into the window behind Lieutenant Jon Nelson's head, causing the Platoon Commander to flinch. This got a laugh out of Jensen, Dennison, and SO2 Marcus Dalton. Nelson blinked, then smiled.

"Lucky day." Nelson said.

"Ain't no such thing, LT." Dennison replied. Now Copre had the M2 trained on the left side of the MRAP, the heavy sounds of the .50 thumping through the thick armor and ratting the men below. They all listened to the radio as the pilot of Six-Two called out that they were hit, and that Hunter Two-One was going to be stranded near the outskirts of Yazd.

"Hey." Vinny said to Nelson. "We should divert and pick up the guys from that bird. We have the room."

"Negative." Nelson replied. It was obvious the Lieutenant wanted to do the same thing, but their Task Unit Commander, Lieutenant Commander Oscar Kensington, was a rare 'Mission First' SEAL that wouldn't divert unless someone was killed or mortally wounded. "Already radioed it up to Neptune Actual. He says let the Army SF team pick them up." Vinny shook his head. He didn't like it. Kensington was a good leader when it came to planning and doctrine, but he was too rigid for most SEALs, both above and beneath him.

"Lima Actual this is Charlie Three-Three, we're going to break away from the column and cover Hunter

Two-One until they get a pickup, over." One of the M1A2 Tank Commanders said over the radio.

"Lima Actual copies." The General replied a moment later. This got scoffs and snickers from the SEALs. They couldn't believe how much the General was involved in small decisions like that. Vinny's eyes shot open as an idea hit him, and he turned to Nelson again.

"We should support the tank. If they get bottlenecked, they aren't going to be able to defend themselves." Vinny said. Nelson shook his head.

"Can't do it, Vin." The Lieutenant replied.

"Come on, Jon. We follow the tank and help get the Rangers out of there, then we hot-foot it back to the X. The rest of our guys can go to the airfield." He stared at his Platoon Commander, his eyes showing that this was no longer just a friendly request. After a moment, Nelson keyed the push-to-talk for his radio.

"Neptune Actual, this is Neptune-Two. We're going to break off and support Charlie Three-Three and Jester Six in getting those guys out, over." Nelson said. The few regular Army soldiers in the back of the MRAP looked at the SEALs with surprise, excitement, and fear. They all waited during the pregnant pause to hear what Kensington would say.

"Neptune-Two, you're cleared to break off. Once you have those guys loaded up, link up with us at the airfield. The rest of Neptune is continuing forward." Kensington's response was terse, but that didn't matter.

"Hey, we're diverting to support the tanks!" Vinny called to the driver.

"Roger that!" The driver called back. Vinny sat back and shot Nelson a nod and a smile. His Platoon Commander replied with a simple thumbs-up. With that, they all began doing final checks of weapons and equipment. It was no secret that they were going to be fighting in the very near future.

36
Yazd Province, Iran

Chief Warrant Officer Three Morgan Tyron flew his Blackhawk through the rising pillars of smoke, looking for a clear LZ to set the bird down and unload the chalk of PJs and Rangers he was carrying. The crew chief behind Morgan's seat, Staff Sergeant Charlie Little, was laying down the heat with his M134 minigun, which screamed as it spat thousands of rounds towards several incoming Iranian trucks.

The fighting at the airport had been going on for almost an hour now. While US forces were on the tarmac and approaching the hangars and control tower, the Iranian Army was making them fight for every inch. Along with the normal radio chatter between pilots and chalk leaders, the tactical net was a cacophony of calls from both ground and air elements. Morgan almost had to switch it off to maintain his focus but was stopped when there was a rapid tapping on his shoulder. He looked over his shoulder to see one of the bearded PJs staring at him.

"We need you to put us down there!" He leaned forward and pointed towards the potential LZ; two shipping containers with two MRAPs parked at a forty-five-degree angle from each container. Ground troops were already pulling security. "They're setting up a triage station and CCP there. Drop me and my guys off as close as you can so we can take care of the wounded."

"You got it!" Morgan replied before banking the helo and starting a wide circle over the airfield towards their new destination. Most of the hostile anti-air had been taken out, but there were a few batteries left scattered. There was no way Morgan was getting shot down today.

"Thirty seconds!" He called out. The call was relayed by the crew chiefs, and then echoed by the PJs.

Half a minute later he touched the bird down fifty meters from the triage area. The Rangers and PJs dismounted, leaving the two crew chiefs and the single █████ sniper sitting in the crew bay of the bird. Once they were out, Morgan got the all-clear from Charlie and they lifted off.

"All stations, all stations, this is Neptune Two. We've linked up with Hunter Two-One, but we have multiple wounded. Need a CASEVAC now!" Someone called over the radio.

"Morgan!" The sniper, Master Sergeant Lee 'Tex' Davids, called out on the bird's internal channel.

"Yeah?" Tyron replied.

"Swing out over the city, see if we can get eyes on our boys down there." The Texas native said in his distinctive drawl.

"Alright, hold on back there." Morgan said, switching frequencies. "C2, this is Super Six-Six, I'm going to move into a holding pattern to provide overwatch for our guys in the city, over."

"Six-Six be advised, we don't have any idea as to enemy disposition or capabilities in the city." C2 replied, calm as ever.

"Six-Six copies all and acknowledges." Tyron said, wincing as a tracer round flew right in front of the bird's nose.

37
Yazd Province, Iran

Vinny took a knee and reloaded his SCAR-L, slapping a new mag in and popping back up from behind the burnt-out car that he and one of the Rangers had taken cover behind. He aimed down the top mounted ACOG scope and put the reticle on the chest of one of the hostiles. On top of having to deal with the Iranian military, the SEALs and Rangers now found themselves being targeted by local pro-Iranian insurgents who fought even more fiercely than their uniformed counterparts. Vinny spotted a guy wearing a black shirt and gray pants aiming an AK down at the Americans. Vinny pumped the trigger twice and the militant fell, a pink mist blossoming from his chest.

"Jensen!" Nelson called from his position behind the MRAP. "Vinny, over here now!"

"You good?" Vinny asked the young Ranger beside him.

"Yeah, I'm good." The guy replied, popping out from cover to fire at another hostile. Vinny broke into a sprint back to the MRAP. Lieutenant Nelson was ducked behind the back of the large vehicle, while Dalton kept busy covering them with his Mk48 machine gun, lighting up insurgents on the nearby rooftops. Nelson sucked water from his CamelBak and pointed inside the MRAP, where a Ranger medic was busy tending to one of the wounded men.

"Shit." Vinny slung his rifle to the side and climbed in. He was careful to step around the seat that Dennison was buckled into. The younger SEAL had taken two rounds to the plate and one to the leg. Jeff had stayed in the fight long enough to get a tourniquet on his leg and begin returning fire before he eventually passed out. Vinny and Nelson had been quick to drag him back to the vehicle and make sure he wouldn't die before sticking him with an IV and getting back into the fight. "What happened?" Vinny asked the medic, who was busy cutting away the shirt of the wounded man on the floor of the vehicle.

"Took a round to the helmet; knocked him out cold. His buddies weren't sure if that blood was his or not." The medic said as he removed the now-torn, bloody fabric of the Ranger's combat shirt and began checking for entry and exit wounds. Vinny helped him roll the man on his side, and both breathed a sigh of relief when neither saw any wounds. At worst, the guy was going to have a bitch of a concussion. "Here, check it out." The medic reached to the side and held up a MultiCam FAST helmet. Still lodged into the helmet was an AK round, which had flowered against the ballistic material.

"Keep it there, I'm sure he'll want it as a souvenir." Vinny said. The medic chuckled. "You good in here?"

"Yeah, I'm good." The medic said. "Here, coupla mags from his vest, figured you guys could use them out there." He pointed to five tan PMAGs resting on the ground beside the Ranger he was working on. Vinny scooped them up and shoved them into his cargo pocket before exiting the vehicle.

The fighting was even worse outside when he hopped back down. Vinny made himself small as he ran to link up with Nelson and Dalton.

"Here." Vinny handed his Lieutenant two of the magazines. Nelson nodded and took a knee to slide them into his vest. "Marcus!" Vinny slapped the SEAL gunner's shoulder. Dalton looked over his shoulder, and just as he did a round *snapped* in front of his face. Both gunner and medic hit the deck, and then Vinny saw Nelson hit the floor, blood leaking from a wound in his forehead just beneath the brim of his helmet. "Jon!" Vinny yelled. Dalton popped up and went cyclic with his machine gun, ripping into the rooftop and top floors of the building where the shot had come from. Vinny rolled Nelson onto his back, but it didn't matter. Their Lieutenant was gone.

38
Yazd Province, Iran

Foaly vaulted over the concrete barrier and landed between Hicks and Major Mark Harlund, the ground force commander for the ████ Teams assisting with the assault. Hudson and Reese followed behind moments later, all of them piling behind the jersey barriers alongside Kilo Team, who were working under Harlund directly.

"You guys good?" Foaly asked. Harlund nodded, reloading his DD Mk12 as he sucked water from his CamelBak.

"Vector Team moved in with two of the Ranger Squads to secure the control tower. Once they're up, they'll provide sniper and machine gun support from above." Harlund said, breathing heavily. His forehead was covered in sweat, which dirt and dust clung to. "The PJs are on the ground and triaging the wounded at the CCP they set up over there. Now we have to clear out these hangars." He pointed towards the cluster of six hangars ahead of them. Gunfire was pouring out thanks to the Iranians that had decided to hole up and make their last stands in the buildings. "Once we make entry, we'll clear them out, then set charges and blow whatever aircraft are in there so we can make space for our own later on."

"C2, this is Neptune Four, we need a fucking CASEVAC now!" The frantic radio call cut through their conversation.

"C2 copies, Neptune Four." The C2 operator replied. "Super Six-Six is on standby but cannot get to your location at this time. Are you able to CASEVAC by ground?"

DECEPTION

"Negative! All vehicles are engaged!" Neptune Four yelled, the gunfire and other voices threatening to drown the man's voice from his own transmission. Foaly looked over at his team, who were keeping busy by drinking water, cramming power bars, or topping off magazines in a rare lull from the non-stop fighting. He looked over his shoulder at Major Harlund, who was peering through the scope affixed to the top of his rifle as he conferred with Vector Team, who were busy setting up on the roof of the control tower.

"Mark." Foaly said, tapping Harlund's shoulder. The senior operator took his eye away from his scope and looked at the Team Lead. "Those SEALs are getting torn up. Let me and my guys go help them out." Harlund looked at Foaly for a moment.

"I don't know Alex; we need all the help we can-"

"This is Jester Three, we just lost one of our vics!" Harlund was interrupted by the frantic transmission from one of the Green Berets. Foaly looked back at Harlund, who nodded.

"Hunter Two, this is Solid Zero-One, can you spare some of your guys? We're going to move in to assist Hunter Two-One and Neptune." Foaly said.

"Solid Zero-One, I've got a few guys to spare. Where's the linkup?" Hunter Two asked. Foaly looked around and spotted a couple of empty pickup trucks that hadn't been blown to hell during the fighting.

"Two trucks just east of the control tower. Meet my team there!" Foaly said, running towards the trucks. His team was right behind him. Hudson and Reese climbed into the cab while Foaly and Hicks got in the bed. Two minutes later they had a squad of Rangers with them, with two hopping into the first truck while the others climbed into the second truck. Foaly slapped an open palm against the top of the cab and Hudson started them towards Neptune's position.

"Solid Zero-One this is Foxtrot Two, we're going to escort you guys into the city." One of the Abrams' tank commanders said in a thick Boston accent. Foaly looked over and saw one of the heavy tanks break away and gun it towards their position.

"Copy Two, thanks for the assist." Foaly replied, facing front again and scanning for any hostiles. While the fighting hadn't spilled out of the city yet, they could all tell they were rolling into a hornet's nest. It didn't matter though; they'd fight every inch of the way if it meant getting their guys out of there.

"RPG!" One of the Rangers in the other truck yelled. Foaly and those in his truck ducked down as an RPG flew by, missing their truck by a mere two feet. Had they been standing it would have likely taken someone's head off.

"Spread out!" Foaly yelled, waving the other truck away. The driver split off, taking his truck twenty feet to the right. By this point, Foxtrot Two, which had the word 'Thumper' painted in block letters on its main gun, caught up with the two speeding trucks, taking the left flank to Foaly's vehicle. As they approached, Foaly looked up and saw the Blackhawk circling above where the Rangers and SEALs were stranded.

"This is Solid Zero-One. Who's in the bird circling the site?" Foaly asked.

"Solid Zero-One, this is Super Six-Six." The familiar voice of CW3 Morgan Tyron answered a moment later. Foaly was relieved to know he had a friend with eyes in the sky.

"Six-Six, what are we walking into?" Foaly asked.

"Heavy fighting. Our guys are surrounded, and bad guys have plenty of RPGs and small arms. We're keeping our distance for now, but they keep trying to swat us down." Morgan answered.

"Crusader, this is Tex. I'm up here with Six-Six to provide overwatch once you boys get closer." Tex said over the radio, using Foaly's unit codename. Foaly looked at Hicks, who pumped his fist in the air. Tex was one of the best snipers in all of A Squadron; they were in good hands.

39
Yazd Province, Iran

Vinny finished helping load Nelson's body into the MRAP before hopping down and joining Dalton in laying down suppressive fire. Almost every seat of the large vehicle was now occupied by casualties.

"Man down!" Someone yelled. Vinny whirled around to see two Rangers pulling another behind cover.

"Fuck!" Vinny yelled. "Marcus, cover me!"

"I got you!" Dalton replied, letting his Mk48 rip and gunning down two hostiles that were readying an RPG to fire at the MRAP. Vinny sprinted through the fire towards the Rangers. One was already applying basic first aid to their wounded man while the other laid down covering fire.

"What happened?" Vinny asked as he crouched nearby.

"Not sure, he was up then he dropped." The young Ranger that had been fighting beside Vinny earlier, yelled.

"Let me check." Vinny said. The Ranger who was helping his buddy paused for a moment, then nodded and let the bearded operator take over. Vinny did a quick check of the guy's vitals; everything was strong.

"Alright, grab him and get him loaded in the MRAP." Vinny said. "I'll cover you, go!" The two Rangers grabbed their buddy and began carrying him as Vinny fired shot after shot into anyone he saw. At this point, the only people making themselves visible were those trying to kill the Americans, and that made target acquisition that much easier.

"Set!" One of the Rangers called. With that Vinny took off and ran towards the MRAP. He tore open the passenger side door and stepped up the ladder to protect his body from the rounds that were *clanging* into the armored side of the now-open door.

"Hey!" Vinny yelled, startling the driver. "As soon as they lock up the back, you haul ass back to the airfield so these guys can get treated!" The driver nodded with wide eyes. "Charlie Three-Three, this is Neptune Four." Vinny said into the radio.

"Go for Three-Three."

"We've got an MRAP that's going to CASEVAC our wounded to the airfield. Can you escort them out?" Vinny winced as a round impacted with the window beside his head, sending a spiderweb of cracks through the ballistic material.

"Roger that Neptune Four, we'll get them out of here." The tank commander answered.

"Charlie Three-Three, this is Jester Five. We've got a vehicle full of wounded that we need out of here as well." One of the Special Forces soldiers called in. The team of Green Berets had originally been the rescue force to get the Rangers back into the fight, but had been bogged down by heavy fire two blocks North and one block east of the Rangers and SEALs. They'd been stuck there since taking contact.

"Copy Jester Five, we'll be on their six." Charlie Three-Three replied.

"Neptune Four, Jester Five, Super Six-Six is moving in to provide sniper support." Super Six-Six's pilot said over the radio. A moment later the sound of a M134 minigun spooling up filled the air, joining the rapid *cracks* of sniper fire from the shooter in the bird.

Vinny slammed the door shut and slapped it with an open palm. The driver put the large vehicle in gear and hit the gas, sending the MRAP leaping forward. The front of the vehicle clipped the corner of a building and almost took down two walls as it sped down the alleyway towards the edge of the city.

"Alright, the rest of you with me!" Vinny said, pointing to a two-story building with blown out windows that would be their rally point. Vinny had chosen the building simply because there wasn't any gunfire pouring out of it at the moment. Dalton and five Rangers moved into a stack on the building. The breacher came up with his compact shotgun and put two rounds into the hinges before kicking in the door. Vinny was the first man through the door and ran straight into an Iranian carrying a rifle.

40
Yazd Province, Iran

Morgan eased off the throttle and swung the bird around to give both Charlie and Tex clear lines of fire as they covered the guys still in the city.

"Super Six-Six be advised: Solid Team and Hunter Two-Four are approaching in Host Nation vehicles. We've marked the top with IR tape." Foaly said over the radio.

"Rog'." Morgan replied. "Guys, check fire before hitting any incoming vehicles; friendlies are using them to move into the city." Morgan relayed over the radio.

"Check." Charlie said, letting the red-hot barrels of the minigun cool down. Tex grunted a reply over the rapid shots from his M110 rifle as he engaged enemies that appeared on rooftops and balconies trying to swat their bird down.

"All stations be advised, CASEVAC vehicles are clear of the city." Foaly reported.

"Shit!" Morgan's co-pilot, CW2 Brett Garriss, yelled as an RPG streaked past the canopy by a mere foot or so.

"Anyone got eyes on that RPG?" Morgan yelled back.

"Nothing on my side!" Charlie replied.

"Wait one." Tex replied, unclipping his safety line and scooting to the other side of the bird. "I got him." He said around a lip full of tobacco as he leaned forward against the retention strap and sighted on the rooftop. Just as Tex put down the guy reloading his launcher, another popped up on an adjacent rooftop, shouldering his own RPG tube. Tex shifted over and put two rounds into the guy. He fell backwards, the rocket shooting straight into the air and well clear of the bird. "Hey, back off a bit! We've got more guys with RPGs coming up!"

"Copy!" Morgan pitched the Blackhawk to the left as another rocket flew past the large helicopter, passing through the space where the bird had been not ten seconds before.

41
Yazd Province, Iran

Vinny yelled out in anger as he brought his fist down on the Iranian that had just shot Dalton, sinking the blade of his SOG knife into the man's throat. The guy gurgled as blood began to pool in his mouth, but still tried to wrestle control of the knife away from the SEAL. Vinny kept the knife pinned with his left hand and drew his Sig P226 with his right, putting two in the hostile's head. Clearing the rest of the room with his pistol, Vinny wiped the blade off on the dead man's shirt before re-sheathing it and backing out. Dalton was being helped to his feet by two Rangers.

"Son of a bitch!" Dalton gasped as he secured his vest over his torso again.

"You good?" Vinny asked.

"Yeah. The plate caught it." Dalton wheezed as the two Rangers helped him. With that, the building was now clear. The current plan was for the seven of them to strongpoint on the second floor and wait for the rescue team to arrive.

"Come on, we'll set up in these corner rooms." Vinny said, giving directions to his guys on who was pulling security where, and taking up a position in the room opposite Dalton while the Ranger with the shotgun covered the hallway they'd just vacated.

"Neptune Four, do you read?" Someone came over the radio. "Any Neptune or Hunter, are you on the net?" Vinny grabbed his push-to-talk.

"This is Neptune Four. Sorry for the delay." Vinny took a moment and leaned against the wall to catch his breath.

"Thought we lost you there. Listen, we need you guys to mark whichever building you're in so the tank doesn't shoot you." Vinny looked around for anything they could use to discreetly mark the building; a rug to hang out of the window or something like that. But there was nothing. The room was empty other than a destroyed desk.

"Uh, wait one. We don't have anything we can mark our positions with inside." Vinny turned to see a Ranger holding a bright orange VS-21 marking panel. "Belay my last, we're going to hang a VS-21 outside of the window of the building we're occupying. Say again, anyone inside the building with the VS-21 is friendly." He took the panel and draped it out of the window, surprised that no shots came towards him. He quickly secured it in place with some 550 cord.

"Roger all, Neptune. We have eyes on the panel. Sit tight, we're on our way." Solid Zero-One replied a moment later.

"Got it!" Vinny replied, checking his ammo, and replacing the mag in his Sig before posting up in a window and opening fire on a group of approaching hostiles. As he swapped mags in his rifle, he looked up to see the Blackhawk circling above, its minigun screaming as the gunner continued to lay into the enemy forces.

42
Yazd Province, Iran

"Six-Six say again, friendlies are occupying the building marked with a VS-21 outside of the window." Foaly relayed.

"Roger that, I've got no visual." Morgan answered. "Brett, you see anything?"

"I've got nothing." Garriss replied.

"I've got eyes on." Tex's cool drawl came over the radio. "Two story building to our four o' clock. Panel is in sight and friendlies are firing from the windows." Tex shifted to the right and re-adjusted his rifle against the retention strap across the helo's door to steady his fire. "Neptune Four this is Kilo Zero-Three. Confirm that's your guys in the second story windows?"

"Neptune confirms!" The response came.

"I've got eyes on." Garriss called out.

"Neptune Four, this is Six-Six, standby while we loop around and-" Morgan was cut off when there was an explosion behind them, followed by immediate autorotation. Morgan and Garriss fought to regain control of the bird, while Charlie and the other crew chief, Staff Sergeant Hal Davis, lunged to the end of their safety lines to grab the back of Tex's vest. The two weren't fast enough, and the sniper rolled over the retention strap and was sucked out of view. They both stared in horror, wondering why Tex's safety line hadn't been secured.

"I've got no pressure!" Garris said, madly pumping his feet on the now-slack pedals.

"This is Super Six-Six, we're hit and going down. Say again, Super Six-Six going down." Morgan grunted into his headset as he wrestled to control the stick, which was moving wildly between his gloved hands.

Despite their best efforts, neither pilot could regain control of the bird. All either of them saw were alternating flashes of sky and the city as they continued to spin further and further out of control towards the ground. Charlie held onto whatever he could, and Davis almost lost consciousness when he was smacked in the face by the butt of Tex's rifle before the weapon flew out of the same door its owner had disappeared through.

"Hold on!" Morgan yelled to his crew, determined to make sure they didn't die in the crash.

43
Yazd Province, Iran

Foaly watched with wide eyes as Morgan's bird continued spinning down towards the city.

"Super Six-Six, you still with us?" Foaly asked into the radio. There was no reply. "Morgan, you still there?" He asked with more urgency. His friend's voice had been the one to tell them the bird was going down, and now there was nothing.

"Boss!" Reese yelled, grabbing Foaly's shoulder and shaking the team lead.

"Yeah?" Foaly replied, his head back in the fight.

"Neptune's team is leaving the building. Are we grabbing them?" Reese asked. Foaly looked around the trucks, then nodded to Reese. The young operator put his hand on his push-to-talk. "Neptune Four, this is Solid Zero-Four. Rally at the base of your building. We're three mikes out."

"Roger that!" Neptune Four's response came, almost stepping on Reese's own transmission. Foaly hunkered down behind the cab as they sped along, and soon they were stopped in front of the building with the marker, which was now being retrieved. The men in both trucks quickly helped the SEALs and Rangers into the waiting vehicles. Foaly reached down to help one SEAL, who had his sleeves cut off at the elbows, into the truck. The man's arms, uniform, and armor had blood on them.

"Are you hit?" Foaly asked, recognizing the SEAL. It was Vinny Jensen. The two had met during a joint operation in Pakistan three years prior.

"Nah, I'm good." Vinny said, still not recognizing Foaly. "Thanks for the ride!"

"Yeah." Foaly replied as he turned around and slapped the side of the truck. "They're loaded let's-"

The truck rocked backwards and tipped up on its back wheels when a massive explosion went off in front of them, completely engulfing the stationary tank that had been providing them with covering fire. A few of the passengers almost tumbled out, but were stopped by those further from the rear.

"Back up! Back up!"

"Holy shit!"

"We've got to help them!" One of the Rangers yelled, moving to hop from the back of the truck. He was stopped when Hudson wrapped his arms around the guy's waist and pulled him back in.

"They're gone! They're gone!" Hudson yelled, an edge to his voice that Foaly hadn't heard in a long time. They all stared at the burning wreckage of the Abrams. No one had any clue what the fuck the insurgents had used to take out one of their tanks, but if it was enough to do that to an Abrams, then another would shred the trucks and everyone aboard. They were still backing off when there was another explosion. A hidden team of insurgents set off an explosively formed projectile from one of the nearby buildings. Had they not backed up; the jet of molten copper would have cut through both soft vehicles.

"Fuck!" Foaly screamed, switching his rifle to full-auto and emptying his mag into the building where the EFP had been fired from to keep the heads of their attackers inside down. "Hudson, level that fucker!" The team lead ordered. Hudson didn't think twice as he loaded a high-explosive shell into his under-barrel launcher and sent it into the building, following it with an incendiary round.

They couldn't see the hostiles, but the desperate, high-pitched screaming that emanated from the building gave them some semblance of satisfaction. One of the Rangers leveled his Mk46 towards the building, but Hicks waved him off.

"Let them burn." Hicks said.

"Lima Actual this is Solid Zero-One. Be advised, Foxtrot Two is down. Say again, Foxtrot Two is down. All crew KIA." Foaly replied. There was a six-second pause before the C2 bird replied.

"Copy. ISR feed shows the wreckage. Standby until CSAR gets on-location, over." Lima Actual himself replied.

"Hold position? Negative, we need to get to Super Six-Six!" Foaly said.

"Negative, Solid Zero-One. We have a QRF spinning up to secure the crash site. Standby for CSAR to reach the tank, then head to Super Six-Six. Over." General Walters ordered sternly. Foaly looked at Hicks, then Hudson and Reese.

"He can't be fuckin' serious." Hudson said. Foaly pressed his lips together in a grimace to stop from yelling into the radio.

"Listen up!" Foaly said, shifting everyone's attention from the screams of the still-burning attackers to him. "I'm going to rescue those guys from the bird. If you want, stay here with one truck, and wait for CSAR. The rest of you, with me." He waited for a response, but no one said anything.

"Marcus, you stay here and wait for CSAR." Vinny ordered the junior operator. Dalton looked like he was going to protest but stopped short of opening his mouth. As much as it chapped his ass not to join his friend in the recovery, he knew that he needed to help get the guys in the tank out of here before being seen himself.

"Solid Zero-One confirm last transmission. You *will* stay with the tank. Over." Lima Actual came over the radio again.

"Lima Actual be advised, your last transmission came in broken and unreadable. Solid Zero-One, out." Foaly said, slapping the top of the truck's cab to get them moving. The driver did so without hesitation. Foaly knew it was a cop-out excuse for his insubordination, but he didn't have time to debate this. Every second counted in getting to Morgan and his crew, especially if they were still alive.

"Solid Zero-One, you will hold position until reinforcements arrive!" Lima Actual barked, breaking his normally calm cadence.

"Solid Zero-One, stay with the tank until the bird gets there!" Harlund's voice cut in over the radio. Foaly thought about responding but decided against it. He was past the point of no return now. "Solid Zero-One, do you copy?" Harlund said again. A moment passed, then Harlund's voice came over the Unit channel. "Alex, what the fuck are you doing? Stay with the tank!"

"No can do, Mark." Foaly said quietly to himself as they continued towards the crash site.

44
Yazd Province, Iran

As Morgan regained consciousness, two things became apparent. The first was that his radio was practically screaming with overlapping transmissions, and the second was that he couldn't move. He craned his neck to the right, grunting from a sharp pain that shot through his left leg, and looked towards Brett. His co-pilot was still, with a trickle of blood running from his nose.

"Brett." Morgan grunted, reaching over and tugging at Garriss' vest. "Brett, wake up." He shook the man again, but to no avail. With a sigh, Morgan took his arm away and tried to look behind him, but couldn't due to him still being strapped in. "Charlie? Davis?" Nobody answered his calls.

Without looking, Morgan patted over his vest until he wrapped his right hand around the handle of his knife. In quick succession, he cut the safety straps on his harness and propped his hands against the ruined instrument panel to turn himself around. This effort was cut short when the pain returned to his leg. That was when he realized his leg was pinned between his seat and part of the cockpit, which had collapsed on impact.

"Fuck." Morgan said through gritted teeth. Trying to not tweak his injured leg any further, he turned himself around, straining his neck and shoulder to look behind him. Davis was lying on his side facing away from Morgan. The only part of Charlie that was visible from the current angle was a limp, splayed arm. Tex was nowhere to be seen, and that gave Morgan a little bit of hope. Maybe the Texan had survived and was setting up to cover the crash from somewhere outside.

With all of his strength, Morgan pressed both hands against the front of the instrument panel against his pinned leg and pushed, hoping to slip his leg out if he gained any purchase. After two tries and zero progress, Morgan let himself fall back and tried to steady his breathing. He switched over to the tactical net and toggled his push-to-talk with his left hand as his right drew the Glock 17 from the cross-draw holster on his vest.

45
Yazd Province, Iran

"Any station, any station." Morgan's voice came over the radio, surprising everyone. "This is Super Six-Six. Bird is down. Four WIA, one possible MIA. We're critical. Need assistance ASAP." They could hear the exhaustion and pain in the man's voice. Vinny looked at Foaly, who had perked up as the transmission started.

"Gun it!" Foaly yelled at the driver, who put the pedal down to the floor. The truck shot forward, almost sending two of the Rangers tumbling out of the back. Twenty seconds later Foaly was once again slapping the top of the truck, yelling for them to stop. The vehicle kicked up a large plume of dust as the tires bit into the sandy road. The vehicle hadn't even stopped moving as Foaly, Hudson, and Vinny jumped off and ran forward.

Lying in the road was a figure in MultiCam combat fatigues.

"Oh fuck." Hudson said. They already knew it was too late. With a sinking feeling, Foaly rolled the man over and they were looking down at Tex, easily identifiable by the large Texas flag patch he wore on the front of his vest. His trademark orange University of Texas hat was nowhere to be seen, nor was his rifle. The sniper must have been tossed when the bird was going down, and they could only hope that the impact had killed their friend instantly. Foaly took a knee and provided cover while Hudson assessed the fallen operator. Solid Team's medic only needed seconds to confirm what he already knew.

"Get him up." Foaly ordered, continuing to cover. Hudson and Vinny carried the operator's limp form back to the truck, where Reese and Hicks helped pull him into the bed.

"Aw fuck." Hicks said. The three jumped into the back and Foaly reached down, tearing Tex's callsign patch from the front of his vest and stuffing it into the admin pouch on his own armor.

"Hudson, call it in." Foaly said, then turned and gave the driver orders to continue before switching over to the tactical net. "Super Six-Six, this is Solid Zero-One. Status." His mind snapped back into mission, compartmentalizing Tex's battered body. Tex was gone, but Morgan was still alive. Foaly intended on keeping it that way.

"Good to hear from you, buddy." Morgan replied, his voice pained. "I'm pinned in the cockpit. Not sure if any of my crew are still alive, no one's responsive. I could really use some help."

"Are you taking fire?" Foaly asked.

"Lima Actual this is Solid Zero-Three. We've recovered one Eagle from Super Six-Six, it's Kilo Zero-Three." Hudson paused during his report to Lima Actual. Foaly wasn't on that specific channel, but he could all but hear the General demanding to know where Solid Team's leader was and why the Captain wasn't answering the comms.

"Negative, no fire yet." Morgan replied. "But I can't really see much from where I'm at. The bird's practically on its side." Foaly's eyes perked up when he saw the dark smoke rising from the crash site.

"Okay, hold tight. We can see your smoke. We'll be there soon." Alex reassured his friend.

"Okay. See you soon." The relief was audible in Morgan's voice. Foaly looked down and did a quick count of his mags. He still had five full and two partials, along with his 'oh shit' magazine that was on his sub-belt. There were also four in a pouch on the back of his vest that his mates could use in a pinch. It wasn't much, but he could make it work. If worst came to worst, he'd use his Glock, then his knife, and his fists if he had to. At that point, they'd also be calling for indirect fire and *very* close air support. Anything to get their boys out.

"Listen up!" Foaly barked over the roaring diesel engine. "We've got one survivor awake and pinned in the cockpit. The other three are unknown at this time. When we hit the crash site, I want two of you with us helping triage the crew. The rest of you are going to pull security until we can get our guys out and loaded on the truck. Then we'll haul ass back to the airport."

"I'll help." Vinny piped up. Foaly looked over at the SEAL, though the recognition in Vinny's eyes was hidden behind his Oakley sunglasses. "His leg is pinned, which might be the only thing holding a femoral bleed together. Myself and your doc can patch him up for movement if he's got anything serious like that." Vinny pointed to Hudson, who had taken off his aid bag and was doing a quick check on what he had available.

"Sounds good to me." Foaly nodded.

"Solid Zero-One this is Jester Five. Be advised, we're coming up on your six." The Special Forces Team Sergeant said over the radio. Foaly and the others looked back to see two Joint Light Tactical Vehicles speeding to catch up with them.

46
Yazd Province, Iran

Morgan was struggling to keep his eyes open. Then he heard vehicle brakes, and his eyes shot wide as he gripped his pistol. Normally he would've had his MP7, but his was lost somewhere in the crumpled metal on his side of the cockpit, and Garriss' was just out of reach. With some effort, he craned his neck and saw two trucks had stopped thirty meters from his side of the bird. There was yelling, then booted feet appeared to jump down from the truck. He raised his pistol and tried to get a good sight picture despite his shaking arms. They weren't going to take him that easily.

"Blue! Blue!" Someone called out as a pair of ankle-high boots under uncuffed MultiCam Arid pants approached. "Friendlies coming in!" It took a moment, the Morgan recognized Foaly's voice. Morgan relaxed, placing the pistol back in its holster. A moment later he was face-to-face with Foaly, who was knelt beside the almost overturned bird. "Hey buddy." Alex leaned in and patted Morgan's shoulder.

"Hey Alex." Morgan replied, grasping Foaly's hand with his own. There were more voices behind them, and the sound of boots on metal as other members of the rescue team moved in. "I don't know how the others are. I haven't been able to get any of them up." Morgan blinked hard. "And Tex, I think Tex is outside. Did you see him?" Foaly's expression told Morgan everything he needed to know about the sniper's fate.

"Door's jammed." Hudson informed Foaly, placing his foot against the fuselage and tugging at the handle with both hands.

DECEPTION

"Is the door on your leg?" Foaly asked. Morgan looked down.

"No, it's the panel. Got pushed in when we hit dirt."

"Okay." Foaly ran a gloved hand down his face, smearing dirt and grime that was starting to cake onto his sweat. "Reese, go see if any of those JTVs have winches."

"On it!" Reese said before taking off towards the SF vehicles. Foaly, Vinny, and Hudson continued trying the door while other Rangers were helping unload the three-remaining crew. There was a loud crack and a round *pinged* off the top of the bird, sending sparks near one of the Rangers.

"Contact!" One of the men of the security element yelled, followed by a long burst from his machine gun. That was when the buildings around them erupted with gunfire.

Reese narrowly avoided getting hit as he ran back with the JTV's winch in-hand.

"Here!" Reese said, handing the winch over to Hudson before getting his DDM4 up and returning fire. It seemed that every window visible from the crash site had muzzle flashes, all aimed towards the downed bird and the rescue team.

The hook was placed on the door and a signal to the soldier driving the JTV had him pulling backwards. The door came off relatively easy, and they quickly went to work on getting Morgan out. The pilot yelled out in pain and Foaly and Jensen pulled him from his seat, each man with an arm hooked under his armpits. As soon as they got him clear, they placed him on the ground behind the cockpit, shielded from the incoming fire. While Hudson and Vinny went to work on making sure Morgan wasn't going to bleed out during the extraction, Foaly brought his weapon up and joined Reese in returning fire.

"Solid Zero-One, this is Hunter Two-Four." The Ranger Squad Leader came over the radio. "The rest of the crew is KIA. The chiefs were killed on impact, and the co-pilot caught a round when they lit us up from the buildings."

"Fuck." Foaly seethed through gritted teeth.

"Any word on the pilot?" Hunter Two-Four asked.

"He's alive, being stabilized now." Foaly said as he reloaded. "Get your guys prepped to move the bodies back to the vehicles. We're going to CASEVAC back to the airport and-" Foaly's transmission was washed out when an RPG impacted the pickup truck that they'd commandeered to first rescue the SEALs and Rangers. Debris and shrapnel shot out at all angles. Foaly glanced back and was horrified to remember that Tex's body had been in the back of that truck.

"Alex. Alex! Where are you going?" Reese called out as Foaly sprinted towards the burning wreckage. Tex's body had been blown out of the bed by the explosion, but parts of his uniform were now on fire, and shrapnel had shredded through his body. Foaly grabbed Tex by the straps of his vest and hauled him to one of the nearby JTVs, hammering his fist on the door. The door opened and a SF soldier looked at him.

"Get him inside, now!" Foaly ordered. The gunner did so, helping load Tex in the back, then went back to manning the console that controlled the Mk47 grenade launcher. "Jester Five, what's your status?" Foaly asked as he made his way back towards the bird.

"Jester Five is hit, standby." Someone replied on the radio. A moment later, Foaly found himself beside a goatee'd SF soldier. It was Staff Sergeant Tim Hollins, a Special Forces medic that Foaly had worked alongside in the past. "What's the plan?" Hollins asked.

"How many of your guys are up?" Foaly asked.

"Three of my guys are hit, including our Captain and Warrant." Hollins relayed.

"Fuck." Foaly said, looking around. He got a thumbs-up from Hudson. "Can you fit wounded in your vehicles?" Hollins glanced over his shoulder.

"Give me a second." Hollins said, keying his push-to-talk. "Matt, Mills, clear out as much space as you can. We're going to move the casualties out in the JTVs."

"Copy!" Mills replied. A moment later the doors were opened, and excess gear was being shoved around while the Mk47 and M2 both went cyclic to protect the men inside. Hollins took off to help load the wounded, and Foaly ran over to help Morgan.

"Alright, up you get." Foaly said, helping Morgan to his feet. Vinny helped Morgan on the other side, and they started walking the wounded pilot towards the JTV while Hicks and Reese covered them.

The forty-meter walk felt like a hundred miles, and Foaly was amazed that none of them got clipped while they moved across the open space towards the vehicles. Vinny held the passenger side open and Foaly helped Morgan in. Foaly took Morgan's pistol and press-checked it to make sure it was loaded before handing the two-toned Glock back to the pilot.

"You coming with?" Morgan asked.

"No, but I'll see you there!' Foaly responded before closing the door. He turned around and joined Vinny in providing covering fire for the other casualties that were being moved. Hollins was fireman's carrying another SF soldier towards the vehicle, while three groups of two Rangers each carried the dead crewmembers from Super Six-Six. One of the Rangers carrying the co-pilot screamed as a round punched through his clavicle, just above his vest. The guy went down, sending the co-pilot and his buddy down as well.

"Shit!" Vinny yelled, taking off to render aid. Foaly moved forward, weapon still up and firing.

"Solid Zero-One this is Granite Zero-Four. We're on approach from your two o' clock." Staff Sergeant Trey Crenshaw said over the radio. Moments later, three Little Birds passed overhead.

"Roger that!" Foaly replied as the small helicopters set down on a nearby street, sending a wash of sand and dust through the crash site. "We've got friendlies coming in from our two o' clock!" Foaly yelled to two nearby Rangers who were laying down suppressive fire with their machine guns. "Hey!" He yelled, clapping a hand on each of their shoulders to get their attention.

"What?" The one on the right yelled, irritated, and startled.

"We've got another team coming in from your three. Watch your fire and cover their advance!' Foaly said, then brought his rifle up and put three rounds into the chest of a fighter with an RPG tube in a nearby alley.

"Solid Zero-One, this is Jester Eight." Someone called over the radio.

"Go!" Foaly yelled, dumping the empty mag, and grabbing one of the partials from his vest. He was getting dangerously low on ammo.

"We're seeing heavy fire coming from that hospital to the southwest. Small arms from almost every window, and lots of RPGs up high." The Special Forces soldier relayed.

"Copy." Foaly said. "Hey! Who can call a fire mission?"

"What?" Someone yelled back over the din of the firefight.

"I need someone to call fire!" Foaly said. "You guys got a SOTAC?"

"Yeah, wait one!" The guy said to Foaly, then turned. "Fortuzzi! Where's Fortuzzi?" A few moments later, they were joined by another Ranger.

"What's up?" Staff Sergeant Devyn Fortuzzi asked. It took a moment, but both Foaly and Fortuzzi recognized each other. The two former high school classmates normally would have shared some pleasantries, but now was not the time or the place.

"You see that hospital? Six story white building?" Foaly pointed.

"You mean the one that everyone is shooting at us from?" Fortuzzi said. "Yeah, I see it."

"Call for fire and level it." Foaly said. Had it been under any other circumstances, Fortuzzi may have second guessed the call. But the amount of fire that was pouring down had picked off more than a few of his friends, and they would die if he didn't do anything about it.

"All nets, this is Hunter Two-Four-Echo." Fortuzzi said into his radio as he looked at the Garmin GPS he wore on his left wrist, above his watch. "Broken arrow. Say again, broken arrow!" Foaly paused mentally. This was the first Broken Arrow call since the 2009 attack on COP Keating. "Expend all munitions on the following grid: Four-Zero-Romeo-Bravo-Alpha-Four-Seven…" Foaly patted the mag pouches on his vest, but they were all empty. He grabbed one of his 'oh shit' mags from his cargo pocket, loading his rifle while listening to Fortuzzi confirm that they were indeed calling a Broken Arrow, and that the point of fire was the building marked as a hospital on all their maps.

"Blue! Blue! Friendlies coming in!" Someone called out. Foaly turned to see Trey and the rest of Granite Team entering the perimeter. Crenshaw made a beeline towards Foaly.

"Did you guys just call that broken arrow?" Trey asked.

"Yeah." Foaly said. They both switched over to the fire support net and realized that Fortuzzi was currently coordinating fire from an orbiting C-130U gunship, callsign 'Spooky'.

"Why am I always the one to end up saving your ass?" Crenshaw asked as he grabbed the spare mags from the back of Foaly's vest and handed them to his friend.

"Always a pleasure, Trey. Thanks." Foaly said as he stuffed three of his empties into his dump pouch, replacing them with the full mags.

Everything seemed to stop when four 105-millimeter rounds impacted with the building in quick succession, sending a plume of dust and dirt that was followed by more explosions about forty seconds later. Fortuzzi was apparently coordinating in artillery as well. It was ballsy to do with aircraft on-station, but Fortuzzi knew what he was doing. That was evidenced by the fact that he now had a full-size topographical map laid out in front of him and held a radio in each hand as he coordinated support across the net.

The dust from the artillery barrage hadn't even settled before it was kicked up by the explosions caused by two incoming Apaches, who came in low and fast, firing a salvo of missiles that punched through the side of the building. This was enough to send the sixth floor pancaking down into the fifth.

Foaly watched through his EOTech's magnifier as the form of a uniformed Iranian soldier was flung from the top of the building and sent plummeting to earth. Good riddance, fucker.

"Spooky, this is Helix Two-Two. We're clear of your airspace." The Apache flight lead said.

"Roger that. Spooky to all ground forces, you're going to want to keep your heads down." The air gunner aboard the C-130 said.

"Check, send it!" Fortuzzi said. "Hey, heads down!" He called out. His call was washed out when the enormous explosion of a 105-millimater round fired from the orbiting aircraft impacted with the lower corner of the building, followed immediately by withering fire from its 40-millimeter gatling gun.

The incoming fire from the hospital had all but stopped at this point. It was obvious that anyone left inside the rapidly-crumbling building was now trying to escape.

Then another 105 impacted from above.

This one was enough to disintegrate what remained of the load-bearing structure on the first two floors' northeast corner, and the building began collapsing on itself.

"Good effect on target. You're cleared to break off. Thanks for the assist, Spooky." Fortuzzi said. He turned around and the two operators grabbed his shoulder and shook him, whooping with praise.   "Nicely done!" Foaly said.

"Killed 'em good." Trey followed up.

"You're buying the first round, Alex." Devyn said, slapping Foaly's shoulder.

"Solid Zero-One, this is Kilo Zero-One." Harlund's voice came over the radio, cutting the celebration short. He was pissed.

"No avoiding him now." Foaly said with a wan smile to Trey before toggling his radio. "Go for Solid Zero-One."

"Status." Harlund demanded.

"Stand by." Foaly stood and did a quick headcount. "Kilo Zero-One: eight Eagles on the deck. One Neptune, Six Hunter. All casualties are off the X, over."

"Roger. Hold position. QRF is six mikes out." Foaly could already hear the heavy sounds of the Chinook's rotor blades approaching. Sure enough, six minutes later, a CH-47 Chinook touched down near the crash site. A group of Marine Raiders, dressed in their trademark woodland camouflage fatigues, rushed off the bird, while Harlund was flanked by the two surviving members of Kilo Team.

"All stations, get on the bird." Foaly said. Without question, the remaining Rangers, the lone SEAL, and the men of Granite and Solid Teams walked up the ramp to take their seats. Foaly and Trey walked up as well, where they were met by Harlund.

"Foaly, what the fuck?" Harlund denied after switching them over to an otherwise empty channel.

"Mark, you know I couldn't just let the bird sit there. They would have been overrun." Foaly said. "And I know that you sure as shit don't want another Mogadishu."

"We almost did!" Harlund said. "And we lost a tank!" Foaly narrowed his eyes. Something about this wasn't right. "I've had a General up my ass since that bird

174

went down and he wants to know why one of my operators decided to go Rambo and call in an airstrike on a hospital." *Ah, there it is* Foaly thought to himself. Harlund wasn't pissed about any of Foaly's actions. He was pissed because a General was on his ass. "Apparently, Walters already has the paperwork for a 15-6 drafted up, and he's going to want your head on a pike."

"Fuck him." Foaly retorted. "I did what I needed to do to get everyone out."

"That's the thing, Alex. You didn't get everyone out." Harlund said. This was Harlund's last deployment where he'd command a team, as he was slated to take over a squadron after this. Tex had been with Harlund for a long while, so Foaly could understand where the Major was coming from.

"We're clear!" One of the Raiders said as they ran up the ramp. With that the bird lifted off, with Foaly and Harlund still standing.

"Make sure you've got your ducks in order, Alex. I don't know how much we'll be able to do, but you'll have our support with whatever comes next." Harlund yelled before turning and taking his seat. Harlund tapped the cup of his Peltors, and Foaly listened to Harlund's filtered voice through the radio. "Regardless of that, we've got a fix on Ghorbani, so get right." Foaly didn't say anything as he took his seat beside one of the Raiders. The Marine, a Captain himself, tapped Foaly on the knee and then pointed out of the open back towards the Black Hawk's wreckage. He held up three fingers, then two, then one. There was a bright flash, and the charges set on the wreckage finished the job the Iranian's had started. Foaly nodded and leaned back, eyes closed beneath his sunglasses.

He wasn't sure what the Army was going to do with him now.

47
May, 2018
Murray Hill, New York

Morgan walked into the apartment and closed the door behind him with his foot. The debrief with State had quickly been hijacked by the CIA and then again by the late arrival of agents from the DIA and FBI. The whole thing had turned into a six-hour ordeal, with each of the three contractors telling the story over and over, only to be asked the same questions again and again. When the government workers would ask them questions they didn't know the answers to, they would point the govvies to the Paoli-provided documentation. That would hold the current agent asking questions off for a bit, until the next agent asked the same thing in a different way, only to receive the same answer from the contractors. It had been tedious.

The flight back to New York had put Morgan home after midnight. *I really need to finish my fixed-wing license.* Morgan thought to himself as he placed his bags down. He didn't want to wake Julia up, since it was a Tuesday and she had work tomorrow. Then the bedroom light clicked on. *Shit.*

"Morgan?" Julia said.

"Yeah babe." He said as he turned on the kitchen light, squinting for a moment before his eyes began to adjust. She walked out of the bathroom wearing a tank top and pajama bottoms, her hair loose around her shoulders.

"Hey." She walked up and kissed him. "How did it go?" She didn't try to hide the fact she was checking his face for any new cuts or bruises.

"The job itself was okay." Morgan said, knowing full well he'd have to explain everything to her in the morning. He didn't want her to stay up worrying about him after this. "Government's a pain in the ass as usual though. Sorry I woke you."

"You don't have to apologize. I'm just glad you're home." She smiled at him. "Come on, let's go to bed." She took his hand, but he didn't move.

"I uh. I'm going to stay up and take care of some stuff. Jet lag and all." Morgan said. Julia looked at him for a moment longer, then nodded and gave him a quick kiss before she went back to bed. The door closed and the light clicked off. Morgan waited a moment, then went over and turned on the computer, then the TV, pushing the volume down so it wouldn't disturb his wife.

Twenty minutes later he sat on the couch, absentmindedly watching a late-night infomercial channel while he ate the meal of eggs, bacon, and pancakes he'd prepared himself. He had no idea why he'd wanted breakfast food at such a weird hour, but he had everything, so he just went ahead and made it. His eyes went from the TV to his pistol, sitting on the cleaning rag waiting for the ritual post-mission breakdown and deep clean.

As he ate, his mind wandered back to right after he'd been selected into the 160th as a pilot in early 2009. He'd lived in a small house just off-base from Fort Campbell, over the border in Woodlawn, Tennessee. It was before Morgan had met Julia, so he was living on his own at the time. One morning, after a long night of night-vision flying, Morgan had woken up to the smell of a similar meal being cooked in his house. When Morgan had walked into his kitchen, Beretta 96 in-hand, he ended up being the one surprised when he saw his father standing in the kitchen, cooking.

"Nice pop gun." Clint Tyron said, gesturing towards his son's pistol. Morgan safed the handgun and lowered it. "Go put a shirt on, breakfast is almost ready."

"Good to see you too, Dad." Morgan said as he returned to his spartan bedroom and pulled on an Embry Riddle t-shirt before returning a few minutes later to find his father sprinkling salt and pepper on the still-cooking eggs.

"Sunny-side up as usual?" Clint asked.

"As usual." Morgan said as he walked over to the coffee pot and added an additional scoop of coffee before turning it on. As much as Morgan loved his coffee strong, Clint Tyron liked his coffee more akin to motor oil. "Toast?" Morgan asked.

"Please." His father replied. Morgan did so, and soon father and son set their respectively prepared foods at the small table. Morgan was glad he'd ended up buying two chairs, or else he would have been eating standing. "Nice place you have here." Clint said as he sniffed the coffee before taking a tentative sip. Morgan knew he'd made it to the old man's standards because he didn't receive a tongue lashing about it. "Reminds me of the place I had when I was at Schofield." Clint was referring to when he'd been a member of the Army's 25th Infantry Division, based out of Schofield Barracks in Hawaii. "I heard from a buddy of mine that you made it into the 160th. Recognized the name and reached out to me." Morgan thought back to who could've known his father. None of his instructors had mentioned it, and the cadre were all too young to have served with him.

Clint Tyron, formally First Lieutenant Clint Tyron, had done three tours in Vietnam. He'd lied on his enlistment papers and had managed to join the Army before being shipped to his first tour in 1967 at sixteen. During his second tour in 1969, the Infantry NCO received a Battlefield Commission. And in 1971, twenty-year-old Second Lieutenant Clint Tyron had been wounded during a nighttime ambush. While pulling his radio operator to safety, Clint had been shot twice, one that grazed his neck, and the second which punched through his right kidney. After being MEDEVAC'd back to the United States, Clint was handed his Purple Heart, a Silver Star, and a promotion to First Lieutenant along with his medical discharge. After months of physical therapy, Clint was able to return to Hawaii to gather his belongings and began the long journey back to his hometown of Schenectady, New York. A few years went by before he came across a cute woman dining at his regular diner in Scotia, and the two hit it off. Clint married Elizabeth Waterton in 1980, and four years after that, their son Morgan arrived.

"What brings you to the neighborhood? It's a bit out of the way for you." Morgan said sarcastically. Clint lived in Osage, Iowa, which meant he'd made a hell of a trip for this surprise drop-in.

"Word on the street is your unit is getting ready to head to the sandbox. I wanted to see you before then." Clint said, focusing on spooning one of his eggs onto a piece of toast. Morgan looked up at his father.

"Now how the hell would you know that?" Morgan asked. The 160th fell under the Army's Special Operations Command, which meant that deployment schedules were kept extremely close to the vest.

DECEPTION

"You know I have my ways." Clint said, giving his son a smirk and a wink. "Have you told your mother yet?"

"No, not yet." Morgan said. The relationship between Morgan and his mother was one that barely existed. She and Clint had gotten divorced in the early nineties, and it had been a messy one. Now she lived somewhere in West Virginia, and Morgan's sister, Katie, had stayed close to their mother.

"Well, do me a favor and at least call her before you do." Clint said. Even with how everything had gone down, he still cared about Elizabeth and knew that she would be worried about their son. He also knew that if anything happened to Morgan, she'd blame him, and he'd never hear the end of it. "I also dropped by to give you this." Clint reached down and grabbed a nondescript black box from his bag, placing it on the table and sliding it towards Morgan. Morgan finished chewing his eggs and wiped his chin with a paper towel before taking the box and opening it.

"Holy crap." Morgan said, eyes wide with awe.

Inside the box was a Springfield Operator M1911 pistol. Morgan picked up the .45 and racked the slide twice to ensure it was empty before aiming upwards and gazing down the sites.

"A lot better than that big-ass Beretta you came in here with." Clint said, smiling at his boy's excitement over the gift. "And a whole different ball game than those piddly Glocks the Army's having you use nowadays. Not as good as the ones we carried back in the day, but I figure since you're part of a special unit now you'd be able to swing bringing that with you."

"I sure hope I can." Morgan said as he set the pistol back in its box. "Dad, this is awesome. Thank you."

"Alright now. Don't get sappy on me." Clint said. They made small talk as they continued eating, and before they knew it, Clint was standing in the doorway, bag slung over one shoulder. "Be safe out there, son." Then he did something that caught Morgan completely off guard. Clint hugged him. "Let me know when you get back. I love you."

"I uh...I love you too, Dad." Morgan said as he returned the embrace. He couldn't remember the last time his father had hugged him or said those words. And with that, Clint was gone.

Morgan wouldn't see his father again until 2012, when they were both invited to West Virginia to meet Clint's granddaughter and Morgan's niece, Danielle. And since then, it had been the sporadic phone call here and there that had kept Morgan and his father connected.

Morgan was snapped out of his memories when his phone's screen lit up and emitted a loud *DING*.

"Shit." Morgan said, quickly muting the iPhone before checking the notification. It was from his banking app, notifying him of a deposit to his account. After inputting his information, Morgan saw that the balance had jumped significantly. Paoli had made good on their word, having paid in full and added a large bonus, just as Greenwood had said. The fact that the money was tax free made it that much sweeter.

Morgan sat back and looked at the pistol still resting on the coffee table. In the nine years since his father had given it to him, Morgan had made a few modifications to the handgun to better its use to him. But overall, it was still the same weapon. It had been strange, reminiscing about his father, but it gave him a good feeling overall. He'd have to reach out to the old man sometime soon.

With that, Morgan picked up the weapon and began breaking it down. While he hadn't used the pistol in Zambia, he was sure that dirt and dust had somehow worked its way into the internals, which would need to be cleaned out. And so, he rolled out his cleaning kit and began the post-mission ritual once again.

48
Upper East Side, New York

Foaly sat on the couch, staring at the blank television across from him, a half-full tumbler of Jameson in his hand. The entire time they'd been down in DC, whenever he hadn't been speaking directly, Foaly had been replaying the events of the previous June in his head.

His eyes went from the television to the framed Distinguished Service Cross write up that he'd been awarded for leading the impromptu rescue operation. Of course, that had been after the conclusion of the 15-6 investigation regarding the strikes on the hospital, in which Foaly was not found guilty due to the fact that the hospital had been cleared out of any civilians by the insurgents. Shannon had insisted he frame it, being that it was the nation's second-highest award. Rumor had it that more than a few people had put him in for the Medal of Honor, but that was shot down as soon as General Walters heard about it.

Under the DSC citation was a framed shadowbox. Centered near the top was a small plaque that read 'Major Alex Foaly' and beneath it was the Unit's signature 'Sine Pari' with the gold oak leaf pin of a Major rank beside a Unit Distinctive Unit Insignia. In each corner was a metal challenge coin from those units involved; 160th Special Operations Aviation Regiment; First Battalion Seventy-Fifth Rangers; and Third Special Forces Group. There was also a letter of commendation, which had been presented to him by an 'East Coast Command' for helping get the SEALs out. The shadow box had been put together by Major Harlund and presented to Foaly in the Unit's cafeteria where the operators said their final goodbyes to him before he left.

All of the awards and shadow boxes didn't make a difference though. Shortly after the promotion and awards, Foaly was called to the Unit's Commanding General, where he was given his honorable discharge. Walters had pushed for an other-than-honorable with the GOMOR, General Officer Memorandum of Reprimand, that had been written up for Foaly. But the praise and character references given by Foaly's fellow operators, those he'd served alongside in Special Forces, and those involved in the rescue operation, had made enough noise to get the General to back down. The GOMOR stayed, with the only condition being that Foaly was discharged. So, with that, Foaly was given his trophies, said his goodbyes, and kicked out of the compound.

Persona Non Grata. Shitcanned. Booted out of The Unit and the Army, the only thing he'd known since he'd joined at seventeen. Two months after the Towers fell, Alex Foaly had signed the dotted line, and he'd never looked back. Now the thing he'd dedicated his life to; shed blood, sweat, tears, and lost friends to, was reduced to some framed documents, a bunch of uniforms hanging in the closet, and scars across his body and mind.

He threw back the rest of what remained in his glass and leaned forward to pour himself another few fingers before deciding to swig directly from the bottle instead.

Shannon stood in the kitchen watching her husband. She wasn't sure if he knew she was there or not, but she was sure that he didn't care. He was in his own world right now; lost in his mind. She knew what he was thinking about too. This happened every few months, ever since he'd been discharged, and it almost always happened during the downtime between jobs.

Shannon had met Alex at the start of both their military careers almost fourteen years ago. Even then, nineteen-year-old Alex had already undergone Special Forces Selection and had passed the Q-Course. They had both been in the National Guard at the time, and had she enlisted or gone through any other training, they would have never met. She would never forget waiting for first formation at her last Recruit Sustainment Program drill when she saw the young man walk in with fresh-pressed BDUs, shined black boots, and a Green Beret sitting atop his head while the rest of them wore plain black berets with blue flashes, which the Army had adopted for every soldier at that point. The two of them had hit it off that final RSP Drill weekend, staying up well into the night talking before finally relenting and going to bed for early morning PT. After that, they were released to their respective units.

She wouldn't see Alex again until almost a year later, when he showed up at her doorstep unannounced at her apartment in Ossining. She hadn't been expecting company, so her boyfriend at the time opened the door. She couldn't remember his name for her life now, all she remembered was that he was some meathead infantryman with the 69th Infantry Regiment, who stayed with her whenever he drilled at the nearby Camp Smith. When she peeked over what's-his-names shoulder to see who was at the door, she was surprised to see a longer-haired Alex standing in the rain, tense and ready to roll with her now-aggressive boyfriend. She quickly defused the situation by shoving what's-his-name back inside and stepping out into the cold fall rain with Alex.

DECEPTION

When she asked where he'd been and why she hadn't heard from him, he told her how he'd just gotten back from a rotation to Afghanistan and was now enrolled in college at Valley Forge. And since he was back in New York for Thanksgiving, he'd wanted to stop in and surprise her. She confessed to him that she thought he'd been killed overseas since she hadn't heard from him, and had met whoever it was she was dating while at drill in Camp Smith a few months beforehand. She then apologized, and insisted they get dinner sometime in the following week to properly catch up.

After bidding Alex a good night, she went inside and was confronted by her boyfriend, who was demanding to know who Alex was. Shannon told him not to worry about it. It was obvious that meathead had wanted to go toe-to-toe with Alex, and while he was bigger, she had no doubt in her mind that Alex would have mopped the floor with him.

A year and a half later, following her medical discharge from the Army, Shannon was present to pin the gold Second Lieutenant bars on Alex's right shoulder, while Richard Gray pinned on the left set. Immediately after his commissioning, their long-distance relationship ceased being long distance and she joined him in moving to Vermont, where he served as an Infantry Platoon Leader while finishing his degree through Norwich University. Ironically enough, Alex had ended up being her then-ex's Lieutenant. She would have loved to have been a fly on the wall when that happened. After that, she followed him back to Bragg, where she stayed with him as he matriculated back into Special Forces, and eventually earned his way into ███.

Shannon watched as Alex stood up and carried the bottle back into the kitchen. He set it on the counter and screwed the cap on before placing it back in the liquor cabinet, then placed the tumbler in the dirty side of the sink. With both hands on the counter he leaned forward, then looked up at her. His eyes were pleading.

"Melatonin?" She asked. His lips pressed together.

"Yeah. Yeah, that'd be good." He said. Normally she would have offered him an Ambien, but he'd been drinking so they both knew it was out of the question. Even though it wasn't necessary, Alex had trusted her in keeping the bottles of his prescribed Ambien hidden so that he couldn't access them in a drunken moment of stupidity. He'd actually had her take charge of all of his prescriptions. And thanks to the VA, there were a lot of them. Tonight, that didn't matter though, so she dug into the kitchen cabinet that held the non-prescription drugs and got two chewable melatonin tablets for her husband. He'd already poured himself a glass of water, which she found amusing. He hated how chewy candy got stuck in his teeth. "Thank you." He said as he took the tablets and chewed them, drinking water as he did so they didn't stick to his teeth too much. When he was done, she took his hand.

"Come on, let's go get some sleep." She gave him a gentle kiss, then led him into the bedroom.

49
Two Bridges, New York

The sun was low in the sky as Vinny pulled his jeep into the parking structure. He saw Álex's Tacoma was already there, so he pulled into the spot next to it. Hopping out, Vinny opened the back doors and grabbed his bags. He'd just pulled out his weapons case when Morgan's Big Horn rolled in, music thumping so loud that Vinny could hear the bass from across the structure. As Morgan pulled in, Vinny gave an enthusiastic wave before slinging a bag over his shoulder and picking up an iced latte with his free hand.

"You and your friggin' lattes." Morgan chuckled as he shook his head.

"Good morning to you too!" Vinny retorted.

"How are you always this chipper after our jobs?" Morgan asked, picking up his own equipment.

"Because I know how to spend my nights, unlike you married fools." Vinny snarked.

"You were married too!" Morgan said as they both started towards the vault.

"Key word being 'were' my friend." Vinny said. While it had sucked when it happened, Taylor divorcing him had probably been the best thing that could have happened to Vinny. She hadn't wanted kids and was always pushing for him to be home. Even with him out of the Team now, he was still leaving on a fairly regular basis. She'd just sped up the process by leaving him while still in uniform.

When the door opened, Alex looked up from the lower receiver of his 416 and greeted them.

"You're here early." Vinny said as he set his coffee down. Foaly stared at the drink for a moment, tried to think of something clever to say, and came up blank. Instead, he shrugged and reached under the table. When his hand reappeared, it held two McDonald's bags.

"Got you guys breakfast." He said as he placed the paper bags on the table. Vinny happily tore into one, retrieving two breakfast sandwiches and hash browns, which he handed to Morgan, before grabbing his own.

"What's in the other one?" Morgan asked as he fumbled to set the Egg McMuffins down on the table without dropping his sling bag.

"Hotcakes." Foaly said with a smile.

"Well, you're just a man after my heart aren't ya?" Morgan said with a chuckle as he set the rest of his bags down before opening the second McDonald's bag and pulling out a Styrofoam breakfast tray.

Despite all the bullshit they dealt with while on a job and dealing with the government, it was moments like this that really brought them together as a team. It felt like they were still in the fight.

Shortly after Foaly had been discharged, Vinny put in his request to transfer into the Navy's Inactive Ready Reserve, which was essentially getting out while still fulfilling the last few years of his contractual obligation. Knowing that Alex was being discharged over doing the right thing, Vinny didn't feel he could morally keep serving, and therefore filled out and submitted his IRR paperwork. After asking three times, and getting the same answer each time, Vinny's leadership signed off on the forms. Three weeks later, Vinny packed his bags from his small home in Virginia Beach and moved to the current apartment he resided in now.

DECEPTION

While this was happening, Morgan was going through some light physical therapy for his leg. It took a few months, but in the meantime, he was able to reach out to both Alex and Vinny and get them all connected while he began laying the groundwork for some of their first contracts. If the Army hadn't approached him with news of a medical discharge, he would have likely followed Vinny's lead and gone into the IRR for the remainder of his contract. Even though he'd been signed off with a clean bill of health, Morgan accepted the Medboard and moved back to New York to live with Julia, who had already been commuting between Tennessee and Manhattan at that point. This worked out for both of them, as her having to travel and his constant deployments had put a serious strain on the marriage. That, and Julia had hated both Kentucky and Tennessee. Morgan had never been a huge fan of Fort Campbell either, and he never once glanced back after he drove through Gate 3 for the final time.

"How's everyone holding up?" Foaly asked. Morgan took a bite full of syrup-soaked pancake and nodded.

"Oh, you know. Living the dream." Vinny said with a shrug as he began disassembling his rifle. Even though he'd spent most of his time assisting the Paoli medical team, he'd still fired off his fair share of ammo when they'd initiated the counter-ambush on the rebels.

"You were singing a different tune just a few minutes ago there, Rico Suave." Morgan said, elbowing Vinny in the side.

"What's the matter, she didn't have enough glitter? I'm sure she's only doing it to pay for nursing school." Foaly said with a snide grin. The two of them always gave

Vinny shit about dating strippers even though he'd never once dated one. "She told me she loves me." Vinny replied, along with a one-fingered salute, which got a laugh out of his fellow former operator.

As they continued to work, Morgan once again put some music on his phone, and each man fell into their own little worlds as they cleaned each weapon down to the smallest components. Along with cleaning weapons, Vinny also had to restock his aid bag that he'd used in Zambia. He was going through replacing components he'd used while helping the med staff and was also taking stock of things he was getting low on so he could put another order in soon.

Both Morgan and Vinny's heads shot up when there was a knock on the vault door, and Morgan reached for his 1911.

"Relax." Alex said, standing up and walking to the door. He pulled it open and smiled. "Hey, glad you could make it. Come on in."

Both men watched and were both surprised and confused when a woman dressed in a pair of tight jeans and a t-shirt under a light North Face jacket walked in. She wore her dark brown hair in a neat ponytail that hung just past her shoulders, and her face was naturally pretty with defined cheekbones and large hazel eyes. She smiled at the two men sitting at the table.

"Guys, this is Andrea Overton. Worked with her overseas a few times. I'm bringing her on as our in-house intelligence analyst."

"Hi." Vinny said with a smile, standing to shake her hand. "I'm Vinny."

"Pleasure to meet you." Andrea said with a friendly smile. Vinny stole a glance down to her left hand and his

192

shoulders slumped ever so slightly when he spied the small silver band around her ring finger. *Damn.*

"Morgan Tyron." Morgan stood and shook her hand as well. "CEO of ISC." Then he looked at Alex. "I wasn't aware we were hiring."

"As the resident Intelligence Expert, I wasn't getting enough done. Andrea went through Intel school with a good friend of mine. I first worked with her in Afghanistan back around oh-seven, when she was an analyst attached to my Infantry platoon. We ran across each other in Bagram back in oh-ten, and again in twelve, both times when she was supporting the Unit and other Special Operations elements. Trust me when I say that she's awesome at what she does." Andrea couldn't help but smile and blush a little at Alex's commendations.

"You guys have quite the collection. I'm surprised the ATF and NYPD aren't trying to beat down the door." She said as she looked over the weapons and equipment laid out. Morgan noticed her eyes resting on his 1911, so he picked it up, flipped it over, and handed it to her grip-first. She took it from him and, in one motion, ejected the mag, pulled the slide back, and caught the ejected shell in her free hand. Vinny whistled. Morgan smirked.

"Looks like you know what you're doing." Morgan said with a chuckle as she handed the mag, round, and pistol back to him.

"This girl knows how to shoot. Outshot most of her class down at Huachuca from what I've heard, and she was pretty shit hot on the ranges out in Afghanistan." Alex said as Andrea took off the black backpack she wore. Then she retrieved the Glock 43 single-stack subcompact pistol she wore in a holster on her hip. The 43 was the slimline version of the Glock 26 Foaly favored, since the 26 had a double-stack magazine that fit better in his larger hands.

"Well, being that Alex has so graciously stepped down from his position as Intelligence SME," Morgan returned his gaze back to Andrea. "What do you have for us?"

"Alex has filled me in on everything that happened in Zambia and Bolivia, along with your other jobs. So, I've already started working on putting together reports that will reflect past performance for the company. I'll also oversee building up products and presenting them to any government agencies, so you guys don't get blindsided like you did when you got back from Africa." Morgan's gaze returned to Foaly as Andrea continued. That was why Alex had gone and hired someone on the outside; to cover their asses when the government came calling. "And for future jobs, I'll be building full intel suites on areas you may possibly end up working in."

Everything she had mentioned had usually been responsibilities divvied up between the three of them. This oftentimes left Morgan and Vinny floundering since both had always been on the receiving end of prepared intelligence briefs. During Foaly's enlisted time, he'd been an Eighteen-Foxtrot, a Special Forces Operations and Intelligence Sergeant, before going the officer route and becoming a full-time door kicker. Intelligence had at one point been his bread and butter, but even he couldn't do everything. The more Morgan thought about it, the more he saw this was a good choice.

"So basically, I see it turning into this." Alex said. "When it comes to planning Morgan handles the business and transportation aspects, Vinny the medical, and Andrea and I split the intelligence stuff pre-mission. Once we get boots on the ground, Vinny and I shift over to operations, with Morgan supporting us as well as providing information to Andrea, who will be acting as our reach back cell. That way, when we get a job, especially if it's a last-minute thing like Bolivia was, we don't have to worry about trying to cram everything between the three of us. Hell, if we need to, we bring her with us and leave her at the staging area, like La Paz or something. She knows how to handle herself overseas, so we don't have to worry about her freaking out because she's away from home or anything."

Morgan looked at Andrea, then Vinny, then Foaly. While he'd been initially caught off guard and irritated by the fact that Foaly had gone outside the normal lines of communication to hire someone, Alex had sold it so well that Morgan was already relishing the fact he wouldn't have to slog through creating his own intelligence reports anymore. He looked back towards Andrea, who quietly stood and waited for his response.

"Welcome to the team." Morgan said. Her smile matched his as Vinny cheered, and Alex applauded.

50
July, 2018
Virginia Beach, Virginia

Vinny watched as four guys charged the man who'd just caught the football, taking off at a sprint down the beach. Marcus didn't get far before another one of his fellow SEALs, a younger guy who must have come to the Team after Vinny had gotten out, tackled him into the shallow surf. As the younger guy popped up with his hands up in triumph, Dalton burst up from the water and wrapped his arms around the kid's neck, taking him back down. The surrounding Frogmen whooped and cheered as Dalton asserted dominance by dragging the kid out of the surf and tossing him into the sand.

Dalton, and a few other former teammates, had reached out to Vinny and invited him to come down to celebrate the Fourth of July with them. While he wouldn't be allowed to attend any official team functions, unofficial ones, such as this, were free game, considering they also invited families to these.

"Look who made it!" Dalton cheered when he saw Vinny standing beside his Jeep. "Good to see you, brotha." The two embraced and slapped the other's backs with excessive force.

"Good to see you too man, glad I could make it." Vinny said as he opened the back door and retrieved a cooler.

"You bring the good stuff this time?" Dalton asked. Vinny had once, *once*, brought a case of Coronas to an event like this, and Dalton had ribbed him for it ever since.

"Yeah, yeah." Vinny said, rolling his eyes behind his sunglasses.

"Come on, I know the guys will be excited to see you." Dalton said, waving for Vinny to follow him. The two walked out onto the sand, and those who recognized Vinny began cheering and clapping at his arrival.

"Look who decided to come back." Dennison said with a toothy grin. "And here I thought you'd started thinking you were too good to hang out with us dirty Frogmen."

"That's because you are dirty!" Vinny said as he clasped Dennison's hand. "Good to see you, bro." Vinny saw the younger operator standing off to the side, staring at them. "What's junior's story?" The fact that Vinny didn't acknowledge the sandy-haired SEAL seemed to irritate the kid, who sneered at him.

"Oh, that's Dave." Dalton said. "FNG; only a couple of months out of ██████████."

"And who would you be?" Dave sneered at Vinny.

"Whoa now." Dalton said, his index finger raised towards the junior SEAL. "Is that any way to speak to your elders?" This got a laugh out of Dennison. "This here is Chief Special Warfare Operator Vincent Jensen. Former SOCM, and someone that you..." Dalton punctuated his point by poking the kid in the chest. "...could learn a lot from."

"You know that picture of the Platoon in the bar that was taken in Iraq two years ago?" Dennison said. Dave nodded. "This guy is Rabbit." Dave's head snapped back towards Vinny.

"You're shitting me. This is *the* Rabbit?" Dave asked. Dennison nodded.

"Oh, come on, don't hit me with that hero worship crap." Vinny said with a dismissive wave. "I'm guessing you're their new medic?"

"You guessed it." Dave nodded.

"Alright, you can kiss his ass while we're working the grill." Marcus said. "New guy, carry the beer." Dave let out a loud exhale and took the cooler from Vinny. It was typical new-guy shit; you get fucked with until you proved yourself. And if you didn't prove yourself, you got booted back to wherever you came from.

"Uncle Vinny!" Dalton's daughter, Kayla, called out as she took off across the sand towards him. Vinny smiled and caught his fourteen-year-old Goddaughter in his arms, spinning her around as he gave her a bear hug. While Vinny had never had any kids of his own, Marcus' kids had always seen him as an Uncle, even though three-year-old Max didn't understand such things just yet. Kayla and Max did know one thing though; whenever Uncle Vinny was around, there were gifts to be had.

After a quick catch-up, Kayla took off back towards the beach to rejoin the other SEAL kids engaged in a game of volleyball. Vinny continued following Marcus and the others to where the families were gathered.

"New kid, beer over there." Dennison said, jabbing Dave in the side. Dave grumbled something and walked the case over to where the rest of the beer was being kept in ice chests.

"Shit, who let this degenerate in?" A gravelly voice said. Vinny turned to see a heavily tattooed man with a thick graying beard approaching.

"Dingo." Vinny said as he received a hard punch to the shoulder, followed by a hug from the large operator.

"Good to see you, Rabbit." Master Chief Special Warfare Operator Eddie Rutkowksi said. "How's life on the other side?"

"Busy as shit, but overall good." Vinny said. He missed his team dearly. Every day he wished he was still out on the sands running in the morning, outpacing the rest of them even in the difficult terrain. That was one of the reasons he'd earned the nickname 'Rabbit'. But he'd made a decision to go with Alex and Morgan, and as much as it pained him to not be with the team anymore, he was sticking with his decision.

"Well, we're better off without you. Now that we've got junior here." Rutkowski said, casting a sideways glance towards Dave. "Sure, he can't lift as much or run as fast as you could, and he can't shoot for shit, but he's a hell of a lot prettier to look at than your ugly mug."

"Hooyah." Dave said, flipping the Master Chief the bird. Vinny chuckled; the kid had spunk, and he wasn't letting the hazing get to him. He'd do just fine with this group.

"Well, well." A woman said from behind the group. Vinny turned around and found himself staring at a shorter woman with shoulder-length brunette hair, narrowed green eyes, slightly pursed lips, and a generally unhappy demeanor. "Now there's a face I didn't expect to see so soon."

"Moira." Vinny said politely to Dalton's wife. While Vinny and Dalton were practically brothers, having gone through selection together, and Dalton's kids adored their uncle, Moira Dalton was less than a fan of Vinny Jensen. She and Taylor had been close, and when the divorce happened, she'd taken Taylor's side in things. "How've you been?"

"The usual." Moira answered.

"Hi Uncle Vinny!" Young Max Dalton cheered from his mother's side.

"Hey buddy!" Vinny replied, lowering himself to be almost eye-to-eye with Max. But before he could, Moira was guiding Max along to go play with the other young children. "You didn't tell her I was coming, did you?" Vinny asked Marcus.

"Honestly, I didn't even think of it." Dalton said, cracking a beer handed to him by Dave. "Thought after all this time she would have been more cordial."

"Don't sweat it." Vinny said. "Thanks." He accepted a beer from Dave.

"Oh motherfucker!" Dennison called out as a jet of foamy beer shot from his can. This got a smirk from Dave, who'd shaken the can beforehand. The other SEALs laughed. "Alright new guy, we'll see how smug you are on the mats on Friday." Dennison said before shot gunning the rest of the can. Even he had to admit that the junior teammate had gotten him good.

"How's your boy, Dingo?" Vinny asked as he settled down on one of the many chairs they'd scattered around the sand near where the vehicles were parked.

"He's currently in Hell Week." Dingo said, beaming with pride. His oldest son, Jack, was currently in what many considered the most difficult portion of BUD/S, Basic Underwater Demolition/SEAL school. "But some of my old buddies out at Team Seven have been keeping an eye on him. I guess he's crushing it." Vinny and Dalton had also been members of SEAL Team Seven based out of Coronado when they'd initially made it through BUD/S. Dingo, having made it into the elusive ████████ well before them, took a liking to them when he found out that the two newest members of his platoon had come from his SEAL 'home'.

"Outstanding." Vinny said, raising his bottle of Dos Equis. Dingo *clinked* his bottle against Vinny's, and the two drank. The small talk continued for a bit, keeping it sterile due to the fact they had families around. Still, there were a couple of war stories traded, mainly from the current SEALs trying to get Vinny to pass on some knowledge to Dave. Then it turned to the question that was on everyone's mind.

"So." Dingo asked, leaning back in his chair. "How hard do we have to beg you to drop this IRR shit and come back to us?"

"What, and steal Junior's thunder? I can't do that." Vinny said, smirking at Dave, who unfortunately now had the nickname 'Junior' thanks to Vinny.

"Bullshit, you know we need all the medics we can get our hands on." Dingo said. "Seriously, what do I have to do to get you back? I can get you your E-9, give you a platoon, whatever. Name your price brother, but we need you back." Vinny took a good ten seconds to absorb the question before he answered. Truth was, he wanted nothing more than to come back.

"I made a commitment to these guys I'm working with after that shit in Iran." Vinny said. "And the pay is damn good, I can't deny that. So why don't we do this." Dingo leaned forward, surprised to hear Vinny was actually considering coming back. "How about after this next job you get me in contact with the readiness folks and we'll work out my coming back. My only request is that I get put back in the platoon as your 2IC." Vinny said, using the shorthand for second-in-command. "And I want my old locker." Dingo smiled, joined by the others.

"I'll fucking cheers to that!" Dalton said, raising his bottle. He was answered, accompanied by several 'here-here's!' as the rest of them joined in the toast.

"Better start getting your shit ready to move, Junior." Dennison said. Dave groaned and rolled his eyes, smiling. Vinny leaned back in his chair, glad that the guys had invited him out, and even more glad that they'd put him on the spot with making that decision.

51
Langley, Virginia

The early morning air was hot as Alex and Vinny waited by the large stone-and-glass archway of the front entrance to the Central Intelligence Agency's headquarters, waiting for Morgan. Foaly and Vinny had gotten out of the car and walked to the entrance while Morgan went to hunt for an open parking spot. As they waited, they were passed by scores of Agency personnel dressed in everything from t-shirts and jeans to business-casual to three-piece suits, and even a couple of uniformed officials. Foaly glanced down at his watch and saw it was eight-forty-five. Morgan was going to have to hustle if they were going to make their nine o'clock meeting.

"Alex!" Someone called out. Foaly looked up and turned to look for whoever had called out to him. "Alex, how are you brother?" He turned to his right to see a man in dark slacks and a button-up shirt with the sleeves rolled halfway up his forearms walking towards him. The man's eyes were hidden behind a pair of William Painter sunglasses.

"Holy shit! Tom!" Foaly said, recognizing his old Team Leader. The two skipped the handshake and went straight into a brotherly hug. The man was Thomas Mason, a former Special Forces soldier and Foaly's first Team Lead. It had been at least three years since Foaly had seen Mason, before Tom had been snatched out of ▮▮▮▮ for some super-secret-squirrel shit.

"What are you doing here? Agency finally decide to pick you up?" Mason asked. Foaly smirked and shook his head.

"Nah, no permanent employment. We got contacted for a contracting gig actually." Alex pointed to Vinny. "Tom, this is Vinny Jensen. Former Frogman and one of my coworkers." The two shook hands and exchanged pleasantries, with a friendly jab thrown in by Mason.

"You guys going GRS?" Mason asked. Foaly shrugged.

"Dunno. Our CEO got called a few days ago with the simple message that someone here wanted to meet with us. You guys have beaucoup bucks, so we sure as hell weren't going to say no to a meeting." Alex said. He was sure that Mason would make a few phone calls and have everything regarding their little company at his cubicle within an hour.

Over Mason's shoulder, Foaly spied Morgan approaching them from across the parking lot. He was making large strides towards them, briefcase in-hand. He did not look happy.

"Literally no spots around here. Feels like I parked half a mile away!" Morgan said as he stopped next to them. He pulled out a handkerchief to wipe the sweat from his brow, then paused when he realized there were three of them.

"Morgan, this is Tom Mason, an old friend of mine." Alex introduced Mason to Morgan. "Tom, Morgan is the CEO of our little group."

"Nice to meet you." Mason said, shaking Morgan's hand.

"Pleasure." Morgan replied, his voice betraying his true feelings at the moment. He looked down at his watch. "Shit, with security we're probably not going to make our meeting."

"Any of you carrying?" Mason asked. They all shook their heads. "Alright, come with me."

Mason led the three into the main entrance, but then cut a left towards a smaller security kiosk. It was a single lane that was manned by three uniformed CIA Security Officers. All eyes turned towards the group.

"Morning Tom." The one behind the x-ray scanner said.

"Good morning, Joe." Mason said as he reached into his waistband and retrieved his nine-millimeter USP Compact pistol, along with two spare mags. He placed his weapon in a gray bin, along with two smart phones, his wallet, watch, and keyring. "Gonna need you to print up three visitors passes for these fine gents behind me." The tray went through the scanner and Mason was waved forward by another security officer holding a metal detector wand. Mason stood there as he was wanded while the third security man stood off to the side, his short-barrel M4 slung across his chest.

"What's their story?" Joe asked Mason, who was busy collecting his things.

"They're here for a meeting at nine with…" Mason looked at the group.

"Thomas Donnelly." Morgan answered.

"Wait one." Joe said, tapping the keyboard to the computer in front of him. A moment later he had a visitor's list pulled up. "Alright guys, I'm going to need some form of ID before I can let you though." They each handed over their respective identification. Joe checked each and nodded, satisfied. "Please empty all pockets and unlock any hand-carried bags." Joe read off the card taped to his monitor. "Once your belongings have been checked you will be issued a visitor's badge. Ensure to keep the badge visible above the waist at all times."

Foaly stepped through the metal detector and it emitted a loud beep. All three security officers looked at Alex, with the one carrying the rifle placing both hands on his weapon.

"Are you carrying anything metal on you, sir?" The one with the wand asked, his free hand hovering near the pistol in his belt holster.

"Probably the shrapnel in my right leg." Foaly replied, slowly reaching down, and pulling his pant leg up to reveal scars sustained from shrapnel wounds by an RPG that came a little too close for comfort along the Afghanistan-Turkmenistan border. "Afghanistan, back in twenty-eleven. Might still be some in my shoulder from oh-seven as well." The guard ran the wand over Foaly's leg, and sure enough it beeped right around his calf.

"Okay sir, go ahead." The officer nodded, stepping aside to allow Foaly to grab his things and waving Vinny forward. "Any shrapnel I should know about?" He asked before Vinny passed through. Vinny paused and thought for a moment, then shook his head.

"Nah, pretty sure they pulled it all out." He said with a smile before passing through without issue.

"Where do you find these guys?" Joe asked Mason from behind his monitors. Mason just chuckled.

"Alex here is an old teammate." Mason slapped a hand on Foaly's shoulder. "The others, I'm not sure about." Morgan passed through without incident, the pins in his leg being made of titanium and therefore not setting off the sensors.

"Thanks Joe!" Mason called out with a wave.

DECEPTION

"Have a good one!" Joe returned the wave, then turned and picked up the conversation with the other guards that must have gotten cut off when the four men arrived.

"So, you're meeting with Donnelly?" Mason asked over his shoulder as they walked across the large lobby. "Surprised he even gave you his name. He's a good dude. Thankfully, doesn't buy into the typical spook shit like a lot of suits here do." Foaly knew Mason couldn't admit it, but he was ninety-nine percent sure that the former operator was now a member of the CIA's Special Activities Division. There was no way Mason was riding a desk. "Hey, I've got to get going. Looks like this is where we part ways." Mason turned to Foaly. "Alex, good to see you again brother. Give me a call and we'll get a beer!" Mason held up a Shaka as he walked away. "And give my best to Shannon!"

"I will. Say hi to Laura for me." Foaly replied with his own Shaka. With that, Mason turned around and disappeared into the crowd of Agency employees swarming around in their respective duties. After a moment, Morgan pointed out three open chairs along a wall.

Five minutes passed and the three men sat in silence, either glancing around or perusing one of the many magazines left scattered on the chairs. Surprisingly, none of them noticed the suited man approaching, until he was right beside them.

"Morgan Tyron?" The guy asked. Morgan looked up from his phone.

"Yeah." He said.

"Please follow me." The suit gestured with one hand. They rose and followed him down a corridor

207

bustling with activity. They hung a left and followed the young officer past a bank of elevators and then a cafeteria before arriving at a smaller set of elevators. There was no one waiting on these lifts. The young man pressed the call button, and they waited for the elevator to arrive.

"How long have you been out of the farm?" Vinny asked the guy, who couldn't have been older than twenty-four. He glanced over his shoulder and smirked at Vinny. The elevator *dinged* and they all stepped in. The ride was silent as they ascended to the fifth floor. Once more there was a loud *ding* and he led them down a carpeted hallway before reaching a nondescript wooden door.

"Here we are." He said, holding the door open for them. They all thanked him as they entered.

The office was decently large, with white-washed walls and dark blue carpeting. An American Flag stood on a brass pole in the corner of the room, and the wall behind the oak desk was covered in framed photographs, diplomas, and awards. The wall to their right was dominated by a built-in bookshelf packed with various titles, and a few shelves held various trinkets from around the world. Tom Donnelly smiled as they each took in his office. All it was missing was a window.

"Hi guys." Donnelly said as he finished typing something on his computer before giving them his full attention. "How're we doing this morning?" He stood and shook each of their hands before settling back into the chair and waving for them to sit. Just like he did at the State building, he looked happy to see them. Almost as if they were meeting for coffee rather than whatever this was about. And whatever it was, seeing Donnelly made Foaly's chest tighten. Ever since his sudden appearance at State, something didn't sit right with Foaly whenever this guy was around.

"We're doing alright." Morgan said. "Yourself?" Donnelly leaned back and gestured around his office.

"New position, new office, new duties." Donnelly replied with a smile. "How's the mercenary business treating you?" Foaly wanted to roll his eyes, and Morgan chuckled.

"Haven't you heard? That's a bad word nowadays." Morgan said. It was Donnelly's turn to laugh.

"Yeah, but we all know that what you three do isn't simple contract work. Call it whatever you want, we know what it really is. That's why you're sitting here with me today rather than pulling gate guard duty at Bagram."

Both Foaly and Vinny had worked plenty with CIA men like Donnelly in the past. It didn't escape either of them that he conducted himself like a former shooter, but neither could place where he could have served. He was a little long in the tooth to have served with either of them, that much was obvious. But this guy had seen his fair share of shit at one point.

"My friend is the station chief down in Bolivia, works right in La Paz. Told me about three Americans that were called in to help nab a high-level target. You three were effective in grabbing him. Almost too effective. Had he gotten popped; you would've ruined a whole lot of intel work." Donnelly smirked as he tapped a folder on his desk. "And after corroborating your reports on what happened in Zambia, you've definitely proven yourselves to know your shit without military oversight."

"This a history lesson?" Foaly asked, finding it irritating that Donnelly was just reading back recent events to them.

"Always a straight shooter. I read that in your file too." Donnelly smiled at Foaly, which doubled his unease. Donnelly picked up a remote from his desk and clicked a button. The screen set in the wall behind him lit up, showing satellite imagery of a docked shipping vessel.

"This is the MV Aguilar. She's a fifth-generation ROCON container ship currently docked at Port Newark in Elizabeth, New Jersey." He turned to face them. "The job is simple. I want to hire you three to guard that ship until it reaches its destination."

"And where would that be?" Foaly asked.

"Mogadishu, and after that the Port of Djibouti. Once you reach DJ, you'll debark and get flown back here." Donnelly said.

"Let me guess, humanitarian supplies." Vinny said. Donnelly smiled.

"Right on the money, Mister Jensen." Donnelly set the remote down and looked at his three guests. "We want you three to provide security because, as I'm sure you know, piracy along the Horn of Africa is on the rise again. The current threat assessment is low, but we want a couple of shooters on board anyway. And we figured we would hire small and keep it low-vis. You stood out as the perfect choice due to your past performance, coupled with Vinny's experience as a SEAL. And it saves us from having to shell out excessive amounts of money for some of the big-name groups out there."

"We don't work for free." Morgan interjected.

"And no one expects you to." Donnelly replied. "We've prepared more than a reasonable amount to be paid out to you. One third before you depart, the rest when the ship arrives in Djibouti." He slid forms in front of each man. Foaly looked down and was unsurprised to see the requisite nondisclosure acts. The direct deposit forms did catch him off guard though. "Travel and expenses will be covered by us. You'll link up with the Aguilar at the dockyard in Jersey next Wednesday." The three men looked up from their paperwork. "So, what do you say?"

"I'm in." Morgan said. His mind had been made after reading the amount they'd each be earning individually. He signed and filled out the forms, sliding them back.

"Looks like I'm in too." Vinny said. With their paperwork done, Donnelly began typing again. A few moments later he looked over at the three.

"Alright, your initial payments have been made." Donnelly smiled and stood to shake their hands. "I'm glad we finally get to do business together."

"The feeling's is mutual." Morgan said with a smile. The door to the office opened and the younger Agency man was standing there.

"I'll walk you guys out." Donnelly said, leading them from the office.

Before they left, Foaly took a detour in the main lobby. He had to stop and pay his respects at the Memorial Wall, knowing his father's name was still redacted in The Book of Honor.

52
Edgebrook, New Jersey

The drive back had been silent apart from the music playing in the cab of Morgan's truck. They'd decided to take one vehicle down, and the obvious choice ended up being Morgan's Big Horn due to its extended crew cab. Morgan was driving, Vinny was asleep in the back seat, and Alex was staring out his open window behind his sunglasses.

"Whaddya think?" Morgan finally asked.

"I don't know." Alex answered honestly. "Something about this seems...off." Morgan glanced over at Foaly.

"How so?"

"Donnelly is one of those Company guys that never sat right with me." Alex said. "Worked with his type in Afghanistan and a few other places, and they've always got some kind of ulterior motive." He stretched his arms above his head until he got an audible *pop* from his back. "First off, why bring in outside contractors to guard a ship when they could just assign some of their guys to it? And building from that, why go with us instead of a more established firm like Trident Group? Yeah, I know. He answered that in his office, but that was him blowing smoke." Morgan closed his mouth, so Alex continued. "And why the hell is a ship being loaded up with 'humanitarian aid' for Africa in New Jersey? Why transport that shit by sea anyway? It would be a lot faster and cheaper just to load it all up in a C-17 and fly that shit over the pond." Foaly shook his head. "Something's off about this whole thing."

"Well, maybe once we're underway you can ask around as to what's really going on." Morgan said. "But if I'm being honest, I think you're overthinking this. It'll be an easy gig compared to everything else we've done so far. The three of us are more than enough to take on some pissant pirates if they even decide to come after us. And having a job for the Agency under our belt will be huge for the company."

"Agree to disagree." Foaly said. He was tired. Morgan could tell that much from voice alone.

"Get some rest dude, we'll switch off when I stop for gas." Morgan glanced down at the dash, which showed they could go another forty miles before the light would even turn on. At this rate they'd be home in no time.

"Sounds good." Foaly said as he rolled up his window to lean his head against it.

53
Upper East Side, New York

"Okay that's great. Thank you so much!" Shannon said before ending the call. She had just gotten off the phone with Julia, who had helped them secure the lease on a new apartment. It was the same one that Shannon had texted Alex about while he had been in Zambia. Her smile turned into a grin as she set her phone down. She picked it up again almost immediately and pulled up Alex's contact, wondering if she should call or text him the news. He was on his way back from Virginia, but he hadn't told her how far away he was when he'd last texted her.

She was about to hit call when the front door's lock clicked and swung open. She turned around to see Alex standing there, bag in-hand.

"Hey!" She said excitedly, running over and embracing her husband before kissing him. He returned the hug with his free arm, and she could tell his mind was preoccupied.

"Hi." He set his bag down and closed the door. "What's got you all giddy?" She couldn't help but break into a grin again.

"We got the new apartment!" She announced. Alex looked at her for a moment, then it clicked. He smiled.

"That's great." He replied, giving her a full embrace. It was awesome news; they'd be upgrading space-wise, and it would give Shannon a room for her office.

"We can start moving in next Friday!" She said. That was when she saw his eyes shift. "What's up?"

"We've got another assignment. It's a government contract." Alex said. He noticed the almost imperceptible slump in her shoulders at hearing this.

"What's the job?" She asked, worry in her voice.

"Ship's security. Heading from Jersey to Africa." He stopped himself from saying anything else, not wanting to break the NDA he'd barely skimmed before signing.

"Africa? I hoped you'd never have to go there again." Shannon said. Then the real concern hit her. "You're usually more excited about getting work. What's wrong?" She asked. It was unconscious for her, but Foaly knew it was her Psychology minor that was kicking in as she inadvertently psychoanalyzed her husband.

"I can't really get into it. Something just feels off about the whole thing. Just my gut feeling, ya know?" He pulled up one of the kitchen chairs and took a seat.

"If it's bugging you that much, why go through with it? Those gut feelings have kept you alive in the past."

"I can't leave Morgan and Vinny to do this alone. We're a team." Alex sighed. "And if I backed out now, I'd have to pay back the initial deposit, and we could use that money." He gave a bit of a smirk. "So, they've already got me on the hook for that. But I'm going to do some research on the ship itself and see what comes up." Shannon reached over and squeezed his hand.

"When do you leave?" She asked.

"Next Wednesday." Alex answered.

"Well at least you'll be home for a few days." She said with a smile. "Though you're going to miss my parents, they're driving down on Thursday. They wanted to take us out."

"You'll have to apologize to them for me." Foaly said. They both knew it wouldn't be a big deal. It wouldn't be the first get-together he'd be absent for. Probably wouldn't be the last, either. "On the bright side, this'll be an easy gig. If any pirates are stupid enough to try and take the ship, they're going to wish they'd stayed in bed that morning. We won't have anything to worry about."

"Yeah I remember you saying something like that before you went to Zambia. And Bolivia. And Nicaragua." Shannon began counting off with her fingers.

"Okay, okay. You've got me there." Foaly laughed.

"I just can't help but worry sometimes." She admitted. That was when Foaly noticed the computer behind her. It displayed the confirmation of an order for a delivery service.

"You must really want out of here." He said. She looked over her shoulder at the screen, then laughed.

"Hell yeah I do! We're going to have an actual office. I can't wait!" Her excitement was contagious, and he stood up and kissed her.

"I'll help pack as much as I can while prepping my own stuff." He said.

"Good, I can get some use out of you for once." She said with a smile.

216

54
Murray Hill, New York

Morgan looked over the clothing he'd laid out on the bed for the upcoming job. According to the ship's itinerary, and corroborated by Andrea's analysis, they were looking at about a month at sea, so he wanted to make sure he had enough clothes to last about a week before they would need to be washed. He had everything laid out, from workout clothes to combat fatigues, and the low-vis regular clothing they'd be wearing as to not draw too much suspicion from any passing ships. He'd set aside a pair of cargo pants and a light jacket to wear the day of departure, since the next two weeks were forecasted to be blanketed with rain thanks to the tropical storms that were hammering Manhattan. He'd also laid out one of his Magnum-inspired Aloha shirts, as he was sure that would make for a fun photo op at some point during the journey.

Satisfied with his clothing selection, he began to fold everything before placing them in the tan rolling duffel bag that sat beside the bed. It was the same bag that he'd taken with him on most of his deployments with the Nightstalkers, and now continued to serve as his 'go' bag in the private sector. As he was packing, Julia walked in and watched as he meticulously folded each piece of clothing before placing them in the bag.

"Excited?" She asked.

"Course I am." He looked up at her and smiled. "I love this stuff, remember?"

"How could I forget?" She returned the smile. He really did love this. "Shame you'll be gone for so long though."

"It's only a month." He said as he picked up his sneakers and placed them into the bag. "Sure, it's a bit longer than our other jobs, but still easy compared to what we went through down in Kentucky."

"That is most definitely true." She said, sitting on a section of bed that was now clear of clothing. She settled beside her husband and rested her head on his shoulder, her gaze drifting to the framed photo of them on their wedding day resting on the dresser.

Morgan knew Julia was happy he was doing something he loved, but he was also all too aware that it killed her not knowing whether he was safe or not. It was obvious that she hadn't fully understood what he'd meant when he'd formed Integral Solutions, likely thinking it was some sort of desk job. When she'd seen pictures of him all kitted up on their first gig, she'd just about had a heart attack. He stopped packing as Julia took his hand in hers and held it. They both sat in silence for a while.

"What's on your mind?" She finally asked.

"How about after this I take some time off?" He looked at her. "The government is paying a pretty penny for this, so we won't be hurting. Maybe we'll take a trip somewhere. I know you've been dying to go to Santorini." Morgan also knew that Julia had been swamped with work, including helping Shannon nail down the details for their new apartment.

"That would be wonderful." She smiled.

"And then after that we can go look for a place down in Florida." Morgan said. Julia hated the cold winters of New York, and being down in Florida would allow her to be closer to her parents, who lived in Louisiana. Honestly, the idea of constant sun and being near the beach appealed to Morgan as well. He'd spent many a summer down in Florida as a kid and had nothing but fond memories down there.

"You keep spoiling me like this and I'm going to think you're up to something." She leaned over and kissed him. "Let me know when you're done, and we'll go get dinner."

"Sounds like a plan." He said before kissing her back. "Love you babe."

"And I love you." Julia said as she walked out of the room, leaving her husband to continue preparing.

55
Allentown, Pennsylvania

Vinny got out of his jeep and approached the Super 8. He spied Dingo's Ford F-150 parked in front of the room and checked his phone to confirm the room number before rapping his knuckles against the door. He was caught off guard when the door only opened about an inch and a voice that was unfamiliar to him asked for the password.

"Huh?" Vinny said, on edge and reaching for his concealed handgun.

"Password." The voice said again.

"You better let him in before he shoots your ass." Dingo's voice said from inside.

"Ugh, fine." The younger voice said. The door closed and Vinny heard the chain lock pull back before it opened again. He found himself staring at Junior of all people, dressed in a plain t-shirt and jeans. "The password was 'password'." Junior said as he stepped aside.

"That's stupid. You've been hanging out with Dalton too much." Vinny said, giving the kid a friendly shoulder check as he walked in. "You brought him with you?"

"Can't be a proper ▮▮▮▮ SEAL without having some skeletons in his closet. Figured this'll get him in line well enough." Dingo said from his supine position on one of the two beds in the room, not looking up from the television, which was playing reruns of Jeopardy. "What is Tallahassee?" Dingo asked.

"What is Tallahassee?" One of the contestants asked.

"Correct!" Mid-nineties Trebek said.

DECEPTION

"How do you know all of these?" Vinny asked. Dingo could always be found watching Jeopardy in the team room or on his phone in the locker room whenever he had some down time. The man was smart as hell, possessing two bachelor's degrees as well as a Master's in engineering physics from the University of Virginia, all of which he'd earned while serving in the Navy. All things considered; Dingo Rutkowski should have been a career Naval Officer. But he hated the politics on the 'dark side' and preferred to chew it up with the rest of the enlisted and non-commissioned officers of the teams.

"Perks of being raised by my grandparents." Dingo grunted as he swung his legs over the side of the bed. "Get the stuff, kid." Junior nodded and walked over to the motel closet, where he retrieved a large black backpack. "Grabbed one of your old bags too. Pretty sure it's one of the ones I loaned to you back in the day, but we have newer shit now." Dingo took the bag from Junior and unzipped it to double-check everything before handing it over to Vinny.

"Holy shit, you were actually able to get it." Vinny said as he retrieved the items from the bag. The first was his H&K MP7 personal defense weapon, which still had the custom tan and brown paint job he'd given it during one of their rotations to Iraq. The Aimpoint CompM3 sight was still attached as well, and Dingo had thrown in three suppressors as well as half a dozen magazines. "How the hell did you pull this off?" Vinny half-expected to get a bored shrug from the man, and he would have been fine with that.

"Had Junior here sign it out for some upcoming training we've got scheduled. Gonna be a real shame when it goes in the drink after he rolls off a Zodiac, but shit happens." Dingo answered. Vinny looked up at Junior, who gave a boyish smile and a shrug.

"He put you up to this?" Vinny asked. "Or were you dumb enough to volunteer?" It had been an incredibly reckless and highly illegal thing to do. If found out it could easily place Junior, Dingo, and Vinny in jail for a very long time, as well as costing the two current SEALs their ranks, and more importantly, their Tridents. That's what made the gesture even more important; they were willing to put life and career on the line for a former teammate. Doubly so for Junior, who hadn't actually served beside Vinny.

"Little of column a, little of column b." Junior said. Vinny nodded as he placed the very-illegal weapon back in the bag.

"Also grabbed you those HEEDs and HITs you asked for." Dingo said. Vinny checked, and sure as shit there were three each of the maritime survival instruments. "Those won't be as missed as the HK though."

"I can't thank you guys enough for grabbing this for me." Vinny slung the bag over his shoulder and stood. Morgan had sourced them plenty of equipment for ground operations, but they had little in the way of maritime gear.

"That sounds great, thanks." Junior said. Vinny and Dingo gave him confused looks.

"Pray tell." Vinny said.

"Offering to take us out for a nice steak lunch? Much appreciated, it's the least you can do after all." Junior's smile turned to a grin, and Dingo started laughing.

"Shithead." Vinny couldn't help but shake his head and chuckle. "Let's go get some grub."

"You're driving." Dingo said, winging his truck keys at Junior's head. The young SEAL almost got hit in the center of the forehead but managed to catch the incoming keys at the last moment.

56
Long Island, New York

Alex sat across from Andrea at her small dining room table, both pouring over the data on their laptops. With such short notice, they'd both been cramming as much work into threat assessments and courses of action in building an intel workup, on top of Foaly having to pack and prep for the job.

"Report out of AFRICOM back last month shows that piracy is on the uptick, but it's more so where the Red Sea meets the Gulf of Aden, as opposed to the Somali coast." Andrea said, sipping coffee from her mug. "Looks like the pirates have moved up there to target the shipping lanes, and a lot of them are using the fighting in Yemen as an excuse to target passing vessels."

"A little too close for comfort." Foaly said as he read over the same report; impressed that the report had been written by, and credited to, an Army specialist. The Red Sea and Gulf of Aden met right around where Djibouti was. They were discharging the Agency's cargo well before they would reach their destination, but it also meant they'd have to be on guard well after the 'hard' part of the job.

"I'm still waiting to hear back from some of my friends over there on any chatter regarding incoming shipments, but so far they haven't picked up anything. And thankfully the Aguilar's itinerary hasn't been released yet." She paused and read through an email that popped up, but that was regarding another project she was working on. "Are you sure you don't want me to come with?" She looked up to see Foaly pause.

DECEPTION

"Honestly, if I could swing it, I would. But I'm sure the Agency wants to keep this one close to the vest. Probably best to keep you as a reach back in case you come across anything important that we'll need to know about. Can't imagine the ship's going to have great connectivity anyway."

"I'm working on something for that." She said with a smile.

"Course you are." Foaly replied. Andrea was one of the best in the business of intelligence, having made a name for herself right out of Intel School.

"Still got reservations about this?" Andrea asked. Foaly nodded. She was all too familiar with how he felt about the CIA and their cloak-and-dagger tendencies. During their last time in Afghanistan together in 2012, Andrea had been part of a small group, mainly consisting of civilian intelligence contractors and an eight-man team from Foaly's ███ element, who'd been hijacked by the CIA to conduct several off-the-books operations into Tajikistan, and one snatch-and-grab that had taken the eight operators and two CIA operatives over the Afghan border into China. Foaly had been vehemently against that cross-border operation, but he knew that the Agency always got its way, and therefore went along with it as the team lead for his people. That way, if shit had gone sideways, it would have fallen on him rather than any of his guys.

"If they didn't hold shit so close to the vest and actually let us in on what was going down, I wouldn't have so much of a problem with it." Foaly said. He understood the whole 'need to know' aspect, but getting roped into guarding something that would likely land them all in prison for a long time and not knowing what it was didn't sit well with him. He'd operated on the black side of things for long enough to trust his gut feeling, and even with all the analysis and risk assessments that Andrea had conducted, the whole thing still stank for him. The fact that it wasn't bothering Vinny as much struck Foaly as strange.

"You worry too much." Andrea said with a reassuring smile. "Even if some shit does go down, it won't be anything you can't handle. Especially with that pretty-boy SEAL on your six." She sneered. Alex rolled his eyes. "I can handle the rest of this. Head home and spend some time with Shannon, I heard that you guys are moving."

"Now how the hell did you hear that?" Foaly asked.

"I have my sources." Andrea said with a wink.

"Of course you do." Foaly said as he powered down his laptop and shut it. "We'll be at the vault tomorrow morning. See you then?"

"I'll be there." Andrea gave a wave, re-focused on whatever was in front of her.

57
Two Bridges, New York

Morgan looked up from his weapons as the vault door opened. A moment later Alex walked in, looking soggy.

"Where's Vin?" Foaly asked as he looked around.

"Good morning to you too." Morgan said. "He's on his way." Morgan went back to checking his H&K MP5 submachine gun. Foaly closed the doors behind him and walked over to his locker, running a hand through his hair. The rain had already started and was only slated to get heavier in the next few days. It wasn't a full-blown hurricane yet, but warnings had already been put out for the citizens of New York to begin preparing for the worst.

"Deck duty's going to be a bitch if this rain keeps up." Foaly said as he pulled out his vest and helmet, setting them both on the table. Next was the soft case for his AN/PVS-15 night vision goggles, which he could mount to the front of his helmet if needed. He normally brought his PVS-14's, which were a monocular design, but he figured if they took contact at night, all he'd have to do is flick on the IR laser, point his rifle, put the line on the target, and shoot.

"I'm sure we'll be fine. Can't imagine this storm will go much further than the Hudson Bay. And it's not like we'll need to start patrolling till we're a couple hundred miles off the African coast anyway." Morgan said as he shouldered the MP5 to re-check the sight picture with the Aimpoint he'd installed on the weapon a few weeks ago. It looked good to him, and his grouping had been even tighter than those with iron sights the last few times he'd taken it to the range. Morgan lowered the weapon and looked over at Alex, who was busy attaching the NODs to the front of the helmet that now rested on his head. Alex had his normal intensity of pre-mission prep, but there was an air of unease around him as well.

"Hey guys." Vinny said as he stepped over the threshold of the vault, interrupting Morgan before he could say something to Alex.

"Hey Vin." Foaly said, checking the counterweight on the back of his helmet.

"Watcha got there?" Morgan asked, gesturing to the black backpack Vinny carried in his left hand.

"Since we're doing ship duty, I wanted to make sure we were prepared." Vinny said as he unzipped the bag and reached in. "A few of my buddies from the Teams came through and got us some goodies." He tossed a black object to Foaly, who caught it with one hand. Upon inspection, he saw there were MOLLE straps on the back of the strange-looking pouch for it to be attached to a vest.

"It's a hydrostatic inflation collar." Vinny explained. "We call them HITs. If you go in the drink it'll inflate and form a collar around the back of your neck and bring you to the surface. It keeps your face above water in case you're knocked out." Vinny tossed one of the collars to Morgan before setting his own on the table. "We used them whenever we'd do helo insertions over water, and whenever we'd take down ships." Vinny set the bag down with a loud metal *clunk* before retrieving a small silver canister, most of which he'd covered with olive-drab hundred-mile-hour tape. "HEED IV mini-scuba bottles. We can attach these directly to our vests as a backup in case the collars fail. Position the mouthpiece, turn the nozzle, and you've got air. Just don't hyperventilate, these things only hold about ten minutes of air for controlled breathing." He set two more bottles on the table. "Gifts from my buddy Dingo." Vinny said with a smile. Foaly was already busy attaching the HIT to the back of his vest. He'd worked a few times with the collars during joint exercises with the SEALs back in the day but was by no stretch of the imagination an expert on their use. It was times like this that he was grateful to have Vinny's SEAL expertise on the team.

They resumed their normal pre-mission prep, with each man going into their own world while music played from multiple phones. Morgan looked over at Vinny, who was swapping over pouches from his regular vest to his Crye Precision JPC 2.0 Swimmer Cut vest, and then to Alex, who was going over his weapons.

"Keeping the ACOG?" Morgan asked, referring to the scope on top of Alex's 416.

"Fuck yeah dude. Any assholes want to roll up on a skiff I want to be able to hit them as far out as I can. Even more so if we get one of those fucking motherships after us." Foaly said, referring to a newer pirate tactic of having larger, better armed boats acting as a launch point for the faster and lighter skiffs that they normally used. "Speaking of which, we should bring at least one long gun with us, and the Mk46."

"I'll grab the RSASS." Vinny set his vest down and went into his locker to grab the Remington sniper rifle. Morgan went to his and retrieved the short-barreled machine gun, along with six soft ammo bags. Foaly also grabbed his own long gun, a Knight's Armament SR-25, and set it on the table. If any pirates did decide to go after the ship, the response they'd be met with would make them wish they'd stayed in bed that morning.

With their primary weapons, the two long guns, machinegun, pistols, two shotguns, and a grenade launcher, the three contractors had enough equipment and experience to stage a coup d'état in any third world nation, and probably succeed, too. With the weapons set, they began piling on boxes of associated ammo, as well as dozens of magazines. Morgan also grabbed a small Pelican case and began loading it with extra parts: firing pins, buffer springs, and other tiny but essential components that would deadline any of their weapons if they broke. He normally didn't worry about this aspect, but they were going into uncharted territory, and he wanted to have all their bases covered.

Hearing the container door open, the three of them turned around to see Andrea crossing the threshold. Foaly smirked; having a fourth person with access to this place was something they'd all have to get used to.

"Hi gang." Andrea said as she slid the hood of her jacket from her head. They all responded in kind while continuing to get their things ready.

"Whaddya got for us?" Foaly asked as he racked his Remington 870MCS shotgun three times before setting it beside his rifle. He figured that if any pirates were lucky enough to board the ship, he'd make quick work of them with the shotgun.

"AFRICOM came back with nil on any chatter, so I reached out to some friends I have at the Activity to see if they'd come across anything." Andrea said as she found a small clearing on the table to claim as her own. She pulled her laptop from her bag and powered it on, quickly pulling up a PowerPoint she'd thrown together that morning. "ISA couldn't pull too much, even on the Aguilar itself. The ship's manifest and crew roster match

DECEPTION

up with what your Agency contact told you, but there's a good amount of cargo space that isn't listed as occupied, yet the ship is sitting at full capacity. Check out the waterline." She rotated the laptop to show them photos of the ship sitting in port, timestamped six hours prior. Even Foaly was impressed. "And there was a last-minute change to the itinerary as of eleven o' clock last night; they've added another week of travel time without any explanation." Morgan looked over at Alex, who sucked his teeth with irritation.

"Donnelly's jerking us around." Foaly said. "Has there been any traffic regarding the ship at all?"

"Nothing stating it directly, though the Activity has picked up a spike in the use of the phrase 'finback' in the past week throughout Manhattan and the tri-state area. They're not sure if it's referring to a ship, or if there's a sleeper cell in the area that just got activated. Either way, everyone is on guard right now." She finished the slideshow and shut the laptop. "You're sure you don't want me to come with?" She asked, then frowned as Foaly shook his head.

"I had a bad feeling about this before, but now there are way too many rogue variables that we can't account for." Foaly said. If it were up to him, they'd pull out of the job right then and there. But there was no way that was going to happen. "What can we use to keep up comms with you for the trip?" She reached into her bag and pulled out an Iridium satellite phone, passing it to Alex.

"All the channels are pre-programmed in. I've also got it to work on certain radio frequencies in case satellite coverage gets spotty. Kind of like those old Nokia phones that you could use as a walkie-talkie." She handed one to

Morgan as well. "Battery life is excellent, and they're basically indestructible. Should be able to keep us in touch the entire way." She paused before smiling. "And in case you get bored…" She reached back into the bag and withdrew a black plastic square that was about as large as a hardcover book. "Portable modem; already encrypted for ISC use only. Think of it as one of the WiFi pucks, except this thing can maintain multiple devices with high-speed internet at once." She placed it on the table, and it was immediately snatched up by Morgan.

"You've really outdone yourself." Morgan commented as he inspected the device. "Alex was right on hiring you."

"Just trying to help fight the good fight." Andrea said with a smile.

"Even though you've already outdone yourself." Alex started as he broke open a box of nine-millimeter ammunition. "Since you're here, want to help us finish loading up?

"I was waiting for you to ask." Andrea replied, picking up a stack of magazines for the 5.56 rifles and breaking open a box of the respective ammo to start loading them.

58
Port Newark, New Jersey

Jake Branson watched through the downpour as the large black pickup pulled into the dockyard parking lot. The truck opened and three figured hopped out. They quickly grabbed bags from under the tarp that covered the truck bed before making their way towards the ship. The lead man was dressed in a pair of navy cargo pants and wore a gray softshell jacket, its hood up over his head.

"You Tyron?" Branson asked. The guy stopped and looked at him.

"No, I'm Alex." He replied through a thunderclap. "That's Morgan." He gestured with his head towards another one of the figures. This one wore a pair of brown cargo pants with a black rain jacket and a tan baseball cap on his head that was being tugged by the wind.

"Mister Tyron, I'm Jake. Nice to meet you." Branson stuck a hand out. Morgan looked at the outstretched hand for a moment before setting down a weapons case and shaking it.

"Same." Morgan said. "You our babysitter?"

"Something like that." He gave a dry, humorless smile. "The other guy is up on the bridge with the Captain, ironing out a few last-minute details before we head off." Branson said.

"Adding another week onto the itinerary?" Alex asked with no attempt to hide his irritation. Branson was about to retort when he looked past the three mercenaries and saw the truck they'd arrived in pull out of the lot. "You had someone drive you here?" He asked. It was his turn not to hide the alert and irritation from his voice. If these cowboys had compromised their presence in any way…

"Relax." Foaly said curtly, growing even more irritated at being stuck out in the heavy rain. "Our driver is trustworthy; been vetted by you guys in the past." Andrea had volunteered to drive them to the dockyard in Morgan's truck so he wouldn't have to leave it in Jersey for the trip. Branson looked at Vinny, who had his head up and was looking around the large vessel.

"Alright." Branson said, grudgingly accepting the response. "Come on, let's get out of this shit." He turned and started up the metal walkway that connected the ship to the concrete dock. As they walked, Branson waved to one of the dockworkers, who was dressed in a bright orange safety jacket while working on one of the ship's moorings. The man returned the wave but continued staring at the group as they made their way onto the ship. He paid particular attention to the long cases and large bags each of the new arrivals carried.

59
Port Newark, New Jersey

The bridge door opened and the sound of howling wind and pounding rain filled the enclosed space. Mike Guardino looked over his shoulder to see Branson lead the three outside hires in. They all looked waterlogged. Branson ran a hand through his long brown hair, which stood up on-end thanks to the water.

"Fucking miserable out there, dude." Branson said. "Mike, these are the security guys." He gestured to the three men loaded down with bags and weapons cases.

"Morgan Tyron, nice to meet you." Morgan said as he shook Guardino's hand.

"Likewise." Guardino said. "Heard a lot of good things about you guys." He said as he made his way down the line, then stopped at Foaly. "Have we met before?" Foaly simply shrugged.

"Maybe. Met a lot of you folks over in the sandbox." Foaly said.

"Ramadi, twenty-fourteen?" Guardino asked. Foaly shook his head.

"Nah, wasn't me. Never got to go there." Foaly said. While strange, it was true. Foaly's career had been a bit of an enigma, seeing as he'd gone to Afghanistan, Iran, Africa, and just about everywhere else an operator could go during the Global War on Terror. Somehow, he'd never ended up in Iraq.

"Alright, this is Jeremy." Branson said, introducing them to one of the crewmembers. Jeremy was in his mid-twenties, dressed in the 'uniform' of the Aguilar; blue button-up tucked into a pair of gray cargo pants. "He'll take you guys down to your cabins. Get your stuff settled and do whatever you want for the next hour or so. Should be right around then that we start underway." Branson informed them. He got three nods, and they all hefted their luggage down the narrow stairwell that led belowdecks.

Guardino looked at Branson, whose face was a mask of irritation and impatience.

"What's your problem?" Guardino asked as Branson lit up a cigarette, thankful for the Captain's allowance of smoking indoors.

"Not a fan of these outside contractors being brought on like this." Branson said as he blew a line of smoke. "We should have pulled from GRS or some green badgers. Too many unknowns about these guys." Mike gave Jake a sideways look.

"Too many unknowns? You know they had the ever-loving shit investigated out of them before an offer was even issued. The higher-ups probably know everything down to their underwear preference." Branson didn't reply, instead opting to take another long drag from his cigarette.

"Whatever. I still don't like it." Branson said. At least they'd only have to deal with these cowboys until they got to Somalia. After that they were the Captain's problem. "I'll be back." Branson opened the door to the bridge and stepped back out onto the rain-slicked deck. Guardino gave a wave, then turned back to finish the preparations for their departure with the bridge crew.

60
Port Newark, New Jersey

"Who pissed in that guy's cereal?" Vinny asked as the three of them walked the deck, following the former SEAL as he got a firsthand look at the layout.

"Hopefully, he chills the fuck out sooner rather than later. We have to deal with that for a month and either him or me are going overboard." Foaly retorted. This got a chuckle out of the others.

They walked past a few deckhands, all dressed in bright safety jackets with reflective silver strips in case they went overboard. The orange jackets were busy moving back and forth finishing preparations, double- and triple-checking cargo straps and scores of other imperative tasks that needed to be done before their trip began. Foaly didn't know how they did this for months on-end. He'd only been on the ship for about half an hour and was already anxious to get a move on.

"I'm surprised we can see the skyline so well in this." Morgan said as he leaned against the rail. Foaly and Vinny turned, both taking in the fairly clear view of Jersey City, and the Manhattan skyline just beyond. Foaly reached up and adjusted the hood of his jacket, his gaze returning to the crew.

"Not a whole lot of crew for a boat this size." He observed.

"A lot of ships like this are automated these days." Vinny answered. "They really only require a skeleton crew of about twenty to maintain essential systems, and to make sure everything is loaded/unloaded at the right places."

"And minimal security, other than us." Morgan cut in.

237

"Yeah, that too." Vinny agreed. "They probably have a couple of pop guns stored away somewhere, but that's about it. A vessel like this would have been an ideal hit for us in the Teams since you don't have to worry about finding a gunman around every corner. I'm sure that other than a couple of pistolas smuggled on by the crew, the only ones packing real heat other than us are our Company friends on the bridge. That's how those four skinnies were able to take over the Maersk Alabama so easily." Alex looked over at Vinny, surprised at the specific and contemporary comparison. Vinny met his gaze, saw the question in his eyes, and gave a sly smile. That was all the answer Alex needed.

The Iridium phone in Morgan's cargo pocket vibrated. He pulled it out and wiped the screen with a thumb, clearing up the words 'FOXTROT-ONE' displayed in black letters against the white background. He extended the antenna before clicking the accept button.

"Morgan." He said.

"And here I thought we were using codenames." Andrea said with a chuckle. "Just wanted to run a comms check before you guys headed out. How's the ship?"

"Wet." Morgan replied, water droplets pouring off the brim of his baseball cap. "Don't suppose you've found anything else for us?"

"Kind of hard to do intel while driving." She replied. "But once I'm back at my place, I'll see if anything has popped up since we left."

"Okay. Thanks for checking in. Alex will shoot you a text once we get word we're leaving."

"Safe travels!" Andrea said before ending the call.

"Comms good?" Vinny asked. Morgan nodded, sliding the wet phone back into his cargo pocket.

"Hey!" Someone called. The three of them turned around to see Branson walking towards them. The soaked Agency man looked even more sour than when they'd first come aboard. "We're leaving soon. Get below decks and hang out there till we're clear of the Bay." He called out. Morgan nodded and gave a thumbs up.

"Jackass." Vinny said under his breath as they began making their way towards the nearest entrance to the lower decks.

61
Port Newark, New Jersey

As the three contractors made their way belowdecks, Branson made a beeline for the bridge. When he arrived, he found Guardino standing near the front with the ship's Captain while the rest of the five-man bridge crew continued their work. There were two pots of coffee burbling on the small counter at the rear of the bridge, and everyone except Branson had a steaming cup of the brown liquid. Branson wiped off his face, then looked at Guardino, who extended a hand with a Styrofoam cup of the black gold to his partner.

"Thanks." Branson said, taking a sip. The coffee was bitter but bold, probably a local blend the Captain had picked up at a port during his years of travel. It warmed Branson up nonetheless. "How are we looking?" Branson asked. The Aguilar's Captain, William Haverton, turned around to face the two government 'employees' he had been charged with transporting.

"All pre-departure checks are complete. Just making sure all of the moorings are off before we head out." Captain Haverton replied coolly. The addition of the two government men and their abundance of 'classified' cargo had initially been a shock to him. That shock had been dampened by Guardino's pleasantness, but Branson's high-strung attitude had quickly degraded the Captain's nerves. Regardless of what they were paying him to not ask questions and ensure the delivery occurred on time per their schedule, Haverton made it explicitly clear that this was his ship, and no one would question that.

"Well let's get a move on then." Branson said.

DECEPTION

"Mister Branson." The Captain turned around, gripping his coffee cup in one hand, and removing his Aguilar baseball cap with the other. "This is the last time I'll remind you that your employers are the ones providing payment for your passage, and my sole responsibility is to ensure safe delivery of you and your cargo. In order to do that I need to make sure everyone, not just you, is safe onboard, and will remain safe. We have another storm rolling in right on the heels of this one, and I need to be perfectly sure that *my* crew and ship won't be put in any danger. Your impatience isn't going to make that go any faster." There was a physical lurch underfoot as the Aguilar moved away from the dock and started its journey from Port Newark into Newark Bay. "As you can see, we're underway. So, if I have your permission, may I run my ship?" Haverton asked rhetorically, his aged eyes drilling into the government man.

Without a word, Branson exited the bridge, bringing his coffee with him as he stepped back out into the storm. He set the cup down and turned his back to the wind, cupping both hands around the cigarette he was trying to light. It took him a few tries, but eventually he got the smoke lit and took a deep drag.

"Shit!" He said as a gust of wind caught both his cigarette and coffee, picking them up for a moment before sending both tumbling to the roiling water below. He pulled out his pack of American Spirits and ducked behind a bulkhead, trying to light another. Once it was lit, he kept one hand on it at all times as he walked back to the railing to look over the passing dockyards.

He failed to notice the four black rigid inflatable boats that were quickly approaching the vessel from the rear.

62
Newark Bay

The lights of the distant Bayonne Bridge were muffled by the dark cloud cover as the four small boats made their way towards the Aguilar's stern. Each watercraft was loaded with six men, four of whom were sitting in the center, with one at the front and the last in the rear, using the small outboard motors to bring them closer.

The men at the front of each boat were armed with FN MK20 SSR sniper rifles, which they used to scan the deck for any movement of crew that may spot them. So far everything was clear. The forward lookout of the first boat reached down with his non-firing hand and held a push-to-talk attached to the front of his vest, relaying the 'all clear' to the rest of the group.

Pulling up to the starboard side of the vessel, the lead boat's pilot pushed the small craft right against the side of the behemoth. The lead man set his sniper rifle down and grabbed a small flashlight from a pouch on his vest. He aimed it upwards and flashed it three times. Moments later, a telescoping ladder was assembled and dropped down the length of the hull, stopping an arm's length above the waterline. The sniper slung his rifle over his back and placed both hands and a foot on the ladder, checking it would bear his weight before he began making his way up.

Upon reaching the deck railing, a deckhand reached over and assisted the sniper onto the slick deck. The sniper thanked the deckhand before turning around and helping the next man over the railing while the crewmember assembled another ladder. Six minutes later, all twenty-four black-clad members of the boarding party were on the deck conducting final checks of weapons and equipment. One unslung the black duffel bag he'd carried up with him and opened it up. He retrieved a helmet, ballistic vest, a spare AK-103 rifle and a Glock 19 pistol, all of which were handed over to the deckhand. The crewmember quickly took off his safety jacket and tossed it over the railing, sending it fluttering in the rainy wind as he geared up.

"Most of the crew is on the bridge or below decks." The deckhand informed the new arrivals as he snapped his helmet's chin strap together. "Might be a few stragglers still on the deck, but they won't see us coming." The leader of the boarding party nodded, then flipped his night vision monocular down over his right eye and signaled for the teams to split up and clear the deck.

The six from the first boat were joined by the deckhand, who stood out from the boarding party with his blue long-sleeve shirt and Carhartt pants, rather than the all-black fatigues and wetsuits worn by the others. The pounding rain hid their footfalls, and their clothing made them practically invisible when sticking to the shadows. If there were areas they had to cross that were illuminated, one of them would use a suppressed pistol to shoot out the lights before continuing.

One unwary deckhand was busy checking the temperatures of several refrigerated containers packed with medical supplies. The combination of the rain pounding against his jacket hood, and the earbuds he had jammed into his ears, meant he was completely oblivious to the intruders. By the time he realized he wasn't alone, it was too late. An arm seemingly came out of nowhere and wrapped around his neck, a gloved hand clamping over his mouth to stifle any cries before the blade of a knife was forced into his throat. He struggled for a moment but was already weakened by shock and blood loss. He could only watch helplessly as he was thrown overboard before everything went black and he was swallowed by the water below.

"Clear." The boarder who'd killed the man said, wiping the blade of his knife off on the leg of his wetsuit before sliding it back into its sheath. The team lead nodded and motioned for them to push forward.

63
Newark Bay

Guardino looked down at his watch and frowned. Branson had stormed out fifteen minutes ago but had yet to even poke his head back in to check in with the senior operative. Guardino couldn't imagine the hotheaded Branson was just out there, sulking in the rain.

"Mister Guardino." Captain Haverton turned around to address the better-mannered government man.

"Yes?" Guardino replied.

"I'd appreciate if you'd inform your colleague that, despite his storied Naval career, this is still my ship. And if he wants to retain full reign of *my* ship and crew, I'd highly suggest he change his attitude. Ricky-tick." The bearded Captain hammered the point home with the cut in his voice.

"I'll relay the message." Guardino nodded, understanding where Haverton was coming from. Branson was a bit of an anomaly; having spent his time in the Navy as an intelligence specialist before somehow making his way into the Directorate of Operations. Guardino hadn't worked with Branson long, but he still hadn't figured out what had given the former Navy man such a chip on his shoulder. But the Captain was right, that shit needed to be curbed now before it pissed off someone important. The last thing they'd need was for Branson to piss off some local warlord when they arrived at-

The door to the bridge opened and three figures in tactical gear rushed in, rifles up and at the ready. It took a moment for the bridge crew to notice that it wasn't any of their own coming in to get out of the storm. By the time they did notice, there was nothing they could do.

"Who the-?" Captain Haverton was cut off when suppressed fire from the intruder's rifles impacted with his chest, sending a spray of blood painting the panels behind him. The rest of the crew were gunned down as the attackers pushed into the bridge. Guardino threw himself sideways, reaching under his jacket to retrieve his Sig Sauer P226 from the holster inside his waistband. The effort was in vain, because the door on the opposite end of the bridge slid open and two more gunmen walked in behind him. They both put three controlled pairs into his back. The first few rounds were stopped by the soft Kevlar vest Guardino wore under his jacket, but the weakened material couldn't withstand the impact of the remaining eight rounds, which tore through his back and punched through his chest cavity. Their exit was stopped by the front of his vest.

Guardino coughed up blood before taking a wheezing, ragged breath. He rolled onto his back and found himself looking up at one of the intruders. This one was one of the deckhands he'd seen around the ship, now dressed in tactical gear over his ship's uniform. The man brought his rifle to bear with Guardino's face and pulled the trigger.

64
Newark Bay

"Bridge secure; four crew down. The Captain is dead, and we got one of the priority targets." The words came over the radio as Team Four proceeded down a stairwell towards the crew's quarters of the ship. Teams Two and Three were busy sweeping the upper deck while Team One got control of the bridge. Now it fell on Team Four to clear out any crew remaining below decks.

So far, they'd come across three crew members. Two of them had been sleeping and were none the wiser when they'd each received a suppressed double-tap to the head. The third had been shaving in the communal head. He'd looked up from the water-filled sink to see an armed figure standing beside him, pistol pointed at the back of the head. He'd managed to let out a startled 'oh' before the nine-millimeter round tore through his head and shattered the mirror, leaving him slumped face first in the now-overflowing sink.

The team lead held up a closed fist, stopping the five other men in their tracks. He looked over his shoulder and pointed at the two men directly behind him, then at two closed cabin doors on their left. They nodded, moving to their respective doors with another teammate in tow. The team lead had the last man pull security before approaching the third door himself, rifle at the ready.

He slowly turned the handle and pushed the door inward, keeping his weapon up as he swept the small cabin. The room was empty, and was much cleaner than the others, almost as if it hadn't been lived in yet. His sweep came to a halt when his eyes rested on the bed.

There was an HK 416 rifle sitting on the bed. The black body of the rifle had a number of scratches on it, and there was an ACOG scope as well as a PEQ-15 laser mounted to the top rail. The team lead slung his AK and picked up the rifle, turning it over and inspecting it. There wasn't a magazine loaded, but he was sure that whoever owned it had some ammo stashed around the cabin somewhere. It was a hell of a step up from the 103's that the boarding party were using, and it would make for a good trophy from this op.

The bolt slammed forward with a smooth and satisfying *thunk*. Whoever owned the rifle kept it in fantastic shape. There was a black duffel bag sitting on the bed beside where the rifle had been. Keeping the 416 in his right hand, he began to unzip the bag. Inside he spied a black tactical vest along with a matching high-cut helmet.

"What the hell?" He asked as he picked up the helmet. Why would anyone on the ship have this kind of gear? Did they have a few deckhands trained to be in-house security? *Well, if they did, they didn't do a very good job.* He thought to himself. But then again, they were prepared to fight off pirates, not this.

Something creaked to his left and the team lead looked to see what had made the noise. He'd had just enough time to register the presence of someone who wasn't on his team standing there before his vision went sideways and it felt like a train crashed into him.

The man had tackled into him, sending them both crashing against the cabin wall. Desperate to get control of the situation, the team lead dropped the 416 and tried to grab his AK, but it was pinned between them. He cried out when an explosion of pain damn near paralyzed him when his attacker brought a knee into his groin. He was fighting the urge to throw up when an open-palmed strike to the side of his helmet sent him stumbling sideways. Unfortunately for the team lead, his attacker followed him to the ground and managed to rip the magazine from his rifle, leaving him with only one round to use if he could just get the weapon up.

The team lead managed to get his hands up, but all he could do was try to deflect the blows that were raining down on him. Then something tugged, clicked, and his helmet went off kilter for a moment before it tumbled from his head. Not knowing what else to do, he scrambled to grab it, hoping to use it to bludgeon this guy who was attacking him with ferocity that no regular crewmember should have possessed.

Suddenly the assault stopped, and he took a split second to pause and take a deep breath. That breath was cut off when he was yanked backwards, the sling of his AK going taut around his neck and cutting off his blood circulation. The team lead gasped and sputtered beneath his balaclava as he clawed at the sling. As darkness began creeping into his vision, he remembered he had his pistol on his vest and reached for the weapons. His hands came up empty and his panicking mind went into overdrive, but then the sling loosened around his neck and he fell forward. Maybe one of his guys had come in and dispatched the crewmember. He wouldn't have heard the shot because his ears were currently filled with the sound of blood rushing back to his head.

His relief was short lived because a moment later everything went black when a nine-millimeter round from his own pistol passed through the back of his head and splattered blood and bits of brain and skull against the bulkhead.

65
Newark Bay

Vinny finished redoing his belt and pushed the cabin's bathroom door open. To his surprise the door bumped into someone, probably Alex or Morgan. Vin realized it was not one of them when he saw he was face-to-face with someone dressed in an all-black wetsuit along with a tac vest and helmet. Their face was covered beneath a black balaclava, though the eyes held plenty of anger. Vinny reached for his pistol.

"Don't move!" A voice to the right said, thick with an accent he couldn't place. Vinny looked to see a similarly dressed figure, this one in fatigues rather than a wetsuit, standing in his cabin with an AK aimed at him. Vinny slowly raised both hands while the guy he'd bumped into took two steps back and drew a pistol on him.

"Listen, whatever it is you want, I'm sure-"

"Shut it." Vinny was cut off by the one holding the pistol, whose voice had a North American non-accent. The pistol one placed his index finger on the Glock's trigger, waiting for any reason to fire. *Shit, this is not good.* Then the AK's safety clicked, and Vinny's eyes darted around as he tried to figure out who he could take out first before getting blasted.

Two suppressed shots filled the cabin, dropping the AK guy. The one with the pistol shifted his focus but a round passed through the guy's ears, just below the helmet, snapping his head sideways and sending his limp form collapsing to the deck. Vinny kept his hands raised and looked to the left to see Alex standing there, smoking pistol in-hand.

DECEPTION

"You good?" Foaly asked, stepping in and putting an insurance shot into each of the intruders' heads to be sure they'd stay down.

"Who the fuck are these guys?" Vinny's response answered Foaly's question.

"Don't know, found one of them snooping around my gear." Foaly closed the door behind him and stepped towards the dead rifleman.

"Where's Morgan?" Vinny asked.

"Not sure, we need to find him though. There were two more of these assholes in his cabin, playing with his gear as well. We need to get kitted up and moving."

"You got it." Vinny said as he walked over to his bag and tore it open. He threw on his plate carrier and helmet, stuffed mags into their pouches, and grabbed up his weapons.

"Vin." Alex said. Vinny turned to see Foaly holding up the assailant's rifle. "Look familiar?"

"Is that a one-oh-three?" Vinny asked, the realization hitting him. There was no way it was a coincidence.

"Yep, same model that our not-so-friendly African neighbors were using." Foaly confirmed. "Cover the hall while I go get my kit."

"Check." Vinny said, reverting to operator mode. Less than a minute later, Foaly was beside him in the corridor in full kit. They both did a quick buddy check, then started towards the upper decks.

66
Upper Hudson Bay

Morgan gripped the cold railing with white knuckles as he leaned into the whipping wind. The rain was coming down so hard that it stung his face, and he'd had to turn his baseball cap around after almost losing it to a particularly powerful gust. He squinted as he thought he saw someone moving towards him. *Why are the lights off in the bridge?*

Someone slammed into him, sending him backwards and landing on his ass. Morgan scooted back, drawing his 1911. He flicked on his gun light and found himself looking up at Branson standing over him, panting heavily and looking directly into the light. The guy's face was drenched from the rain, and his eyes were wide.

"Kill that fucking light!" Branson hissed. He had his pistol out.

"Branson? What the fuck?" Morgan clicked off the light but didn't re-holster the pistol. Seeing that Branson wasn't offering to help him up, Morgan grabbed the rail and pulled himself to his feet.

"Did you see them?" Branson asked.

"See who?"

"Don't fuck with me!" Branson jabbed a finger towards Morgan. "Did you see the bridge?"

"No. I was on my way there now."

"They're dead. They're all fucking dead." Branson inhaled sharply.

"What the fuck are you talking about? Who's dead?" Morgan demanded.

"I don't know! I didn't get a good look at them, but they're all tac'd up. I think one of them saw me." Branson ran a hand through his hair. "Fuck. Fuck!" He turned to face Morgan. "We hired you guys to pull security, then this shit happens!"

"Hey, calm the fuck down." Morgan took a step forward. "What the hell are you talking about? Who is on the ship?"

Morgan's question was somewhat answered when Branson jerked violently and a splash of warm blood hit Morgan's face. It was quickly washed away by the pounding rain, and Morgan saw a shape appear a few feet behind Branson. It was a silhouette of someone wearing tactical gear, staring at Morgan through monocular NODs. Whoever it was, they were almost invisible due to the combination of low-light and their all-black clothing. Before the shooter could react to the secondary target behind Branson, Morgan had brought his pistol up and put three rounds into the attacker, the loud report cutting through the rain. They went down, and Morgan stepped forward and delivered a final headshot to ensure they stayed that way.

With his weapon still up, Morgan knelt beside Branson and did a quick check for vitals. There were none.

"Shit." Morgan looked around to make sure he wasn't being flanked by any unexpected guests. With the coast clear at the moment, he wasted no time in getting to the nearest entrance below decks. He needed to get his gear on and find the others.

67
Upper Hudson Bay

Alex and Vinny both snapped their weapons up when someone stepped through the entrance from the upper decks.

"Blue, blue!" Morgan said, startled. His hands shot up to show he was unarmed while they confirmed that he was indeed friendly. "What the fuck is going on? Who are these guys?" Morgan asked, referring to the bodies they'd dragged out of their cabins.

"No idea. Get kitted up, we're heading to the bridge." Foaly said bluntly, falling back to his instincts as a battlefield commander.

"Ran into Branson on my way there. He said these guys killed everyone on the bridge." Morgan said as he pulled on his vest.

"Where's Branson?" Vinny asked.

"Dead. Got clipped by one of them topside." Morgan grabbed his helmet and pulled it on.

"Get Andrea on the phone and see if she can figure out what the hell is going on." Foaly ordered as he covered down the corridor. Vinny continued pulling security down the other end while Morgan grabbed the sat phone and clicked Andrea's number. When he held it to his ear, all he heard was a wash of static. He ended the call and tried again. Same thing.

"Sat phone's down." Morgan announced, sliding it into an empty utility pouch on his vest.

"Shit." Foaly grunted. Keeping his rifle up with his right hand, he fished his iPhone out of his pocket with the left and called Andrea from there. The call immediately ended, returning Foaly to the Contacts screen. A quick glance showed a simple 'X' in the top left corner. No signal. "No signal on cell either."

"Probably a jammer." Vinny theorized. "Stop any outgoing comms, encrypt their own so it works fine. It's what I'd do." He looked over at his teammates. "Whoever they are, they're using legit tactics." He omitted the fact that they reminded him of what he and his guys did while on the Teams.

"We need to get to the bridge and try to figure out who these guys are and what they're after." Foaly said. He'd already pulled off the balaclavas and taken pictures of the faces of the dead men in the cabins. Once he had a signal, he'd send them to Andrea to pass to her contacts for identification. "I'll take point. Vin you cover our six."

"Check." Vinny said. With that they all made sure their weapons were topped off before making their way towards the upper decks once again.

68
Upper Hudson Bay

Foaly stopped and swiveled his NODs down over his eyes before stepping out into the dark upper decks, sweeping across the gray-green world with the IR laser on his rifle. The lights from the Bayonne Bridge directly above the Aguilar were bright through the NODs, giving better illumination to their surroundings. Once all three of them were on the deck, Foaly gave a hand signal for them to follow him forward. He got two nods of acknowledgement in response.

They slowly and quietly made their way across the deck, stopping and sweeping the 'alleys' between the rows of shipping containers. This place was a CQB nightmare and reminded Vinny of the many years he'd spent fighting in Iraq. Every corner opened up a new fatal funnel; every container a possible sniper's perch. He didn't want to think about the possibility of some asshole with a long gun keeping watch from the bridge tower's mast.

Vinny almost ran into Foaly, who had stopped suddenly. Looking over his partner's shoulder, Vinny saw Foaly had painted a target with his IR laser. Vinny wondered why Foaly hadn't taken the shot, then remembered that Alex's 416 didn't have a suppressor on it. Vin raised his rifle and painted the target with his own laser while Foaly drew his suppressed Glock. A moment and a double tap later, the sentry was down, the heavy rain basically rendering the suppressed pistol's report mute. Once the area was clear, Alex motioned for them to continue.

Morgan reached the bridge first and pulled the hatch open while Vinny and Alex rushed inside, sweeping to ensure it was clear.

"What the?" One of the intruders standing at the main console said. That was all he got out before they both put a controlled pair through him, sending him to the ground and mixing his blood with the rest of the bridge crew. Morgan followed in, his MP5 raised as he helped sweep the rest of the bridge.

"Ah shit." Morgan said, lowering his weapon when he came across Guardino's corpse. He had multiple gunshot wounds through his torso and had been executed with a bullet to the head. Foaly closed the hatch and pulled security while Vinny began tapping away at the main console. As Vin did that, Morgan tried the sat phone again. Nothing. Maybe if he sent a text message...

He began tapping away at the keypad. *Aguilar boarded by unknown hostiles. Bridge crew dead, both Agency contacts dead. Contact Donnelly, have him send backup.* Morgan hit send and could only hope there would be a break in the jammer's coverage for the message to go through at some point.

"Anything?" Alex asked.

"Phone's still dead lined." Morgan said.

"Hold on, I've got an idea." Vinny said, looking around. "There it is." A moment later he had a push-to-talk radio held in front of him. "Mayday, Mayday. This is the MV Aguilar. Our position is four-zero-point Six Degrees North, Negative seven-four point zero-three degrees West. We have been boarded and multiple crew members have been killed. Say again, Mayday, Mayday. This is the MV Aguilar. We are moving southbound in the Upper Hudson Bay, requesting immediate assistance." He paused and looked around. "Now how the fuck do I...yes!" He said, flicking several switches and pressing a button, then repeating the message once more. "The jammer shouldn't affect radio traffic. If it doesn't, I just set that message to repeat and blast out on all channels. Someone will hear it eventually." Vinny said.

"Brilliant." Morgan said, genuinely impressed by Vinny's quick thinking.

"Anything on the main console?" Foaly asked.

"Yeah, they changed the destination from Somalia to a spot about forty miles southeast of the Hudson Bay." Vinny said. "Best guess? These guys want something on the ship, probably whatever the CIA was transporting. I'm thinking it's weapons, but who knows at this point. Anyway, they're probably going to swap everything over to their own vessel and then scuttle this one."

"Let's test that radio theory." Foaly said, reaching for his push-to-talk. He couldn't believe he'd forgotten about radio comms till now. "Foxtrot-One this is Yankee-Three." He rattled off their respective codenames, hoping to raise Andrea on the radio. There was nothing but static in his Peltors. "Foxtrot-One, comms check. Over."

"Come on, let's go." Someone said from the stairwell leading to the lower decks. Morgan and Vinny darted to the side while Foaly stepped back into a small alcove beside the door, knocking over a few half-filled Styrofoam cups and spilling their contents on the floor. A moment later two of the gunmen walked on the bridge, weapons up.

"Looks clear to me." One of them said in a Pacific Northwest accent. He lowered his weapon slightly and looked at the dead crew.

"Oh shit." The other one said, voice tinged with a Boston accent. "Fuck, someone's been here!" Looked like he'd found his friend. "Fuck, it's Phil." He knelt beside the dead man at the main console. "Call it in."

Both men were cut down with suppressed shots from multiple angles. Foaly had just finished putting a bullet in each man's head when the radio on the Bostonian's belt crackled.

"Team Two, status." Someone said into the radio. It may have just been static from the storm, but it sounded like whoever was speaking into the radio had an Eastern European accent. Foaly unsnapped the radio pouch and lifted it to his face, lightly holding the transmit button for maximum interference.

"Team Two here." Foaly said in his best Boston accent. "Came across a crew member on his own. Nothing to report." There was a pregnant pause as they all waited, listening for more bootsteps charging up towards them.

"Roger that, return to your posts." The radioman responded, resulting in a collective sigh of relief from the three men on the bridge.

"Copy." Foaly said, then slid the radio into his back pocket. Now he had access to their comms. "Alright, we seriously need to figure out what the fuck is going on and who these assholes are, because they've obviously got Americans working with them. As much as I hate to do it, we need to split up." He looked at his two colleagues. "Morgan, get to communications and see if you can find and lift whatever the hell is jamming us. Vinny." He turned to the former SEAL. "You know how these things operate. What are we looking at below decks?" Vinny mulled over the question for almost half a minute.

"Based off the schematics that Andrea pulled, along with what she told us about the waterline, they've probably got a couple of storage holds below decks. My bet is that's where they're keeping the weapons or whatever the fuck it is they're transporting, which means we're going to have a bunch of their goons down there to move the stuff. And who knows if they just came in one wave or if they've had more show up since the initial board-" There was a metallic *clunk-clunk* and two black cylinders bounced up from the stairs, coming to a stop against Guardino's body.

"Down!" Foaly yelled. Vinny tackled into Morgan, sending them both tumbling down the stairwell as Foaly landed behind the console, the Captain's body softening his fall. The less-than-lethal grenades detonated, and Foaly was thankful he'd put on his ear protection. Had he not, he'd have had two blown eardrums. He picked himself up and moved towards the stairwell that Morgan and Vinny had disappeared down.

69
Upper Bay, Hudson River

Morgan's head was spinning from the blast, and his left ear was ringing something fierce. He could barely make out the shape of an armed figure heading towards him. Then he felt something on his belt tug. He blinked his eyes and realized Vinny, pinned beneath him, had grabbed his 1911 and was firing it at the approaching hostile. The gunman twitched and dropped to the floor, so Morgan rolled to the side.

"Hey." Vinny said, slapping Morgan's cheek to get his attention. "Hey, you good?" Morgan blinked, exhaled, then nodded.

"I'm good." Morgan coughed.

"Guys?" Alex called from the stairs behind them.

"We're up!" Vinny called out, helping Morgan into a sitting position. "Come on buddy, up you get." They both stood at the same time. Morgan wobbled as Vinny handed the 1911 back.

"Come on, we need to get moving before they send more assholes our way." Foaly said. Vinny nodded, shouldering his weapon. Morgan reloaded his pistol, sliding the half-empty mag into the now-empty pouch on his vest. Right about then he wished he'd brought a battle belt with a dump pouch for when he started getting empties.

There was a spot of blood on the floor, and Foaly spied another a few feet further down the corridor. They had a bleeder.

"Come on, this way." Foaly pointed, then returned both hands to his weapon and continued. As he rounded the corner, he saw a smear of crimson on the bulkhead, and then the uniformed gunman struggling to rotate the circular handle of the watertight hatch that led to the next section of the ship. "Put your hands in the air. Now." Foaly ordered, his rifle's laser holding steady in the center of the man's neck. He stiffened, then slowly raised his right arm. "Both arms." Foaly barked.

"I'm bleeding…" The man responded in accented English. Alex took a step forward.

"On your knees, hands behind your head and fingers interlaced." Foaly growled.

"I told you I'm bleeding."

"Bleeding's going to be the last thing you'll have to worry about if you don't get on your knees right now." Foaly said, patience gone. After a moment, the guy lowered himself to his knees and placed both hands against the back of his head. Blood dripped down to the floor from his torso; Vinny had only winged him. "Turn around." Foaly ordered. The gunman awkwardly did so, rotating himself so he was facing them. His already dark uniform shone with blood from the right side of his torso.

"Don't you fucking move." Vinny growled, stepping beside Foaly with his own rifle raised. Alex moved forward, rifle still up with his right hand, and used his knife in his left to cut the sling of the man's AK before kicking the weapon back towards Morgan. After sliding the knife back in its sheath, Alex reached to the thigh holster and pulled out the guy's pistol, turning it on its owner as he took a few steps backwards.

"Start talking." Foaly said.

"Who the fuck are you guys?" The gunman asked. That was when Foaly recognized the accent; the guy was a fucking Canadian.

262

DECEPTION

"Why'd you take the ship? Who are you with?" Foaly asked. Their captive said nothing, just glaring up at Foaly. His face was still hidden behind a balaclava. Foaly aimed the pistol at the guy's head. "Give me a fucking answer." Morgan watched as the guy's eyes focused on the pistol in Alex's hand, then he tried to make a move for it. The Canadian wasn't fast enough, and Foaly popped him right between the eyes.

"So much for splitting up." Foaly said, retaining yet another stolen Glock from the boarding party. "Door says it leads to the holds. Vin."

"On it." Vinny said. Alex and Morgan covered him as he rotated the handle before pushing the hatch inwards.

It led to a hallway that was dimly lit by singular lightbulbs hanging at regular intervals. Most of the bulbs had been shot out, probably by the intruders. Vinny tapped a finger against the quad-tubed GPNVG-18 night vision goggles on the front of his helmet, and Alex nodded. They all flipped their NODs down and powered them on. The combination of the NODs and the ambient light lit the corridor up like it was daytime to the security team.

As they continued down the corridor, Vinny hissed and held up a closed fist. Foaly and Morgan both froze in place, watching as Vinny took a tentative step forward before getting on one knee. He slung his rifle and retrieved his multitool before slowly tracing his finger along a nearly invisible tripwire. The line led to a box affixed to the side of the corridor. Wires led from the box to a fuse box higher up on the wall.

"Early warning system." Vinny said as he carefully snipped the wires. "We tripped that, and it would have sent a signal to the box that probably would have shut off all the lights and let the bad guys know someone was coming.

"And we already know they have night vision." Morgan said. "This whole thing is a shit show."

"Just keep your eyes up." Foaly said, bringing his rifle to bear as they continued down the corridor.

To everyone's surprise, they met no resistance the rest of the way, and reached the hatch at the end of the corridor without issue. Foaly nodded to Morgan, who stepped up and began to slowly turn the handle on the hatch to make minimal noise. Once it was open, he pulled it towards him. Foaly and Vinny pied the corner, weapons up, and saw it opened to a catwalk. Once on the catwalk, they realized they were about thirty feet above the floor of the holds; well inside the belly of the ship.

"God damn…" Morgan said. Foaly lowered his weapon slightly and peered over the catwalk's railing to see what had caught Morgan's attention.

There were at least thirty similarly uniformed men moving around the floor of the hold. Guess than answered Vinny's theory on them sending multiple waves. From what Foaly could see, they were all busy hauling multiple crates in the direction of a freight elevator located on the port side of the ship. He reached into his vest and pulled out the small Nikon waterproof digital camera from a pouch on his vest and zoomed in, looking at the images on the small screen.

The dark green cases contained tactical equipment, as Foaly saw two of the intruders had broken one open and were holding up older models of ballistic helmets, and one man held up two ballistic plates. There were a few boarders who carried a rack of M4 carbines out of a Conex box that seemed to have sacks of rice spilling out of it.

"So, they weren't lying about the 'humanitarian supplies'." Morgan said.

DECEPTION

"Smokescreen. Color me surprised." Vinny said. Foaly snapped a few pictures, then swiveled to a group of intruders who were re-packing a wooden crate full of M67 fragmentation grenades. If the twenty or so containers down here all held weapons and equipment, then the CIA was gearing up to supply an entire army somewhere in Africa. And now they were supplying whoever these assholes were. Foaly quickly snapped a couple dozen pictures, ensuring he got any weapons or equipment they pulled out clearly, then moved onto the groups that seemed to be overseeing things. A few of the intruders had set up small 'field desks' by putting their Toughbook laptops on top of overturned crates. It was like they were using the holds as a makeshift forward operating base. Likely holding off on using the elevator until they reached their destination.

"Alex, look at that." Vinny tapped his shoulder, then pointed where to focus. Foaly zoomed in the camera and saw two men carrying a crate of AT4 anti-tank rockets between them. Then something else caught his attention. There were three men making busy arming blocks of C-4 plastic explosive, sticking primers in the blocks of plastique and setting them to the side.

"Whatever you do, do not engage." Foaly said slowly to make sure his point was made. "Be on the lookout for anyone who looks like they're running the show." He snapped a few pictures of a guy priming a brick of explosives, then a few of a passing fighter carrying two M249 squad automatic weapons by the carrying handles. Morgan nudged Foaly's shoulder. "Whaddya got?"

"That dude looks important." Morgan pointed. Foaly focused the camera and saw who Morgan was talking about.

The guy was wearing a pair of black combat pants and a matching softshell jacket beneath his plate carrier. Unlike the AK-103's that the rest were carrying, this guy had what appeared to be a Draco AK-47 pistol slung across his chest. Foaly zoomed the camera's lens, hoping he could get a clear shot of the guy's face. Thankfully, the picture cleaned up, and Foaly memorized the details as he snapped away. The guy had sharp, Slavic features, with dark eyes and equally dark close-cropped hair. The camera even picked up the scar that started just below his right eye and ran horizontally across his nose, stopping just before it reached under the left. He was standing beside one of the makeshift desks, occasionally glancing down at the Toughbook beside him before being approached by more boarders carrying either clipboards or pieces of paper. They received either a head nod or shake regarding whatever they showed him before moving on.

"Definitely some kind of shot caller." Foaly said as he snapped a burst of photos. "You guys head topside and see if you can secure a way off the ship without these assholes coming after us. Looks like word of our presence hasn't gotten down here yet, and I'd like to be long gone when it does. Once we're off the ship and out of the Jammer's bubble, we'll radio Andrea to get in contact with Donnelly or whoever so the Coast Guard can retake the ship."

"What about you?" Vinny asked. Foaly held up the camera.

"I'll be right behind you guys. I want to get as much as we can to give to Donnelly so they can figure out who these guys are and how they knew to hit the ship." His eyes met both Morgan and Vinny's. "I'll see you topside." Both nodded before turning and staring their way back topside.

70
Lower Hudson Bay

The rain was coming down even harder when Morgan and Vinny stepped out onto the deck. Morgan wished he'd thrown on his baseball cap under his helmet, because it was doing nothing to stop the rain from pelting his eyes and face.

"Shit." Vinny said.

"What?" Morgan asked, bringing his MP5 up to the high-ready. Vinny pointed behind them at a barely visible glow through the storm.

"That's the Verrazano." Vinny said. "That means that's Fort Hancock over there. We're right in the middle of Lower Bay." He said to Morgan.

"So?" Morgan asked.

"We need to get off this ship and away from the jammer ASAP. Once they hit the Atlantic, they're going to power ahead and reach their rendezvous in no time." Vinny explained. Morgan grabbed the sat phone and looked to see the messages to Andrea was still sitting in the outbox.

"Shit." Morgan said as he looked around. "How the hell are we going to get off this thing?"

"Vessels like this always have lifeboats, we just have to…" Vinny trailed off and Morgan stared at him, waiting.

"Have to what?" Morgan asked. Vinny held up a finger to silence him. Morgan cocked his head to the side in confusion, then he heard it. That unmistakable sound that he'd spent his whole career around. The distant sound of helicopter rotors. And from what he could hear now, it sounded like two birds. He turned around and spotted the distant running lights of the approaching helos coming from the mainland. A few moments later, he could see the orange-and-white painted MH-60T Jayhawk helicopters approaching.

"Make sure your strobe is on!" Vinny called out, reaching up behind him and turning on the infrared strobe attached to the back of his helmet. Morgan did the same as he watched the birds close the distance.

Out of nowhere, Morgan was blinded by an intense light. He held up his left hand to block the light and realized that it was the spotlight affixed to the bottom of the birds.

"This is the United States Coast Guard." A voice boomed from a speaker on the helicopter. "Put your hands in the air and remain where you are." Morgan looked at Vinny, who squinted in the light as he slowly raised both hands over his head. One of the birds maintained its hover, keeping them lit up in the spotlight while the other circled towards the stern to drop off its boarding team.

71
Lower Hudson Bay

The pilot of the second bird brought the helicopter to a hover above the deck, and the crew chief kicked out the ropes. Chief Petty Officer Frank Mendez, the first member of the Coast Guard boarding team, grabbed ahold of the rope and slid down, struggling to maintain his grip in the whipping winds and slick rain. As soon as he hit the deck, he brought his M4 up and moved clear for the next man to come down.

"Last man!" The final member of the boarding team called out forty seconds later. Mendez turned and signaled the crew chief they were good. With that, the crew chief let the ropes loose, and the boarding team moved towards where the two men were still spot lit.

"Hands!" Mendez barked as the two men came into view through his NODs. "Show me your hands!"

"Hands are up, dude." The one with the quad-NVGs flipped on his helmet said. "We're on your side, I'm the one who sent out the mayday."

"Drop your weapons!" Petty Officer Third Class Donald Galen yelled.

"Listen!" Quad-goggles said. "We're not the ones you need to worry about, we're the ship's security. There are about thirty armed assholes below deck that are responsible for taking the ship."

"Shut it!" Petty Officer Second Class Tyler Morris yelled. There was a loud *boom* followed by a flash above that startled everyone on the deck. Mendez saw quad-goggles' face take on a look of horror, then he heard the high-pitched sound of one of the Jayhawks' engines whining. He looked over his shoulder to see the bird with the spotlight burst into flames, spinning towards the deck.

"Move, move!" Quad-goggles yelled, grabbing his friend and Morris by the front of their vests and shoving them clear, before following himself. Mendez followed them, keeping his weapon trained on the men in plainclothes and tactical gear in case they got froggy on him.

"Voo…si…ro…hit!" Someone said, their transmission choppy. Mendez reached to his push-to-talk but was met with a wash of static.

"Shit!" Mendez yelled, watching as the bird continued to spin. His NODs made it clear as the two rescue divers were launched out of the bird by the centrifugal force of the spinning before it crashed into the dark water below. The other helo hovered above, keeping its spotlight on where the other bird had gone down. "What the fuck just happened?" Mendez yelled to the two guys.

The two rescue divers on the second bird had just jumped into the water when there was another *boom*, which Mendez now recognized as the sound of an AT4 being fired. The rocket must have missed the second helicopter, because there was no follow-on explosion. The pilot yawed to the side, bringing it to a higher altitude and starting an orbit around the Aguilar, leaving the two divers in the water. They would have to wait for the incoming ships to recover them.

"You got our mayday?" Quad-goggles asked.

"Who the fuck just took out my bird?" Mendez yelled, aiming his weapon square at the guy's chest, despite the fact he was wearing a plate carrier.

"The same assholes that took over our ship. Listen, we need to get this secured before they get out of-" Vinny was cut off when loud gunfire rang out. Bullets impacted the deck and sent sparks flying, and one of the boarding team members let out a grunt before dropping to the deck.

"Contact!" The other plainclothes guy yelled, bringing his MP5 up and returning fire.

"Cover, get to cover!" Morris yelled as he dragged Galen's limp form behind a bulkhead.

Mendez and his boarding team scrambled for cover while the two plainclothes men began returning fire. From the sound of it, the intruders had broken out the M4s and a couple of the 249s and were now hammering the Coasties with their new toys.

72
Lower Hudson Bay

Foaly had exited the holds and was making his way back down the long corridor towards the upper deck. He took it slow, moving forward at a steady but cautious pace, his weapon up and at the ready. He paused when there was a muffled *thud*, followed by another only seconds later. *What the hell was that?* After a moment, he continued forward.

A burst of gunfire rang out and sparks hit the side of his face. Alex slammed himself to the side, pressing up against the bulkhead as more rounds ripped through the air where he'd been standing. Switching his rifle to a left-handed grip, he brought the 416 up and pumped the trigger, returning fire as quickly as he could. There was a lull in fire from his attacker, so Foaly drew his pistol and side-stepped across the corridor, firing to keep their heads down. Now that he was on the other side he could reload and regain his right-hand advantage from behind cover.

The lone gunman popped out from behind cover down the hall. His suppressed AK was slung behind him and he held one of the stolen M4s, aiming it at where he'd last seen Foaly. Luckily for the contractor, the last burst from the intruder's rifle had taken out a few of the small light bulbs in the ceiling, engulfing Foaly in darkness.

Staring down the back-up iron sights built into the top of his ACOG, Foaly watched as the gunman slowly reached up and swiveled his NODs down over his eyes before taking a step out from cover and starting towards the darkened portion of the corridor. Foaly let him take a few more steps before putting three shots into the guy's head, dropping him instantly. Foaly took a step forward and put another two in his face just to be sure, then returned to cover. He leaned his head back and let out a long exhale, gloved fingers touching the stinging skin on his face where he must have caught a ricocheted piece of metal from the incoming fire.

A small, barely visible red light blinked above him. This caught Foaly's attention, but he wrote it off as a trick of the light. Then it blinked again.

The hell? He thought to himself as he grabbed his small penlight and clicked it on. The cone of white light revealed a block of plastic explosives like the ones they'd seen being armed inside the holds. Foaly moved the flashlight down and saw one, then two, then three more of the charges, all laid out at even intervals along the ceiling of the ship. They were all blinking; armed and waiting for the signal to detonate.

He dropped the flashlight and took off at a run, clearing the ship's knee-knockers as he did so.

"Morgan, Vinny!" He called out into his push-to-talk, praying that the transmission was going through. "They're getting ready to scuttle the ship. Get the hell out of here, now!"

73
New York/New Jersey Bight

Vinny reloaded and posted behind one of the refrigerated shipping containers, squeezing the trigger and dropping another gunman. They seemed to be using a combination of their own AKs as well as the M4s stolen from belowdecks. A few of the bastards had broken out the linked ammo for the 249s, which were doing a hell of a job keeping the Coast Guard team pinned down. As Vinny drew a bead on another hostile, something *snapped* and his head whipped backwards, sending him to the ground.

"You hit?" Morgan yelled.

"Fuck!" Vinny replied, feeling his forehead for any blood. The impact had given him a near-instant headache, and his neck felt tweaked. Further inspection showed one of the tubes to his NODs was now a jagged mess of plastic and metal; one of the rounds must have caught it. *There goes forty-three grand.* He thought to himself. "I'm good." He said through gritted teeth. He unclipped the ruined goggles and let them clatter to the deck. "Any word from Alex?"

"Nothing yet!" Morgan yelled, firing his pistol with one-hand while he used the other to reload his MP5. "Hey, I'm down to my last mag!"

"Check!" Vinny acknowledged. He was just happy the Coasties had realized they weren't the bad guys and were now assisting them in the firefight.

"...off the ship!" Someone yelled. Vinny looked away from his rifle to see Alex sprinting towards him. One of the Coast Guardsmen near Vinny drew a bead on Alex, so Vinny tackled into the guy, knocking his weapon out of line with Alex.

"Blue! Blue!" Vinny yelled, swatting away the fist the guy threw at him.

"What?" Morgan yelled.

"Get off the ship, they're gonna blow it!" Alex yelled, waving his left arm frantically towards the stern of the Aguilar.

"Who the hell are you?" The Chief Petty Officer yelled as he reloaded his rifle. That was when they noticed that the incoming fire had all but died down. A cursory glance showed the black-clad attackers scrambling down and heading towards the ship's bow.

"They're going to scuttle the ship; we need to leave now!" Foaly said. The color washed from the CPO's face and he turned to the rest of his Boarding Team.

"Angel Two this is Alpha One-One, we need an immediate extract!" Mendez yelled into his radio.

"Roger that, coming in hot." The second helo's pilot said. With the backup team on standby in the second bird, it was going to be packed. The pilot expertly brought the Jayhawk down to the level of the deck, holding it steady as the Boarding Team inside shifted over to try and make room for the men on the ship.

"On the bird, go!" Mendez yelled. He glanced backwards and watched as Galen launched himself over the railing, landing in the crew bay of the helicopter. Morris was on his heels.

A long burst of gunfire rang out and sparks raked the canopy of the Jayhawk's cockpit, shattering the windscreen and killing both pilots. This sent the bird out of control, with it wobbling away from the ship. Morris had already jumped, but the bird drifted far enough that he was sent plummeting into the stormy water below. He was quickly joined by two others, who'd also jumped. Mendez let out a guttural scream as he charged forward, diving off the boat to save his guys despite the cries of protest from the three contractors.

"Come on, we've got to move!" Foaly yelled. There was a rumble beneath his feet, and moments later an enormous explosion ripped through the large ship, sending the three men tumbling to the slick deck. Fire and debris shot up hundreds of feet in the air, and soon it would be coming down on them. Just another hazard to worry about.

"Holy fuck!" Vinny yelled.

"Get up! Get up!" Morgan yelled as he grabbed Vinny by the back of his jacket and pulled him along. It only took seconds for the former SEAL to snap back into action. "Where's Alex?" They both looked around, stomachs knotting up. Had he been blown overboard? Had he been disintegrated?

Another explosion sent shudders through the ship, which was beginning to groan as the structural integrity degraded.

"He'll catch up, keep moving!" Morgan gave another glance around but didn't slow. If they stopped, they'd be dead too.

A third explosion sent them both stumbling, and the deck was beginning to angle more as the ship began to tear itself apart. If this kept up, it would threaten to send them both tumbling end-over-end into the water below. And if that happened, they'd both be sucked down into the depths with the ship's wreckage.

"Lifeboat!" Vinny called out, pointing as he vaulted over a safety railing. Morgan followed, but slipped and fell. He lost grip of his MP5, and it would have been lost to the drink had it not been slung over his chest. Vinny reached the door to the smaller vessel and pulled it open, waving Morgan inside. He dove in and climbed into the pilot's seat while Vinny closed and secured the door.

They were in an eight-man freefall lifeboat mounted in a bracket on the side of the Aguilar. These were designed to shoot away from the ship, putting as much distance between the evacuees and the ship in minimal time. With the way the ship was listing, they would be dropping almost straight down. Morgan looked back to see Vinny strapping himself in, then gave a thumbs up.

"Hold on!" Morgan triggered the release mechanism. Both of their stomachs rose as the lifeboat took the two-hundred-foot plunge. The sensation came to an end when they were violently jarred upon hitting the water. Morgan blinked and tried to clear his vision as he checked the boat's systems while Vinny unbuckled himself and walked with wobbling legs to the door.

The Aguilar was on fire. Morgan climbed from the pilot's seat and joined Vinny as they watched another explosion rip through the bowels of the ship. Flames shot high in the air, and the terrible screech of metal-on-metal filled the air as the ship split in half. Both halves rose high into the air near the center, the few pieces of connective metal screaming in protest. When those pieces gave, both ends began crashing back towards the ocean. Morgan and Vinny held onto the safety straps just inside the lifeboat as the two enormous halves of the ship came crashing back down, sending a wave towards them. This time it was Vinny's turn to yell 'hold on' as he grabbed ahold of Morgan's vest to make sure neither of them fell out when the wave hit.

And hit it did.

DECEPTION

Morgan was thrown off his feet and tossed around the inside of the lifeboat as it lifted out of the water. He impacted the floor and felt like he was going to throw up before he registered the coppery taste of blood in his mouth. He jammed two fingers into his mouth and sighed in relief when he confirmed he hadn't bitten off his tongue. Now that they weren't being thrown around, he looked over his shoulder to check on Vinny. His friend wasn't in the lifeboat.

"Vin?" Morgan called out as he crawled towards the door. "Vinny!"

"Here!" The voice called out, followed by rhythmic splashing. Vinny had been tossed clear of the boat. Thankfully, the HIT collar worked as intended and shot him right back to the surface. Morgan stayed in the door and helped Vinny up onto the platform, then both of them turned around and stared at the now-sinking, still-burning wreckage. Neither of them knew if Alex had even made it off the ship. And if he had, how had he survived that wave?

They continued watching, the knots in their stomachs growing tighter. Then they saw it: a brief flash of white light. It was between them and the wreckage. It blinked again, closer. That was when they realized what they were looking at.

74
New York/New Jersey Bight

Foaly gasped for air as he swam the last few meters towards the lifeboat. Morgan was practically hanging off the back of the boat while Vinny hopped in and swam to meet Foaly. He hooked his arm under Alex's and swam them both back to the craft. Foaly weakly raised his arms onto the platform and was dragged on by the back of his vest thanks to Morgan. Vinny was about to ask why Alex hadn't installed his HIT collar, but then saw that the device had been shredded, likely from when the Aguilar went up. That meant that Alex had swam the whole way weighted down by his clothes, armor, and weapons.

"Come on buddy." Morgan said as he helped Alex into a seated position. Foaly gasped for air, his lungs burning from the effort of the swim. He'd nearly drowned when that wave had knocked him around and sent him under. Had it not been for the burning wreckage illuminating the surface, he wouldn't have known which way was up.

"You good?" Vinny asked. "You okay?" Foaly nodded, trying to get air in his lungs. "Morgan, check the first aid kit. Should be a bottle of oxygen in there." Foaly turned his head to look at the wreckage. This was bad. Really bad. "Hey, take a breath." Vinny said, holding the mask attached to the oxygen bottle's nozzle to Foaly's mouth. Alex took a deep breath. The purified oxygen felt like sweet relief.

"Thanks for the save." Alex croaked out. He reached up to his push-to-talk but didn't even get static back. His radio and Peltors had likely been fried by his dip.

"How the fuck did you make it out of there alive?" Morgan asked.

"Waited till the rear was almost in the water and then I jumped. Collar worked fine at first till it all came crashing down." Foaly said, then grabbed the oxy bottle from Vinny and took another breath.

"What do we do now?" Morgan asked.

"Give me the sat phone." Alex said. He'd lost his in the swim. Morgan patted down his pants and his heart raced for a moment. Then he found the phone and handed it to his friend. Somehow, it still worked.

75
Long Island, New York

Andrea was startled from her work when the Iridium phone began beeping loudly. She snatched it from her nightstand and extended the antenna before hitting the answer button.

"Hello?" She said, her voice urgent and worried.

"Andrea, it's Alex." Foaly's voice came through. It was riddled with static and sounded like he was speaking from inside a soup can, but it was him.

"Alex? How are you-?" She paused and took a moment to calm down. "I thought you were dead. What happened?"

"Whoever took over the ship set up some kind of jammer. We tried to get ahold of you." He paused for a moment. "What do you mean you thought we were dead? Do you know what's going on?" There was an edge to his voice.

"Everybody knows!" She turned to see the news footage of the still-sinking wreckage of the Aguilar, now surrounded by Coast Guard helicopters and ships. Her eyes widened when she saw their names appear on screen. "Alex, they're blaming you three for it."

"What? How is that possible? Who else would have our names other than Donnelly?" Alex demanded.

"I don't know!" Andrea replied. "I...maybe they had someone on the inside. I'm not sure. I'll reach out to Donnelly and-"

"No." He interrupted. "If they're pinning the blame on us, they're going to be looking for any and all traffic regarding where we are. Frankly, I think Donnelly sold us out, and I don't want you roped into this. Take the battery out of the phone and kill it. Delete your drive, destroy the company computer; get rid of anything and everything that could tie you to us. You're not officially on our books yet, so you should be in the clear." She couldn't believe what she was hearing.

"What should I do after that?" She asked.

"I'll let you know." Alex said, then the phone hung up. She took the phone away from her ear, still staring at the television in confusion. Why the hell was someone blaming them for the attack on the ship? Who would even know about it other than her and the CIA?

She shoved those questions to the back of her head; she'd have time to think about them later. For now, she had to scrub everything, following Foaly's orders to make sure she couldn't be tied to the team or the incident. She popped the phone's battery, then removed the sim card and snapped it in half. Next, she unlocked the Surface Book laptop that Alex had provided her on behalf of the company and initiated a complete drive wipe, which would even delete the machine's operating system.

While the program chewed, scrambled, and then destroyed every shred of information on the laptop, she went through and deleted their numbers and text chains from her iPhone, then did a factory reset to the backup just before Foaly had brought her in. Sure, she'd lose pictures and some other text chains from the weeks since she'd joined them, but it was a small price to pay to avoid getting sent to Sing Sing or somewhere even worse for something they didn't do. She'd seen how the Army had handled Foaly's case after what had happened in Iran and could only imagine what the federal government would do to a group of civilians implicated in something like this.

After gathering up the few dozen folders of hard copy documents she kept for the team, she saw the Surface Book now displayed a blue screen of jumbled characters and symbols; the system had finished deleting itself. She threw the papers in her kitchen sink and turned on the water, letting it pour over and soak into the sheets. Then she picked up the laptop and brought it into the bathroom. Holding it at the corners, she smashed the face of it against the corner of the bathroom counter, sending shards of plastic and metal flying. She continued to bash it until the computer was split down the middle, hanging together by a few wires. Using one of her knives that she kept stashed in the medicine cabinet, she worked the blade between the broken screen and ruined internals, wedging it up and down until the casing split apart.

She returned to the kitchen and dumped the ruined components of the laptop into the sink, where they splashed into the water that was pooling over the soaked paper. The nonessential parts of the laptop went into her kitchen garbage while the snapped sim card and important components went into the sink. Satisfied the paper was a pulpy mess, she kept the water flowing and switched on the garbage disposal. It ran fine for a few moments, but then the sound of the motor turned to a loud squealing and crunching as it began to take in the electronics; chewing and grinding the metal and plastic against its blades until they were broken into small enough fragments to be sucked down the drain. With a final wet squelch, the last of the waterlogged pages chased the computer parts down the drain, and the disposal returned to its normal sound.

Doing a final sweep of her apartment, Andrea was sure she'd left nothing behind that could tie her back to the team if someone came snooping around. She tied up the garbage and threw a hoodie on before sticking her Glock 43 in the sweatshirt's front pocket in case someone had put two and two together and was coming after her. If they did, they were going to have one hell of a fight on their hands.

76
Upper East Side, New York

Shannon watched in horror as the news continued to cover the sinking ship in the Hudson Bay. Overlaid over the footage were three black and white photos that were supposedly Alex, Morgan, and Vinny. At least, that's what the talking heads were saying. The pictures were too blurry to confirm they were actually the guys, or if the pictures had even come from the ship.

"At this time, there has been no confirmation as to who was responsible for the attack on the MV Aguilar." The newscaster said. "It has been reported that three Manhattan residents; Alexander Foaly, Vincent Jensen, and Morgan Tyron had boarded the ship and killed the crew before sinking the vessel. It's an unprecedented show of piracy right here off the coast of New York, and officials are already saying that the environmental impact the oil spilled from the vessel could be catastrophic to the bay…" Shannon lowered the volume and sat on the couch, staring at her phone. There was still nothing from Alex.

It couldn't be true. There was no way that Alex would have allowed for something like this to happen, much less be involved or responsible for it. She held the phone up and dialed Julia.

"Hello?" Julia answered just as the phone began to send Shannon to voicemail.

"Have you heard anything from Morgan?" Shannon asked.

"No." Julia replied. "The police are on their way. Have they called you yet? It can't be true, right?" Shannon pressed her lips together and shook her head.

"Absolutely not. There's no way any of them could be behind this. They were hired to protect…" She trailed off, knowing that her phone was likely being monitored at this point. "Let's keep trying. Let me know if you hear anything."

"Okay." Julia said, then the conversation clicked to an end. Shannon stood and walked over to her desk, where Alex had left a note for her on the computer's keyboard. It was a post-it note with a number written on it, and below it was Andrea's name. Shannon quickly tapped the number into her cell and hit call.

"We are sorry. You have reached a number that has been disconnected or is no longer in service. If you feel you have reached this recording in error, please check the number and try your call again." The automated female voice answered Shannon's call.

"Dammit." Shannon said, ending the call. She looked at the note and made sure to double check the numbers before hitting call again.

"We are sorry. You have reached a number that has been disconnected or-"

77
Arrochar, New York

"-is no longer in service. If you feel you have reached this recording in error, please check-"

"Fuck!" Foaly yelled, ending the call.

"No luck?" Vinny asked from the front seat of the stolen car.

"Nothing." Foaly slid the burner phone back in his pocket and looked out the window. Had it not been for the dry bag he'd kept the phone in, that probably would've gotten killed in the water as well. He'd been trying to get ahold of Donnelly, but none of his calls were going through, and the single call to Shannon's cell had gotten him a busy signal.

After successfully piloting the lifeboat to the beach of a small peninsula south of Staten Island, the three had managed to sneak to a nearby parking lot where a few cars had been left unattended. Morgan had quickly broken in, silenced the alarm, and hotwired the car. Now Vinny rode shotgun, and Alex was in the back while Morgan drove.

"Oh fuck." Alex said as a realization suddenly hit him.

"What?" Morgan and Vinny both asked. Vinny turned around to see if Alex was okay while Morgan's eyes flicked to the rearview.

"The long guns and Mk46. They were in our cabin." Foaly said.

"Shiiit." Morgan seethed through his teeth. "We're already being fucking blamed for this shit, now they're going to find weapons registered to us in the wreckage. Fuck!" He slammed his fist against the steering wheel.

DECEPTION

"What's the plan?" Vinny asked. Despite the difference of their previous commands, Vinny was confident in asking Foaly since Alex had been a boots-on-ground Officer, and a Mustang at that. Vinny knew Foaly would know what decisions to make next. Foaly exhaled and ran a gloved hand over his face.

"We need to get back to Manhattan. Make a beeline for the container and grab our bugout shit. I'll try to get in contact with Donnelly and see if we can sort this whole mess out."

"Why don't we go to the police?" Morgan asked.

"Our names are plastered all over this thing. NYPD and the Feds are going to be snooping around for us." Foaly paused, thinking. "With how quickly they put our faces to this thing, I'm thinking someone set us up. We can't go home. That's the first place they'll look. Hell, they probably already have PD and FBI on the way to talk to Shannon and Julia." Morgan's eyes narrowed at Foaly's statement. "We need to get to the vault and grab weapons and go-bags. We'll make a decision from there."

"Check." Vinny said. Morgan was silent as he continued the drive to the city.

78
Two Bridges, New York

It was almost four in the morning when they finally got to the vault. They'd decided to leave their vests and weapons in the car, as it would look a lot less conspicuous to send one of them out with a duffel bag rather than all of them walk in kitted up. Morgan quickly opened both doors and the three of them filed into the room. After disarming the alarm, Morgan walked over to his locker and turned on the small satellite television sitting atop it, tuning in to Fox News.

The news showed aerial footage of the bay where the Aguilar had sunk. Bits of the wreckage were still burning at the surface despite Coast Guard vessels being on-scene and spraying everything down. Most of the massive vessel was deep underwater now. The tagline at the bottom of the screen read 'Domestic Environmental Terror Attack Sinks Relief Ship in Hudson Bay."

"...and five hours after the initial Mayday call was received, there has been no sign of the three individuals believed to be behind the attack. While at least seven lifeboats were launched from the vessel, no survivors have been found." All three of their chests tightened. "The MV Aguilar began its voyage to the Horn of Africa from Port Newark last evening, where it was transporting several tons of relief supplies for humanitarian assistance in areas such as Somalia and Eritrea-"

"Son of a bitch." Foaly growled.

"Fuck." Morgan said under his breath. Vinny was busy breaking open one of his aid bags.

"Morgan, come here and let me check you for a concussion." Vinny said. They'd all been banged up pretty badly, and the medic had already splinted his sprained ring and pinky fingers on his right hand.

"Law enforcement agencies have already contacted the families of the three men who are said to be responsible for the sinking, but so far initial interviews have shed little light on the situation. The United States Coast Guard has deployed vessels and helicopters on-scene at the site of the sinking, and crews are already coordinating efforts with FEMA and the EPA to contain the massive oil spill that has resulted from the sinking. Our correspondent, James Holder, is currently on one of the vessels arriving on-scene. James, what can you tell us so far?" The view cut to a newscaster wearing a bright-orange rain jacket with the Fox logo on it. He held his microphone with one hand, the other gripping his jacket's hood as the howling rain tugged at it.

"Kiera, I'm here on a ship that's currently surveying the area around the site for any survivors that may have made it off the Aguilar. While seven of the lifeboats were reported as being launched by their GPS locators, all but one appear to have been disabled. They're still trying to figure out if this was a technical error, or if any of the lifeboats were sucked under with the ship-" Morgan turned away from Vinny, wincing in pain as the medic dabbed more antiseptic on the cut on Morgan's forehead that he'd had no idea about until he'd seen it in the rearview mirror.

"GPS transponders? Shit, that means they know where our boat went." Morgan said.

"We can't go home." Alex said bluntly, having waved off Vinny's check-up to begin packing. "We can't go home; we can't use our vehicles. Shit we can't even call anyone in our families right now." He knew all too well that by now every federal agency would have their families' lines of communications tapped and actively monitored, looking for any signs of proof of life for the three of them. Once they smelled a drop of blood in the water, they wouldn't stop until they had all three of them in custody. Shortly after that, the black vans and helicopters would be on them in no time. "Start packing, we need to get out of Manhattan."

79
Murray Hill, New York

The ringing phone woke Julia with a start. She rapidly blinked as she looked around for her cell. She found it face down on the coffee table next to the couch, its vibrations sending it shaking across the table.

"Hello?" She said, failing to hide the fatigue in her voice. She looked at the wall clock and saw it had only been twenty-some minutes since the police had vacated her apartment. She'd fallen asleep watching the news, which was still covering the sinking ship.

"Is this Julia Tyron?" A voice she didn't recognize said on the other end of the line. Tears welled in her eyes, likely another police call. Thankfully, the threats hadn't started coming in yet, though she was sure that her information would be made public for that soon enough.

"Yes, this is Julia. I've already spoken with the State Police and the FBI. The NYPD just left my apartment maybe thirty minutes ago." Her voice sounded defeated.

"No ma'am, that's not why I'm calling." The man said. She narrowed her eyes. If this was a threat, she would-

"Who is this?" She demanded.

"I'm calling because I found something of yours that you dropped at Fugett Park. I just wanted to make sure I had the right number. I'll drop it off sometime next week." He said, then the call ended. She felt her chest tighten. Was someone stalking her? Should she get out of town? No, the police explicitly told her not to do that.

Then it hit her.

Fugett Park was the park in West Chester where she'd first met Morgan. No one would have known that detail and called her unless...unless that was a message from him. He was still alive!

She let out a loud sigh of relief that turned into sobs. She didn't know how or where he was, but her Morgan was alive. She took another look at her phone, staring at the lock screen. It was a picture of the two of them from two Fourth of Julys ago, one of the few times he'd actually been home for the holiday.

"...and still no word on the recovery of the three men now confirmed behind the attack. Though several bodies of the crew as well as members of the Coast Guard boarding teams have been recovered. The bodies indicate that the crew and a number of the Coast Guardsmen were killed by gunfire..." The reporter's voice came back into focus. She closed her bleary eyes and shut CNN off. At least now she could sleep a little easier.

80
Two Bridges, Manhattan

Morgan woke with a start to a knocking sound, instinctively bringing his pistol to bear. He got up from the chair and approached the door, both hands on his 1911. Vinny had his P226 at the ready as Morgan pulled open the door.

Foaly stood there, a duffel bag in each hand. He'd gone and pulled their weapons and equipment from the car. Alex looked down at Morgan's pistol, then stepped around it and entered. Morgan closed the door as Foaly put the duffels on the table, unzipping one and withdrawing his gear as well as his rifle.

"Did you get in contact with Donnelly?" Morgan asked. Foaly shook his head.

"Tried on three burners. Nothing." Foaly set his gear down on the table and pulled open his locker. Morgan slammed his fist against the table.

"What the fuck do we do now?" Morgan asked as Foaly retrieved a gray-and-blue non-tactical backpack from his locker and placed it on the table.

"Like I said before, pack whatever you need, and get out of Manhattan. Hell, get out of New York." Foaly said as he stripped off his rain-soaked clothes and replaced them with a pair of jeans and a gray flannel shirt beneath a Carhartt jacket. He grabbed a nondescript gym bag and tossed three extra pairs of clothes in it. Morgan sighed and began doing the same.

The three of them worked silently in a morbid facsimile of their normal pre-mission preparations. Each man grabbed whatever clothing and equipment they might need for the foreseeable future, packing as much into their limited bags as they could. Foaly stuffed his MP7 in a soft case along with half a dozen mags and the respective ammo at the bottom of his duffel. Next, his Glock 19 and HK P30. Then he retrieved a small metal lockbox from his locker, which contained numerous documents for his many aliases. Passports, driver's licenses, social security cards, foreign visa forms, credit and debit cards, and even business cards, all contained in different plastic bags to keep matching sets together. He grabbed two American personas, and one British, courtesy of a contact he had in the SAS, and dropped them on the table. He took out his actual identifying documents and dropped them loosely in the box before locking it and sliding it back into place.

With everything set, Foaly placed two of the document bags in the backpack while storing the third on his person. After triple checking he hadn't missed anything tradecraft related, he zipped up both the backpack and duffel and picked them up. His Sig P228 went into an IWB holster behind his right hip, which was covered by his flannel and jacket. Morgan looked up from his own preparations to see Foaly sling the duffel over his left shoulder and start towards the door, carrying his backpack.

"Where are you going?" Morgan asked. Foaly looked back at him.

"It's best we don't know each other's location. If one of us gets pinched, we can't out the others." Foaly moved his gaze from Morgan to Vinny. "Something tells me that if anyone gets their hands on us, they're not going to be playing by anybody's rulebook."

"Good luck, Alex." Vinny said, stepping forward with a hand extended. Foaly took it and squeezed tight.

"Thanks Vin, safe travels brother." Foaly gave a nod to his SEAL counterpart. "Morgan, stay safe. You guys better hurry, the sun's going to be up soon." Morgan stared at Foaly. "I'll be in touch." And with that, Alex was gone.

Morgan looked over at Vinny, who stared at the vault door a moment longer before returning to his own preparations. Like Alex, Vinny had a duffel bag and a large backpack. He also had a small computer bag, which he'd placed his P226 in, and now wore his SIG P365 on his hip.

Vinny had packed similarly to Foaly, though he'd opted to take food items with him as well. Morgan wasn't sure how Vinny was planning on bugging out, but however he was going to do it, he was prepared. Hell, Morgan didn't even know how *he* was going to get out of New York, or where he'd go after. He'd have to come up with a plan. Now.

The former pilot, and CEO of the now-condemned private military group, continued to pack as Vinny changed from his own waterlogged clothing into a nondescript outfit. Vinny wished Morgan the best, then stepped out. That left Morgan to pack alone.

81
Fort Lee, New Jersey

The ride had been almost entirely silent after Andrea had picked Foaly up outside of the storage facility. He'd given her an address and she'd started driving while they both sat in silence after he'd made a quick, curt phone call. The air in the car was thick with anxiety as they drove. Neither of them knew what to say, while simultaneously wanting to ask a hundred questions all at once.

"So, what do I do now?" Andrea asked, breaking the unbearable silence. Foaly blinked, brought back to the present by her question. He looked over at her.

"I don't want you to do anything. You burned all ties to us, right?" He asked. She nodded, her lips pressed firmly together. "Have any authorities contacted you?" She shook her head. "Alright, at least one thing has gone right so far." He took his hat off and ran a hand through his hair before replacing it.

"I know you don't want me involved, but I can still help out." She said as she merged into the left lane. "What happened was a complete shit show. I don't know who leaked what to the media, but from what you've told me, everybody has it wrong. I mean, I know that none of you were responsible for what happened. It isn't fair, and I can't in good conscious sit by while you're blamed for this. You're literally going into hiding!"

"The longer I'm presumed dead or missing, the more time I have to put together a plan and figure out exactly what happened." Foaly responded. "I don't have anything for you to help with off the top of my head right now. Hell, I've already asked too much of you by asking you to drive me. Some overzealous Trooper trying to make his quota pulls us over, you're right in the shit with me." He was mentally kicking himself in the ass for dragging her along with this. It was obvious that answer wasn't enough for her. "If anything comes to mind, I'll let you know." She looked over at him. He may have had her delete all their information, but he'd kept hers for future use. Smart.

"What if I keep an eye on Shannon? Run some CI to see who is looking into her and what they're looking for?" Foaly's eyes widened slightly at Andrea's proposal. It wasn't a terrible idea; have Andrea working under the guise of an old friend of the widow's husband to console her, all while secretly running counterintelligence. *That may just work*. "Hell, I'll even look after Julia."

"No, you can't have any direct contact with Julia. If you get involved with both, some egghead in the Bureau is going to put two and two together and question your association with Morgan, seeing as you two never worked together in the past." Foaly paused and took a sip of the coffee that Andrea had ordered for him during a pitstop to a Dunkin Donuts drive-thru. After a moment of silence, he simply said. "Thank you." The small glance she gave him was answer enough.

The rest of the drive to Teterboro Airport was silent as Alex finally succumbed to his body's needs and fell asleep. Andrea looked over at him. There were times that she wished that things had developed further between them beyond the drunken kiss shared on New Year's Eve in Afghanistan all those years ago.

She pushed that thought out of her mind and returned her eyes to the road. She had a job to do helping her friend out, and she was not going to let him down.

82
Virginia Beach, Virginia

Marcus Dalton was busy sitting in the sand building a sandcastle with his son, Max, when the cell phone in his shorts vibrated. He grabbed it and looked at the screen, expecting to see one of his mates calling. Instead, it was an unlisted number. He clicked the ignore button and went back to playing with his son. The phone rang again, and he saw it was the same number.

"Whatever you're selling, I don't want it." Dalton said angrily before moving to hang up.

"Marcus." A familiar voice said. Dalton paused, then brought the phone back to his ear.

"Vin? Is that you?" He asked.

"To your left." The voice said, then the phone clicked off. Dalton turned and saw a lone figure standing just off his property.

"What the fuck?" Dalton said to himself as he got up.

"Daddy said a swear!" Max said from his seated position behind his own sandcastle.

"Yeah, sorry bud." Dalton said, his mind elsewhere. "Stay here, Dad'll be right back." He looked his son in the eyes to make sure his message was clear, then started towards his property line.

Vinny stood there in a hoodie and shorts, his hood up and sunglasses on to obscure his face. He looked rough.

"Vin, what the hell are you doing here man? I thought you were dead. What's all this bullshit about you sinking a cargo ship?"

"The whole situation is fucked, Marcus." Vinny said, looking over Dalton's shoulder towards the young

Max. He hoped his Godson wouldn't recognize him, but the boy was busy destroying the sandcastle in front of him while making roaring noises.

"What the hell were you even doing on that ship? Was that your contract?" Dalton asked, still not believing that he was seeing his best friend-turned fugitive standing in front of him. The fact that Vinny was still presumed missing, and possibly dead, only worried Dalton more.

"Yeah." Vinny answered. "Dude, you know me. You know I wouldn't do something like that."

"So why are you here? Why haven't you contacted someone to clear your name?" Marcus asked.

"Hey." Vinny gestured over Dalton's shoulder. He turned to see Max was up and walking towards them.

"Max!" Marcus barked, stopping the child in his tracks. "Just stay there, buddy. I'll be right back."

"Okay Dad!" Max turned around and went back to stomping on the ruined sandcastle.

"I wish it was that simple dude, but this thing, whoever it was that hit that ship, they were well-armed and well-equipped. They hit it just like we would have, and I need to figure out who the hell they are." Vinny explained as much as he could. Dalton looked up at him, then leaned his head back and sucked his teeth.

"Dingo and the rest of the guys are a mess right now. No one can wrap their heads around what's being said about you on the news." Dalton said. "Junior's basically written you off, and Dennison wants to lead the search effort to find you." He paused. "Well fuck, I guess this means you're not coming back to the team." Neither of them laughed. "What do you need?"

"I need a boat. With enough fuel and supplies to make it to Cuba." Vinny said. Dalton scoffed and rolled his eyes. "Look dude, I don't need your boat. I just need *a* boat. With all the heat I've got on me, anywhere in the US is too risky for me to stay. I need to get to the island and lay low while I figure this shit out. Once I've got all that set, I'll come back and pay you whatever it is that you want for helping me out." Vinny stared at his former teammate, who placed his hands on his hips and was looking out towards the ocean. There was a long moment of silence between the two of them. The only sounds were the breaking waves, squawking seagulls, and Max's giggles.

"You can use my boat. I'll load her up and you can take her tonight. Cut the mooring lines so it looks like she was taken by the storm." Dalton said. "Consider it paying you back for saving my ass last year."

"I appreciate it, brother." Vinny said. "Here's a number you can contact me at. Just text me the time and location for the pickup. I'll be there." He handed a piece of paper to Dalton, then started back towards his vehicle.

"Vin." Dalton said. Vinny looked at him. "Watch yourself. And be careful tonight. If Moira sees you, she'll probably call the cops. And then I'll get chewed out for helping your dumb ass." That brought a slight smirk to Vinny's face.

"You got it." Vinny said before climbing into the rental and disappearing onto Atlantic Avenue. Dalton watched his former SOCM drive away. His buddy was in a world of shit, but Dalton owed him his life from Iran. Looking back at Max, Dalton was reminded of that debt once again.

83
Plattsburgh, New York

Morgan gripped the steering wheel of the stolen van tightly as he drove in the right lane, keeping his speed right at sixty-five as he drove up I-87. Along with what he'd brought from the vault, he'd also made stops at several camping and sporting goods stores, loading up on extra survival equipment that was now piled in the back of the vehicle.

The plan was to leave New York and head to Canada. His father owned land and had a cabin northwest of Fort Severn, ironically located near the shore of Canada's own Hudson Bay. He would hide out in the cabin until he got word from Alex. Not knowing where Alex and Vinny were going didn't exactly give Morgan a warm-and-fuzzy, but he had to admit that he wasn't nearly as skilled in tradecraft as the two former operators, so he didn't question it.

Having to leave Julia to deal with the aftermath of this shitshow, now being dubbed the 'Hudson Bay Incident' by the media, had Morgan pissed. Thankfully Alex's buddy Mason, who had sworn to keep their whereabouts on the down low due to higher loyalty to Alex over the CIA, had heeded Morgan's request and left Julia with his cryptic message to let her know he was alive. The thought of the NYPD, and especially the FBI, questioning his wife while reporters and online vultures hounded her for information pissed him off, and the fact that he couldn't do anything about it pissed him off even more. He knew that in just a few hours, their faces would not only be plastered all over the news, but also by every two-bit 'reporter' with a webcam and green screen spewing their opinions on the matter all over YouTube, Reddit, Twitter, and Facebook.

His knuckles turned white as he gripped the steering wheel, his lips peeling back in a seething grimace. He thought back to how Alex had voiced his concerns about the job, and how he'd said that something hadn't felt right to him from the get-go. Morgan should have listened and questioned Donnelly about the details of the job, or just outright refused. After all, with the payout from Paoli, they could have lived comfortably for a while before needing new work. But instead, he'd been selfish and had stonewalled Alex and pressed on, knowing full well that even with his doubts, Alex wouldn't have left Morgan and Vinny to take on the job themselves. Morgan shook the steering wheel, grunting in anger. His selfishness and exploitation of his friend's loyalty had landed them all in this situation, and he was pissed off about it.

Half an hour later, Morgan had calmed himself down enough to make a call that he knew he had to make. Keeping one hand on the wheel, he clicked on the Bluetooth speaker in his ear and waited for the beep. Then he spoke into the device, telling it to call one of the five saved numbers on this burner.

"Call Clint Tyron."

This was going to be one hell of a reunion…

DECEPTION

To be continued in…

Wetwork

Acknowledgements

This novel would not have been possible without the support and encouragement of my vast support network of family and friends. If it weren't for their support in the almost decades-long pursuit of this project, Deception would likely still be sitting in a folder on a dusty hard-drive, and I'd be sitting around feeling sorry for myself in a 'shoulda-coulda-woulda' cycle of never having actually published anything I've written. Deception would not have been possible had it not been for the following:

To my father. While at first skeptical of my writing, my Dad was always honest with me. He told me that, while I enjoyed writing, I should only do so as a hobby and focus on what would put food on my table and money in my wallet. Because of that advice I was able to balance everything from work and school and continue writing. And because of that balance, here I am. Despite that, he also saw just how much I truly enjoyed writing, and after hearing from outside sources who had read some of my work at the time, encouraged me to continue doing so. I also owe it to my Dad for being the one to get me into reading the thriller genre, having started me off by loaning me his hardcover copy of Tom Clancy's Rainbow Six, and then the paperback copy of Red Storm Rising. I still have both of those books on my bookshelf to this day. No, you're not getting them back, Pops. Thanks for everything, Dad, I love ya.

To my stepmother. While she may sometimes get confused by the scores of military terms and acronyms (both in-fiction and reality) used by myself, my brother, and our Dad, she has been a pillar of support when it came to my writing. She saw that I finally had a creative outlet that I was both invested in, and decent at (seeing as my hobby as an artist never took off, but thank you for all of the drawing books!). She also played an instrumental part in piquing my interest in the action thriller novel, through the many novels written by Chris Ryan that she'd purchase for me whenever she went to visit family back in England. And last, but certainly not least, she provided the ultimate litmus test on whether Deception was a good novel, as she helped with the proofreading and editing process prior to publication. Thank you, Mum!

To my mother, for introducing me to Brad Thor's novels, and for reading the many, many, *many* different iterations of Alex, Morgan, and Vinny's adventures before I finally settled on the current path. I know printed copies of all the older versions have littered the dresser and night table in your bedroom for years now, and I appreciate you sticking with me as the stories have evolved from goofy set-pieces set in a semi-realistic world to the modern thrillers that the series has transformed into. Our shared love of writing has allowed you to be incredibly supportive as this project nears ten years in the making (nine and change as of the official publication), and I'm grateful for all the support that you and Mike have given me over the years. I love you guys, and I hope you enjoy the new direction I took the book.

To my Grandma Eileen and Grandpa Ron, whom this book is also dedicated to. My love of reading wouldn't have been nearly as strong as it was without your support. It never failed to excite me when we would come to visit you and you would have a bag of books from Tom Clancy, W.E.B. Griffin, and more, waiting for me. New, used, it never mattered to me. You guys knew what I liked, and I loved receiving and reading them. This book would have never been possible had it not been for the reading, and subsequent desire to write, that was possible from all of your gifts. My only regret is that I wasn't able to get Deception out before Grandpa passed. I love you both very much, thank you for everything.

To Grandpa Ralph and Grandma Judy. I also have you both to thank for so many books over the years as birthday and Christmas gifts. And thank you for the support and interest when it came to my writing. I can remember many a weekend spent at your house, sitting at the dining room table with my laptop as I wrote page after page of one of my many projects in high-school that would form that basis for what the series to follow this book has become. Thanks guys, I love you.

To Grandpa Jack and Grandma Judy. Thank you both for your interest in reading and providing feedback on my manuscripts, particularly for Deception and Occupant. I know that I haven't been around all that much in recent years, even before I'd started working overseas, and I apologize for that. I hope that in the coming years I am able to see you more often and to make up for lost time. I truly hope that you enjoy this book, and look forward to sitting down and discussing it with you in the future. I just wish I'd known that you guys enjoyed fiction sooner!

To Mami and Papi. While the topic never came up during our few visits together, I know that I would have had your support with my writing. Thinking about it now, I'm sure that the fact that Papi had published multiple books had a subconscious impact on my desire to write and publish my own works. I miss you both and would love to have had the opportunity to sit down and discuss the global goings-on as an independently thinking adult. *Le monde est un spectacle, le vie un passage; tu es venu, tu as vu, puis tu t'es en allé.*

And to my Grandma Ginny. As I said earlier, my only regret about this novel was that I was not able to write and publish it before you passed. It's hard to believe that it's been fifteen years (as of this writing) since I last saw you. I miss and love you so very much.

To Davis, Don, Cody, Patrick, Rod, Matt, James, Antonio, and all the other great folks I had the pleasure of working with overseas. If I were to write out everything about how awesome you guys are, and all the shenanigans we got into during our times overseas, this section would likely end up about a hundred pages long. You guys know who you are and what you did, and I can't thank you enough for helping me keep my sanity with all the mundane, and less-than-mundane, shit we did together. Cheers, boyos.

To Whispers, Jack, Trey, Matt, Isaiah, and all the other 'cool' guys I've had the privilege to know and call my friends. You guys have served as true-life inspirations for how characters like the men on these pages conduct themselves, both in and out of uniform. You've all shouldered the burned of being the tip of the spear for our great nation. And for that, I am both honored and humbled to call you my friends.

To authors Brad Thor, Brad Taylor, Jack Carr, the late Vince Flynn, Dalton Fury, and of course, Tom Clancy. While I initially began writing in earnest in the early 2010's, my early style was awful. Having taken the time to read/listen to your works over the years, I've been able to practice and refine my writing style into its own cohesive method, rather than being a smashed-together mess of pop-culture references and cliché set pieces. Thanks gents, I look forward to reading and re-reading your outstanding works.

To Brian Andrews and Jeffrey Wilson, authors of the ███████ Thriller Series (Yes I know, but the DoD says I *have* to black out that term). I've greatly enjoyed reading the exploits of John Dempsey and Task Force Ember, even if I did have a late start getting into the books in 2017. Listening and re-listening to your work while overseas was a great way to escape and kill time when I wasn't working. Your guys' tactical and technical knowledge was extremely helpful in shaping my style of writing. Keep up the good work, guys!

To John Dell. While we didn't have too much direct contact while I was a cadet at Valley Forge, it's been awesome keeping in touch with you in the years since. Whether it was you educating me on the 'Army of Northern Virginia' (you know which one I mean), talking shop on our various writing endeavors (which I think you should still pursue, you had some great stuff!), and you reading this book in advance of its release date. Stay salty, Big Sarge.

To my writing buddy, Ryan Aslesen. I'm glad I decided to reach out to you via email after re-reading Undead. Little did I expect a simple fan email to turn into a great friendship with a fellow veteran. Since then, I've greatly enjoyed the continued saga of Max Ahlgren, and the War's Edge series. Keep up the great work buddy, looking forward to talking shop with you in the future.

And to everyone else who has supported and encouraged me over the past ten years with this project. Chris Sr., Caitie, Andrea, Jillian, Devyn, Shannon, TJ, Matt, Mark, Ricky, Zack Y., the Afghan crew, Augie,

DECEPTION

Jamie, Judy, Kelly, and everyone else. If I could write a paragraph to each and every one of you, this section would be just as long, if not longer, than the actual book. Thank you all so much for your support (and in many cases, the inspiration for many great characters in this book and the ongoing series). I hope that you enjoy the read, and that I will have the opportunity to cross paths with you sooner rather than later.

And last, but most certainly not least, to my German Shepherd, Heidi. While you're no longer with us, you were my writing companion for many days and nights when I was juggling work, school, military obligations, and struggling to find time to write just a page, or even a paragraph, among everything else. I miss taking a moment from writing to look and see you sleeping, usually after you'd messed up my recently-made bed. I'd give anything to have you with me as I continue this journey. I miss you girl.

The typical view of Heidi 'joining' me while writing

About the Author

A veteran of the United States Army, Zach James has firsthand experience working in the Horn of Africa, Afghanistan, and Cuba. While not a Special Operator himself, Zach has had the privilege of providing mission support to members of the SOF community, and the honor to call a number of those operators his friends. When not writing, Zach is still active in the defense industry as a private contractor. If you would like to get in contact with the author, you can reach out to him at the 'Contact' page at authorzachjames.com, or through his social media: @authorzachjames.

Art by Teo Alex. @teoalexart on Instagram